That Treeplanting Story

Stories by Dan De Vries

IF
SF
publishing

Cover Photography by Dorian Hawkey

First Edition

ISBN 978-1-7333864-0-1

Published by IF SF Publishing.
San Francisco, California
www.ifsfpublishing.com

Cover and Book Design by
David Barich, San Francisco, California

for Christine Zupanovich (Stella Pacifica)
and in honor of the memory of Bernard Van't Hul

And I saw you in my nightmares
But I'll see you in my dreams
And I might live a thousand years
Before I know what that means

Now the earth was a formless void,
there was darkness over the deep . . .

(epigraphs from the Jerusalem Bible and songs by Neil Young)

TABLE OF CONTENTS

That Treeplanting Story

. . . see the sky about to rain . . .

It was late afternoon when Alex arrived. The narrow clearing was dusted with fine snow, and a low cloud hung over the little plateau, seeming to rise up the mountainside, whiteness joining whiteness at some point and hiding the peak. Alex stood for a long time on the wooden bridge gazing down the mountain at the arm of water that led eventually to the city whose lights were beginning to sparkle beneath the cloud.

Two switchbacks down the road a waterfall dashed a refracting mist into the air, and there the truck with the house on its back crossed another bridge. The rest of the crew followed on foot. When he saw them coming, Alex advanced into the clearing.

He dropped his pack beneath a tree and pitched his tent on a flat place overlooking the river. Its rushing noise promised solitude and sleep.

As he finished, the truck with the house on its back rumbled into the clearing. Vern got out and asked him what he was doing.

"This was the first flat place I came to," Alex replied. "There might not be another one for miles."

"That's for Vern to say," Ray told him, and turned to Vern. "How close are we to the site? That's where we should camp."

Vern pondered the map. "We just passed mile three. The site is at mile seven." He and Ray got back into the truck and drove it slowly toward the steep grade at the end of the clearing. Again, with weary feet, the crew trudged along behind. Only Catherine remained with Alex, staring up the road, as though she should be following as well.

"We can't stay here by ourselves," she said.

The cloud seemed to be lowering over them. The truck was nearly lost in mist by the time it stopped on the grade. In the damp twilight, the sounds of a struggling engine and tires grinding on gravel reported down the mountain. "If that thing falls off again," Alex said to Catherine.

"Vern chained it down this time," she reminded him. The house rested precariously on the back of the truck, and from their distance it was impossible to tell if its weight had shifted. The tires ground more sharply against the road and then the engine coughed and died. Ray jumped from the passenger door and stepped back to examine the situation. He said something, inaudible to Alex and Catherine at their distance, and waved his arms. The crew scattered into the bush, returned with armloads of branches, and laid them in front of the tires. "We should help," suggested Catherine, but Alex did not move and neither did she. The engine grumbled again, and they could hear the clawing noise of gears failing to engage. For a moment it looked as though the truck was going to move forward once more, perhaps it briefly did, but then mountain silence reigned. Ray circled out of their line of vision to the driver's side and was gone for a while. By the time he reappeared, the two young men were kicking the branches off the road. When they had finished that, the truck inched backward toward Alex and Catherine. She began unpacking and arranging her sleeping bag in the tent. Vern parked in front of an open space that looked as though it had once, long ago, been a campsite. "You can all camp here," he told his crew.

"Shouldn't we put the cookshack there?" suggested Alex.

"This is just for tonight," Vern told him. "We'll camp at the site tomorrow." It was growing dark, and snow was beginning to fall. Alex's feet were getting cold. Vern opened the door to the house and Alex could see the rubble of gear thrown into a chaos when it had fallen off the truck. His shoulders still ached from helping lift it back up. Vern climbed inside and rooted for packs among the boxes and bags and barrels. Each time he found one he handed it out to Alex, who stacked them against a boulder. The crew members eventually each found their own and wandered into the area Vern had indicated. Tents rose in the gathering darkness. "Shall Cookie and I try to make some supper?" asked Virginia.

"I'm not hungry," Vern decided. "Don't we have something that people can eat without cooking?" He pawed inside the house. "Here," he said to Alex, handing out a wooden box. "There's food in here."

A bag of flour had burst and everything in the box was covered with white dust. Alex scooped two handfuls of granola and brought them to Catherine, still inside their tent. "Are you hungry?" he asked her through the screen, proffering the granola.

"You shouldn't go off by yourself like that," she warned him. "You're part of this crew too."

"Would you like some granola?" he repeated, squatting at the door. Catherine had rolled out her bag and lay on her stomach, staring at him.

"I'm not hungry," she decided.

"Well, can you take this, so I can get in? It's cold out here."

"Jesus Christ, Alex," she muttered, "what a mess. Can't you eat it out there?"

He stood looking over the river, chewing carelessly. The snow seemed to be falling harder, and the wind was beginning to blow. When he finished the first handful he threw the second into the water. Finally, he was allowed into the tent. "Shall we zip these bags together?" he wondered.

"No," she replied. "I'm already settled."

He unrolled his bag and pad, undressed, redressed in heavy underwear, and crawled into the bag. It was stiff with cold, and he pulled it over his head, shivering, waiting for his breath to warm the space inside it.

"I heard Vern and Virginia arguing on the boat," Catherine told him when he peeped out. "They're supposed to have four-wheel drive. She's worried about it, but he says the nine-ton can make it up the hill."

"It took us all afternoon to climb three miles," he pointed out.

"Well," she answered sharply, "if you think negatively about this, it will never happen. Now I'm tired." And she turned away from him.

Alex's shoulders and back were very stiff when he awoke the next morning. He struggled into yesterday's clothes. The jeans were frozen around the ankles. He crawled out of the little tent, leaving Catherine mumbling in half sleep. Vern and Ray were standing by the truck smoking something, and Ray was also eating bright yellow powder from a plastic bag. The ground was covered with snow, but a fine mist filled the air. "Find some wood for a fire," Ray told him.

A fire sounded like a good idea and Alex did as he was told. He went into the bush and gathered an armload of dead

twigs and branches for kindling. When he returned, one of
the crew, a shortish man with wire rim glasses and a black
walrus mustache was smoking with Vern and Ray. A chain
saw lay at his feet. "Find a log and Stoner will cut it up," Ray
told Alex, who did as he was told and returned with a wet
dead one. Stoner passed the pipe to Vern and fired up the
saw. He quickly reduced the log to lengths. Alex was returning with a second when Stoner tipped the saw over the pile of
kindling and poured out fuel. Vern lit the pipe and tossed the
match at the brush pile, and it exploded in flame. As the first
pieces of log took fire, Catherine came around the corner.
"What happens now?" she asked Alex.

"I don't know," he replied. "Ask Vern."

Vern and Ray were still leaning against the truck. "Gee,
ah, I dunno . . ." said Vern. "What do we do now, Ray?"

"Is everybody up?" wondered Ray.

Virginia and Cookie, the two young men, French Pierre,
and the guy named Nick were not. Vern reached into the
cab and blew the horn. A high-pitched undulating scream
echoed back and forth across the valley. "That'll get 'em,"
said Vern.

Virginia stuck her head out of the house. "Cut that out!"
she cried.

"Time to get up," Vern shouted back. "We need breakfast. We didn't get any supper last night and I've got the
munchies . . . Cookie!" he called across the clearing. "Get
up and cook!"

People emerged from the tents in the clearing. The two
young men arrived together. "Good morning, Vern," said
one. "What should we do?"

"Got a little fire going here," Vern replied.

"Good morning, Vern," said the other. "Can we help?"

"We're going to have breakfast," Vern told them.

"I don't s'pose," said the first, "you have any a'that hash?"

"Shouldn't we build a cookshack?" wondered Alex.

"Hey, Ray," called Vern. "Should we build a cookshack?"

"Listen," said Ray. "Building a cookshack is downtime. And we don't have any time to waste. We don't make any money for downtime. We have to get to work right away. This isn't like working for MacMillan Blowjob where you can just fuck off all day and still get paid. And we don't have to punch any timeclocks or take any orders from assholes. Building a cookshack is downtime and we have to get to work."

Alex turned his eyes up the road to the mountain, which stretched high, snow-dusted, into the lifting mist. He heard voices, Nick's, whom he had not seen arrive, and then Virginia's.

Virginia said, "We can't cook without a cookshack."

Nick said, "We can't work without trees, and the trees are down at the landing."

"I agree," said Ray. "And it's all downtime. We don't get paid for getting the trees. We're not working for MacMillan Blowjob."

"Do you know what's going on here?" Alex asked Catherine.

"Don't be so negative," she told him.

It seemed to occur to Vern that in order to get the trees they would have to get the house off the truck. He said as much. "But that's more downtime," said Ray. Still, it had to be done, and it took time. First, they had to take out all the remaining gear, and Vern and Virginia's personal belongings. Then they had to gather logs to wedge under the house's back corners already sticking off the truck bed. When that was done, Vern put a jack under the third corner. "Everyone over there," he said, and pointed at the fourth. Ray stood back and waved his arms as Vern inched the truck away, leaving the house perched on a foundation of logs, jack, and humanity.

"Vern," thought one of the young men, "we can't hang on t'this all day."

Alex thought his back might crack.

"We better get more logs," Vern said to Ray. "You women help us." It took them an awful long time to get enough. "Hang on!" Vern told them all. "Come on! Lift! Higher!"

"This is fun, Vern," said the other young man. One by one the lifters fell away and the house wobbled into place on what was jammed beneath it. Alex stumbled over to a boulder and inventoried his pain: fingers, wrists, forearms, elbows, calves, ankles, heels, toes, all complaining extravagantly.

"It's crooked," noticed Catherine.

"I'm going to die," he told her.

"No you're not," she reassured him.

No one had even noticed the red pickup parked on the road. There sat two men with orange hardhats and puzzled expressions. A representational map of the province graced the door facing the crew. "I'm Dick and this is Rick," said the man with the red hair when they approached. "Are any of you Simon Phillips?"

No one batted an eye at that. "Oh, heh heh, that's me," said Vern. "Are you our checkers?"

"Yes," said the man with the red hair. "I'm Dick and this is Rick. The trees just came in. They're down at the landing. Is that your only vehicle?" He looked the least little bit askance at the nine-ton flatbed. No one said anything so he went on. "The specifications call for four-wheel drive. The road ahead is pretty steep."

"I had one," said Vern. "But it broke down on Saturday."

"Hey," said Ray. "Why don't you let us use your truck to haul up the trees?"

The red-haired man stopped for about a tenth of a second. "But that's against regulations," he told them.

"Well listen," Ray insisted. "We're all in this together. I mean, don't we all want the same thing, to plant those trees?"

"Yes, I mean, we just want to do it," agreed Vern. "We've just got to get out there and plant those trees."

Dick and Rick looked at one another and shrugged their shoulders. "We really can't," explained Dick.

"So that's the way it is," Ray realized. "All the way by the book. We're gonna be out here bustin' ass but nobody's gonna help us. C'mon Vern, let's go down and get those trees. This talking is all downtime. We aren't working for MacMillan Blowjob."

"What about a cookshack?" Alex asked tentatively.

"We aren't here to build cookshacks," Ray shouted at the mountain, hopping from one foot to another. "We got to get out there and plant the trees."

"Yes but . . ." Alex tried.

"Listen here," Ray shot back, "We're all in this together. We're not working for MacMillan Blowjob. You better do what you're told."

Dick the checker turned toward Vern. "But you can't plant until the snow melts," he pointed out. "It will be even heavier further up the mountain. You should use today to get the trees and make your camp."

"I plant trees in the snow," Ray insisted. "When I was working for . . ."

But Vern interrupted him. "Does anybody here know how to build a cookshack?" he inquired.

"I build lots," said French Pierre.

"Nick's a good carpenter," Vern remembered to himself.

"How do you want it built?" asked Nick.

"You guys figure that out," Vern told him. "All the stuff

is in that pile there. We have to get organized."

"We sure do," agreed Ray, still hopping from foot to foot. "This is all . . ."

One of the checkers turned to Vern. "Well, I guess you got that thing up here once, you can probably do it again, eh? But you still have to go four more miles to get to the site."

"Of course we'll make it," insisted Vern. "Listen here. Pierre and Nick and the women stay and make a camp. The rest of us will go get the trees."

Meltoff ran down the road and toward the stream in rivulets. Vern and Ray got into the front seat of the nine-ton and Alex, Stoner, and the two young men climbed on the back. "Got any dope, Stoner?" asked one of the young men, and Stoner inserted a joint between the shafts of his black walrus mustache. The air lay heavy around them as they headed down the mountain. Had they been moving faster, it would have been very very cold; as it was, the truck crept, and it was simply damp and miserable. Alex huddled inside his raingear and held on as they bounced along. The mist was too thick for him to see the water below, or the mountains across the water, or the peak of their own mountain.

There was no snow on the ground for the last mile down to the landing and the dock there. The tree boxes lay stacked in a pile by the dock. The checkers' red pickup was parked by a ramshackle cabin in which the two of them had taken up very temporary residence – a thin wisp of smoke rose from the chimney. Vern backed the truck to the pile of boxes and Rick or Dick approached him with a clipboard and told him to sign for receipt of the trees. Alex ached from the day before, and it hurt to pick up the boxes; their length taxed his entire reach and they were heavy. The cardboard was wet, and the hand slots on the ends had a tendency to tear from his grasp when he lifted. It seemed like a long time before the entire stack had been transferred from the ground to the bed of the truck.

Vern and Ray stood and contemplated it.

"Think we'll make it?" wondered Vern.

"Oh yea," said Ray.

Vern pulled the little wooden pipe out of his pocket and scraped hashish into it with his fingernail. They passed it around, huddled against the side of the truck away from the checker's cabin. The hash hit Alex like a hammer. It made him more aware that his feet were wet and cold, but also seemed to numb his aching joints a little, and he pondered the wet gravel at his feet with infinite appreciation as he began the long walk back to camp. The truck started up the hill well enough, and Alex was hardly noticing it until he heard a thunk as of tire hitting pothole and looked up in time to see it stop and then lurch. The boxes swayed forward, then backward, the straight lines of tension between them gradually bending and increasing in width, this all so slow he felt as though if he could just shout **Stop!** the load would shudder and settle back into place. Instead, Vern gunned the engine, the back tires spewed mud and gravel, caught something, and the mountain of boxes came tumbling down, piece by piece, at Alex's feet.

Vern climbed in great amusement from the truck. "How do you like that?" he chortled. "We got further than this yesterday. We should have tied them down."

Rick and Dick were coming up the hill. "What happened?" they wanted to know.

"You and your regulations," said Ray. "See, if we could use your truck, none of this would happen."

The checkers contemplated the situation. "Separate out the broken boxes," they finally told Vern. "And this time tie them down."

There was nothing to do but start over, and a new set of problems had created itself. The truck was parked on a steep vertical and although it was not terribly difficult to layer the bed one, and then two, deep with boxes, at the third layer gravitational forces exerted themselves, and the boxes having been in some cases bent out of shape by their fall, things just generally had a tendency to tumble back down the hill. Ray and Vern gradually became aware of this and they discussed the situation over more hashish. Apparently, the only solution at which they could arrive was to pile as many boxes as would stay there back onto the truck and then to take that load down the hill. The rest had to be carried by hand. There was some complaining about this since the boxes weighed a great deal, and it was at least a quarter mile back to the landing. But, as Ray was quick to point out, it was down the hill all the way, and besides they weren't working for . . . Most of the boxes on the truck made it safely to the landing and, although it took a while to carry the remainder, sometime around mid-afternoon all those that had not broken open were piled on the bed and roped in place. This accomplishment was celebrated with some hashish. Rick and Dick drove their pickup slowly up the mountain and the crew tagged along behind, throwing the broken boxes and trees that had been in them into its bed. Ray and Vern, Stoner, and the two young men started back down to the nine-ton. Alex jumped into the back of the pickup truck for the ride up to camp. As the pickup disappeared around a switchback, Vern shouted something he couldn't hear.

The first thing Alex noticed when he arrived at the camp was that the snow had pretty much melted. The second was that a small frame for a cookshack had arisen where the tents had all been pitched. The third was that Catherine was deeply disgusted. "What took you so long?" she wanted to know. "And where's everyone else?" Alex began to explain about the trees falling off the truck. "I don't even want to hear about it," she stopped him.

Dick, or was it Rick, approached. "We have to take these trees up to the site and someone has to heel them in," said the checker. "Can you come with us?"

"Sure," said Alex. "Coming along?" he asked Catherine.

"I may as well do something useful," she agreed.

Again he attempted to tell her about the trees falling off the truck and she still did not want to hear about it at all. She did want to tell him about building the cookshack, though. She and French Pierre, who was not French at all, but Dutch ("They think anyone who doesn't speak Canajun is French," she explained), and Nick could have used some help. The other two women were no use, although they had sorted out all the cooking gear and food. "It looked pretty small," said Alex.

"Well, there's only ten of us," she pointed out.

"Eleven, I think," Alex corrected her.

She counted. Herself and French Pierre and Nick, the two women, the two young men, Stoner and Vern and Ray made ten. "And me," Alex reminded her. "Oh," she said, "I guess you're right."

The truck climbed steadily higher into the mist. The top of the mountain was still covered, invisible, seemingly no closer for their climbing. More snow appeared on the ground and the fog thickened and finally adhered to their sweaters in droplets. The truck cleared a steep grade, turned a switchback, and entered a precipitous deforested mountain valley. "This has to be it," said Alex. "Look at that slope."

"It doesn't look too bad," decided Catherine.

The pickup followed an only slightly graded road along

the side of the mountain, turned down into a valley, crossed a bridge over the river, and headed for the north face. It climbed a few hundred yards, cleared a crest, and stopped on a flat open patch of gravel. The mountain loomed massive above them, still revealing no trace of its actual height in the cloud.

Alex and Catherine jumped down from the back of the pickup. "We have a problem," said Dick, or was it Rick? "Or rather, you have a problem. All those loose trees . . . Well, we have two different varieties, a spruce and Douglas fir. Rick and I can separate them out, but you have to heel them in in separate places, and keep them straight. One goes above this road, and the other goes below. Can you keep that straight?"

It was a legitimate question, Alex agreed. Catherine was quick to point out that none of it was her fault. She would know enough to tie down the trees, especially after watching the house fall off the day before.

"It may not be your fault, but it's going to be your problem," the checker told them firmly. "We can fine the contract for what happened today. Abuse of the trees, eh? We won't, because I don't think any real harm was done, but we have to issue a warning. Next time, we'll be required to fine you."

"Listen," said Alex, "I can keep two piles of trees straight, but I can't speak for everyone else."

Rick and Dick seemed to understand what he was driving at. "Don't you see," said one of them, "that everyone has to keep it straight?" He did not mention fines again. "This has all been carefully planned." The two checkers began sorting the loose bundles of trees into two groups. Catherine and Alex layered them neatly, bundle atop bundle, against the banks on either side of the road. They covered the roots with dirt and packed it firmly, she the spruce below the road, and he the Douglas fir above it. Dick and Rick left in the pickup after they finished sorting. "What do we do when we're done?" Alex asked Catherine. "Why don't we worry about that when we're done?" she returned.

They were done soon enough. "Did you count the bundles?" she asked him. "I did actually," he told her. "We should remember in case it matters."

"Now what?" Catherine wondered. "Do you think they'll try to get the rest of the trees up here yet today?"

"And what if they can't? The truck couldn't make it yesterday."

"Vern said something about mud chains."

"Well, there's no point standing around here," Alex suggested.

"There's also no point walking four miles if we're just coming back up."

"There's really no point standing around in the rain," Alex maintained. The cloud seemed to have crept further down the mountain again, and the mist had turned to drizzle. It was hard to tell whether the gathering darkness signified dusk or more rainfall.

"Well I'm staying here," she decided.

"Jesus, Cathy, we could be here all night. My feet are cold. I have to keep moving."

"So get moving," she told him. There were a lot of things he wanted to say just then, about him, about them, about planting trees. He might even have chosen one finally had she herself not muttered, "Oh, all right," in feigned disinterest, and started moving down the road.

"You know," he suggested as they crossed the bridge and headed up the hill toward the main road, "we don't have to stay on this contract. There must be some boat traffic up and down the Arm. You could probably get a job cooking for Frans. I know I can't go back to work for him, but I could catch on somewhere. We don't have to be on the same contract."

She turned sharply to face him. "Goddammit Alex! Do you have to quit everything you do? I've got a commitment here and so do you. I intend to stick to mine." She wheeled and stalked away, surprising him with her speed.

They walked most of the four miles in stiff silence that was finally broken with the by then familiar sound of tires grinding against gravel road. When Vern saw them come over the hill he made a violent motion at the ignition key and jammed on the emergency brake with a force that shook both the truck and its load. He stormed out of the cab toward them. "Where have you been?" he fairly screamed at Alex. "You can't just be wandering all over this mountain whenever you please. We're all in this together, one for all and all for one, and you keep disrupting our group harmony."

"Yea, listen here," Ray joined in, jumping up and down from one foot to another. "How'd you like to be working for MacMillan Blowjob and have to punch a timeclock and work for some asshole?"

Alex stopped for a moment and scratched his head. He turned and looked back up the road for the mountain, hardly visible at all now in the falling darkness. Not far below, the cookshack frame was nearly half-covered with plastic and a stovepipe spewed smoke graced by an occasional flurry of orange sparks into the grey night. It was a welcome sight. "Is there any supper?" he asked quietly, and walked past them toward the camp.

"Alex!" Catherine's shout cut the thick air like a steam whistle. "You come back here and talk to Ray and Vern." Wearily, he turned and leaned against the truck, and waited for them to approach him. "We needed you down here to work on the cookshack," Vern told him.

"I was heeling in the trees that fell off your truck," said Alex.

"What's this your?" Vern challenged him. "I thought I told you we were all in this together."

"All for one, one for all," agreed Ray.

"Did the bozos talk to you?" Alex asked them.

"The what?" cried Vern and Ray in unison.

"You know, Dick and Rick, the checkers," said Alex.

"What did you call them?" demanded Vern.

"Bozos. That's what we always call them."

"Well I don't know about that," said Vern.

"Did they talk to you?"

"Who?"

"Dick and Rick, the checkers."

"No, they waved as they went by. They said they'd talk to me in the morning."

Alex began to explain about the spruce and the Douglas fir. "What a couple of Noofs," said Vern.

"Everybody knows the difference between spruce and Douglas fir," said Ray.

"Well anyway," said Alex, "I know how many of both are up there."

Vern looked at him blankly. "Well don't be going off by yourself like that," he insisted.

"But they told me to," Alex answered foolishly. He resumed his way toward the cookshack and, before entering, stopped and shouted back at them over his shoulder: "Shouldn't you try your chains if we're ever going to get up that hill?" Ray was saying something to Catherine about all for one in a fairly loud voice.

"Well, you sure had a fine day," she told him later when they were alone in the tent. "Look, I told them that you were just hungry and tired, but, really, you should be more cooperative."

"I suppose," he said. "Shall we zip these bags together?"
"Not tonight," she said. "I'm tired."

The next day saw no sunlight, but did at least find some definition of dry land as the snow melted off, and Alex had a chance to plant a few trees. On the one hand, there was some consolation in that, since it was what he had come to do in the first place. On the other, it did not happen immediately, or conveniently, and certainly not easily. First of all there was the matter of getting the trees up to the site and that took all morning. Right after breakfast – and it had been good for everyone's spirits to have a breakfast, even if it was only porridge and raisins – Ray and Vern jumped into the truck, backed it to the bridge at the beginning of the clearing and roared through the camp at the mountain. The two young men shouted in unison and followed running up the hill, their long slender legs flailing at the gravel almost as though they were a single pair. The truck ground to a halt perhaps a hundred yards further along than it had progressed the night before, and still a full hundred yards short of the first crest. The two young men reached it there as its tires spun in the mud and hit it like football players, as though they would shove it the rest of the way themselves. Instead, Vern chose that very moment to throw into reverse, and they bounced off hard. Fortunately, they kept their footing and careened outside the truck's path or they would have been crushed by the wheels. They jumped up and down and howled with glee.

Vern finally remembered his chains. It took nearly an hour to find them in the piles of gear spread around the cookshack, partly because the two chains were in two separate piles. When he and Ray got them on the tires, the truck rumbled up the hill and over the crest with little difficulty. A spontaneous cheer rose from the people watching by the cookshack, and there was a mad scramble for hoedads and tree bags as the crew scrambled up the mountain after the truck. With some momentum finally going, Vern never did stop driving, so the rest hiked all the way. The four miles were, of course, a much longer walk uphill than down, and Alex and Catherine were the last to reach the site. As they started down to the bridge over the river, they could see Vern and Ray and the two young men unloading the boxes. Heading uphill from the bridge were Stoner, Nick, and French Pierre. "I wonder," said Alex, "If Vern and Ray remembered their bags and hoedads."

"Someone should have thought of that," said Catherine. "Why didn't you?"

"Did you keep the spruce and Douglas fir separate?" Alex asked when he reached the truck.

"Listen to this!" Vern hooted from the bed. "Last one here and he's telling us how to unload."

"Let's take care of these," said Ray. He dragged one of the boxes across the road to the place where Catherine had heeled in loose bundles the night before. "Arty, Jerry," he called to the two young men. "One of you guys feed me." They both jumped over the road and started throwing bundles at him. "No, no, not at me," cried Ray. "Hit the dirt here." They threw the trees into layered rows with extraordinary accuracy. "Are those spruce?" Alex called to him. "Cathy heeled spruce in there last night. They go on different sides of the road."

"And these are spruce?" marveled Ray, pointing at his feet. "Hey, these aren't spruce. Who told you these were spruce?"

"The bozos did," said Alex.

"What?" Vern jumped down from the bed. "What did you call them?"

"Bozos," Alex repeated.

"Listen here," Vern told him angrily, "I'm not into calling them bozos. What's a bozo? A bozo's a clown. Listen, we can't be calling our checkers clowns."

"So I won't say it around them," conceded Alex.

"Don't be saying it anywhere," cried Vern. "You might slip. Bozos! A bozo's a clown with big floppy ears! Bozos! Listen, you call them Sir!"

Alex threw up his hands. "OK," he agreed, and walked over to where Ray was still heeling in trees. "Ray," he said, "these are Douglas fir in this box."

"What do you mean?" Ray jumped down from the bank. "You think I don't know Douglas fir from spruce? Do you know how long I've been planting trees? For years! I've been planting trees for seven years and you're trying to tell me Douglas fir from spruce. How long have you been planting trees, just tell me that, how long have you been planting trees?" He waved his hoedad in Alex's face and awaited his answer.

Alex's calmness, his virtual passivity, amazed him. "Ray," he sighed. "It says Douglas fir on the box."

"Where?" Ray spit out the word. He leapt at the box and read the side panel. "No!" he protested, and Alex ducked as the little man swung the hoedad at the box like an axe, splitting it wide open, sending trees tumbling out onto the road.

"Look at this!" Vern stormed at Alex. "Is all you do is make trouble? Is that all you do?"

Alex's sense of calm struck him as all but preternatural. He spoke quietly, deliberately measuring his words. "The . . . that is Rick and Dick told us last night here that if we screwed up any more with the trees the contract would be fined." He gestured to his right, where the two young men stood on the bank below the road, where Ray had been working. "They told us those were spruce. Those, on the other side, are Douglas fir. The box here says Douglas fir. We have to keep them separate. We're not making enough money to get fined."

"You can say that again," said Vern.

Alex took a bundle from the far end of the layered stacks. After glancing to make sure that he was out of Ray's range, he compared it with a bundle from the box labeled Douglas fir. "The Douglas fir," he told Vern, "are a year older. You can see the difference in size."

Ray and Vern stood side by side looking at him. "So the spruce are on one side and the Douglas fir are on the other?" realized Vern. "Well what's so tricky about that? Why don't you pull out all the spruce that Ray heeled in and put them where they belong?" Without correcting them, Alex did what was necessary. "Can't tell Douglas fir from spruce," Ray muttered to Vern as he walked away.

It was early afternoon by the time they finished heeling in the trees. Mounds of wet snow still clung to the rocks and fallen logs on the slope. The air hung dead and heavy over them, promising a drizzle that was not quite happening yet. But there was a problem. Ray and Vern had not remembered their own hoedads and bags. On the face of it, it seemed only to mean that they would be the ones not to plant, but the issue was apparently not that simple.

"Maybe Catherine and someone else should skip it today if no one else minds," suggested Vern.

Alex watched Catherine's jaw tighten. "Catherine's a very good planter," he said. "And she remembered her equipment."

Vern and Ray trained significant stares upon him. "Well, uh . . ." said Vern. A little grin crossed Ray's face. "She is, huh? Well, well."

"Look," said Vern. "I just think we should all be working together out here. We're all in this together."

"But we don't have the tools to all work together today," said Alex. "And I'd like to get the feel of the land. At least get a few in, you know."

"Well if you don't mind some of us not working while you do . . ." said Vern.

Alex looked at him blankly, meaning to say "Why should I mind such a thing?" but having talked a great deal, and not seen all of it responded to pleasantly, forbore. "OK," said Vern. "I've got things to do in camp. We can make this an optional. Who's coming with?" The two young men jumped into the truck.

So Alex finally got to plant a few trees. There was some consolation in this since it was what he had come to do in the first place. On the other hand, it did not happen easily. There was the matter of Ray's leadership. "Everyone take two hundred trees," Ray shouted. "Get in line eight feet apart. Everyone follow me." Alex made it a point to get as far from Ray's end as possible. Only Catherine was further away, on his own right side. They climbed the bank and Ray jitterbugged into the muddy slash. Alex felt a little charge, something like before a big ball game. He always felt like that before a contract's first trees. He hit the mountain with the hoedad and it cleft the muddy soil with a thwack. "Good ground," he called happily to Catherine and she grunted in agreement over her own first tree. Alex kicked his tight and strode forward, but noticed that Nick was still struggling, clawing at the soil with the hoedad. He had a tree by its roots in his fist and seemed to be trying to scrape soil over it. "Have you ever planted before?" Alex paused to ask him. Nick shook his head no. So Alex and Catherine gave him a quick lesson. "Thanks," said Nick when they were through, and nailed the perfectest straight little Douglas fir into the mountainside. "Eight foot spacing," Alex reminded him. "We'll be going faster than you, so we'll get ahead, but we'll keep the line straight. Just follow it up and plant eight feet from each tree in our line." He and Catherine shifted left, leaving Nick on the end. "Try and keep them obvious," Alex called back. "Someone else will have to follow them down." He and Catherine planted slowly two or three more times in order to watch Nick, and then Alex took off with her right behind. Pierre's line was a little ragged, but Alex could follow it without much difficulty. The slope was fairly steep, although it looked like one of the flatter on the site. The burnoff was recent and clean, and the wet clay was covered with a layer of sand. All in all, it was the best ground he'd seen in a year. A drizzle had begun to fall, but not hard enough to demand rain gear, which was down at the shack anyway. Alex felt familiar rhythms surging back. He was swinging the hoedad with a snap. Halfway up the mountain, he overtook Pierre. "Coming through," he called, and stepped in front of the other man to continue. Pierre shifted into Alex's line, and a moment later Catherine passed him too. Stoner's trees were a little more erratic than Pierre's, but he was only three or four ahead, and Alex followed him by sight. He caught up and called out to him: "Coming through."

As Alex came up from planting Stoner nearly ran him down. "What are you doing in my line?" Stoner asked quietly. "I passed you," explained Alex, and started back up the mountain. "Passed me?" Stoner inquired in bewilderment.

Ray turned and saw them. He stopped planting, and advanced. "What's going on here?" he demanded to know. By then Alex knew what was coming and that it couldn't possibly work out right, but he tried anyway. "I passed Stoner," he said. "I was planting faster than he was."

"Passed him? Passed him?" cried Ray. "What do you want to do that for? Can't you do anything simple? Listen here, we're not working for MacMillan Blowjob."

"No one ever passed at MB," Stoner reflected quietly. "But it's not a bad idea. Why shouldn't we pass if we're going faster?"

It looked for a moment as though Ray might burst a capillary. His thin face flushed red at purple, his eyes bugged, his words came sputtered and spit. "Don't get fancy on us!" he hissed at Alex. "Do as you're told! Here we are standing around on more downtime when we could be planting the trees. Now follow me, hear?" Alex and Stoner looked at one another as Ray started back up to his bag. Stoner gestured, before me, to Alex. Catherine and Stoner exchanged words that Alex did not hear. Alex picked up his bag and began to follow Ray's line, which was hardly a line at all. The only reason he could make any sense of it was that they were planting virgin slash. Ray's trees were the only ones on the mountain. Unfortunately, they were spaced a bare three feet apart. Alex watched the strange little man and his frantic speed. On the surface, at least, Ray's trees were workmanlike, adequate. If not elegantly planted, they were more or less straight, with no bare roots showing. He never screefed, but the soil was good, and there was no real need for it. The problem was that he planted one, hopped left and ahead, planted wherever he landed in that stride, then hopped right and ahead and planted again, and in that fashion zigzagged up the hill leaving a weird trail of seedlings spaced far too closely together. "Ray," Alex called ahead, but Ray either did not hear, or ignored him. Alex called once more to no response. He planted hard until he caught up, which was not difficult, because Ray planted on every stride, and Alex on every other. He had to shout from three feet away to get the little man's attention, though. "Your trees are too tight," he told Ray when he finally had it. "They are not!" cried Ray. Alex thought for a moment, corrected his words,

and returned, "You're planting them too close together!"
Ray just looked away, and kept planting. Alex slowed and
waited for Catherine. "See that?" He pointed to the zigzag
trail. "If they take any plots through there . . ." She looked at
him intently. "Haven't you had enough arguing for one day,
Alex? Maybe some people have to figure things out for themselves."

"But," he protested, "these guys don't figure things out."

"Maybe that's not your problem," she answered grimly.
"Let's get moving."

They planted until their bags were empty. Ray had long
since finished and disappeared. Nick was still going up as
they passed him coming down. "How's it going?" Alex asked
him.

"I'm tired," answered Nick. "How many you got left?"
asked Alex. "A bundle," said Nick.

"Heel them in and come with us," Alex told him. "It's
getting late. Today was just a warmup anyway."

As they walked back, Alex talked treeplanting with
Nick. The talk may have been the thing he liked best about
the work. Comparing notes on terrain, weather, and wildlife
encountered in different parts of the province. The planters'
yearly odyssey from coast to the interior, to Prince George
and points beyond. The strategic varieties of footgear,
raingear, headgear, even the different sorts of gloves (he
preferred leather, although it wore out fast in the rain), the
different kinds of hoedad (the whip or baseball bat handle, it
all depended on terrain), and that was the thing, that everything depended on something else, and this expressed in
the infinite variety of conditions and situations that always
surrounded the same basic form of cookshack and logging
slash and waxy brown boxes with Trees for Tomorrow, Keep
Cool stamped in green ink on their sides. It was really, this

afternoon, his first chance to talk about it in a while, and Nick was full of questions. Catherine kept very quiet, but for Alex the four miles back to camp flew by quickly. He was happy, and had forgotten every hassle by the time they got there.

Vern and Ray were smoking hashish with the two young men in the cookshack. Vern stood up with what was either a hitch in his gait or a swagger. "So," he said with a smile, looking at Alex, "I hear we had some controversy out on the slopes today."

Alex's body stiffened as though it had been doing so for years. "We have to get some things straight," Vern continued. "First of all, whose contract do you think this is?"

"Yours," Alex admitted.

"Wrong," Vern told him. "It's ours. All of ours. All for one and one for all. So we can't have everyone fighting all the time. And I'm in charge. And Ray's in charge of planting. Any questions?"

"But it makes sense to pass on the line," Alex maintained. "Otherwise it only moves as fast as the slowest person on it."

Vern looked at him incredulously. "What are you talking about? Passing? Listen, here we are having a perfectly good conversation and you start talking about passing!"

"But . . ." Alex attempted, shaking his head, and then Catherine grabbed him by the arm and dragged him outside. She stood with her hands on her hips and ordered him, "Stop arguing with those guys, Alex. I can't take any more of it." Then she went to the tent. Alex looked up the road at the mountain, but it was still covered with cloud.

In the tent that night she was in a somewhat better mood. They had, after all, finally had some supper, and one could now sit, if not totally comfortably, on log rounds near the airtite stove, and she had even been able to read for a while.

"Well I talked to Virginia and found out what Ray's problem is," she confided.

"What's that?" asked Alex.

"He's totally burned out on planting trees."

"He's burned out on something," Alex agreed. "I mean, hashish for breakfast?"

"That's pretty funny coming from an old pothead like you," she nailed him.

The next day, thanks to the sun finally mercifully appearing in the eastern sky – a great orange circle on a bed of blue – Alex got to see the mountain. It was sort of a disappointment, really. What he had been expecting he couldn't quite say, but it was such an ordinary mountain. After breakfast, with a cup of coffee in one hand and a cigarette in the other, he sat outside the shack in one of the folding chairs that Vern had brought in his house and stared up to the first crest and past that to the next ridge. The two sides of the valley rose in series of ridges with crests running like spread legs toward each other, converging at the mountain. Yet, it was quite an ordinary mountain, not even snow-capped, although there was plenty of snow on it just then, as well as on the V-shaped converging crests. But not peak snow, not like towering mountain majesties, not even like peaks he saw from the city, which were part of the park, which lay somewhere to the east of this, his mountain. He had somehow expected it to have a face.

Just to remind him that there were no unmixed blessings, even on the day that both sun and mountain chose to reveal themselves, Ray came walking out of the cookshack to talk to him. It was quite literally the first time that had happened, that Ray had tried to talk to him, and it turned out not to be bad. "Vern and I were thinking," said Ray. "We thought there would be more harmony if we worked in two crews in different areas. Why don't you and Catherine take

Frenchy and Nick and work beneath the road?"

"That's a good idea," agreed Alex, and felt guilty to be examining the suggestion for an angle. The terrain below the road was steeper than that above, and plunged to a narrow strip of timber at the bank of the river, but the ground had to be roughly the same as above, and at least he would be able to plant in his own style. "That's a very good idea," he concluded, and smiled.

He described their conversation to Catherine on the back of the truck as they headed up the mountain. She even smiled. "Good," she said, nodding. Then the truck ground to a halt and spun its wheels. "We haven't got enough weight back here," realized Nick. The two young men jumped down and tried to push, but it did no good. French Pierre pounded vigorously on the cab window to make sure Vern knew they were back there. Ray jumped out and squatted next to the rear wheels, shaking his head. "We need more weight," Nick told him. Vern and Ray stood in the road and lit a pipe. Alex felt a dull ache in his stomach. More than anything else he wanted to plant trees, even for only seven cents a tree. The word downtime kept echoing in his mind and he tried to force it back. He looked at Catherine, her white freckled face inscrutable, there might have been ice in her veins, and yet it felt as though heat were flowing from her rigidly composed silent body. What were they going to do?

Ray and Vern had an idea. Why not pile rocks on the truck bed? So they did that, despoiling the road's shoulder of every boulder of a size to be lifted four feet and carried ten, until there was a rock pile, pyramid fashion, over the rear axle. It took time, and more than that, energy. Alex found his legs and arms aching hard – much too hard for beginning a day's planting – when he finally pulled himself up onto the bed. He stood back against the truck's cab, out of the way of falling rocks, which rattled and bounced down off the pyramid into the road as Vern spun the chained tires hard in first gear and the truck heaved and coughed and the chains caught, and they resumed their weary, creeping progress upward. Alex turned around and leaned over the cab, watching the mountain approach, slowly.

Tired as he was, it was a good day to plant trees. The sun was by then several degrees overhead, past the mountain, and the sky's blue so high, so lucid, that its only texture was one of pure color, rarified blueness that intensified the greens and whites around him. He felt that mountainous sensation, as though he were so large he could embrace the whole thing, reach out an arm in either direction, grab a handful of hillside and pull the valley to him. He wanted to sing, he wanted to dance, he was ready to plant trees.

Catherine led the way down. She was getting further and further away from him, but he thought he could tell by her motions that even she would enjoy this today and he loved the way she planted when she was right – short compact motions not so much graceful as controlled and careful. How easy it was to forget just looking at her standing or sitting or trying to be girlish how tough she could be. The ground, starting to dry on the surface, was soft and clinging beneath. French Pierre followed her, gangly, unconcernedly awkward, tree for tree, his two steps to her three. In the perfect yielding soil the trees went in straight and stood that way, roots extended full length, already grabbing at the earth as Alex kicked tight. He allowed himself to fall behind, planting a double line and keeping an eye on Nick who, although struggling a beginner's struggle, was still fundamentally sound, was just being careful to do it right. "You don't mind advice?" asked Alex. "No! I want it," said Nick. They planted, talking, down to the river, where Catherine and Pierre were leaning against boulders, waiting. Nick offered Alex a cigarette that he waved away. "We're about set to head back up," said Catherine. "We'll be coming soon," said Alex. "Now I'll have one," he told Nick as Catherine began planting again. "I'm supposed to have quit," he confided.

Alex had planted four hundred trees when they stopped for lunch, Catherine three, Frenchy three-fifty, Nick two-fifty. "Not bad for a late start," he decided. "Nick's doing good," he told Catherine. "We'll all be planting a thousand in no time. That's seventy bucks."

"Oh," wondered Nick. "You mean we get paid by the tree?"

"Yes," said Alex. "Didn't Vern explain that?"

"He was rather vague," said Nick. "He said we'd all make about a thousand dollars."

Alex squinted into the sun and glanced over to Catherine. She continued to look at the mountainside, expressionless.

"What did he tell you?" he asked Pierre.

"He was vague wit' me too. He said 'bout seven cent a tree," Pierre told him.

"About?" asked Alex.

"Ja, I t'ink so. 'Bout seven cent."

They all planted more slowly in the afternoon. Alex's two weeks of loafing around Vancouver waiting for a contract were showing a bit as the day wore on and he noticed a few familiar old aches and pains. The four of them had returned back to the road, each trying to decide how many more to take for a last run, when Pierre said something that sounded like, "I t'ink I get a hate up," and Alex burst out laughing. "Yes!" he cried. "Hate will motivate you if nothing else does."

"He said eight hundred," Catherine corrected him.

"Oh," said Alex. Their break dragged on as no one made the

first move to stand up and get more trees from the bank.

And no one had when Ray approached and stood over Alex. "Well they checked our plots from yesterday," said the little man. "How were they?" asked Alex. "Too many trees," said Ray. "Way too many trees."

"Well look, Ray. I told you you were planting them too close together."

"This took more than one person," said Vern, arriving on the scene.

"Not if one person was planting them three feet apart," Alex shot back. "And they took the plots right through his line. Shit. I wouldn't be surprised if there were twice too many."

"It's not that bad," said Vern. "And anyway, since it was our first day they're giving us a break." He turned away.

"Great," said Alex. "That's right of them."

"Right," said Ray. "So we thought you and Catherine could go back in there and straighten it out."

"Whaaat?" cried Alex.

"Well, I mean, you're two of our better planters and you seem to know what the Forestry wants and . . ."

"Whaaat?" cried Alex. "We're not the ones who messed it up!"

"What?" marveled Vern.

"Ray . . . Ray was planting three feet apart through here . . ." Alex sputtered. "I saw it! I told him, he ignored me. Now I'm supposed to clean it up for him? I can't believe it . . ."

"Well!" shouted Vern. "We're all in this together!" He threw down his hoedad in disgust. "The contract gets fined, we all lose money, right?"

"Yes," Alex cried back at them, "but that's why we have to make sure we all plant well, so this kind of stuff doesn't happen, but does anyone listen to anyone else, no, you just wander around stoned planting wherever you want and then ask the only people who aren't so fucked up that they can't tell eight feet from three to straighten it out . . ."

"Listen," Ray informed him. "I've planted trees for nine years and everybody knows you plant better when you're high."

"Do I get paid for correcting your trees?" demanded Alex.

"Do I get paid for supervising planting?" Ray shot back. "Does Vern get paid for driving the truck up the hill? Did Frenchy and Nick get paid for building a cookshack? Does anybody get paid for picking up tree boxes when they fall off, or for loading rocks on the truck?" He gestured at the nine-ton with his hoedad. "Or for heeling in the trees?" He gestured at the bank. "And do we do it for love? No, we do it because we have to! We get paid for planting trees but we have to do all that so we can plant trees, but we don't get paid for it, it's downtime!"

"Yes, but I could be planting trees, right now, making money, finally," Alex protested.

"What!" Vern challenged him. "What's this about making money? How many times do I have to tell you, we're all in this together?"

"But what do you mean by that?"

"What do I mean by it? What do I mean by it? Don't you understand English? I mean we're all in this together!"

Nick stood up slowly. "Look," he said, "we were all in there yesterday. Why don't we all go through it again?"

Vern looked at Alex in anger. "There! See what I mean? Nick knows that we're all in this together. Why didn't you suggest that? But no, instead you have to argue about whose fault it is. You were all in there together, I wasn't, but see, I'm even willing to go in and help out because I know we're all in this together. Come on, let's do it."

All French Pierre said was "Shit."

Nick looked at Alex. "Coming?"

Alex looked at Catherine. "I guess we were all in there together," she said.

"Fuckshit," muttered Alex, but he went along.

When they got back to the tiny cookshack, Alex contemplated his growing isolation. He knew that he ought to be developing some sort of rapport, if not intimacy, with these people. But, except for Nick, quite the opposite thing was happening, he was getting further and further away from them, which was the wrong direction. But none of the normal forms and rhythms seemed to apply. He needed the cookshack to be the place where he sought and found comfort and companionship. This first full planting day ought to leave him hurting and happy, but instead he was walking on tiptoe trying literally not to bump into Vern or Ray. The two young men sat together on the old battered sofa, which had apparently come up in the house and found its way into the shack, and there was space there for a third person, but every time they looked in Alex's direction one would whisper something to the other and they would start laughing. Alex took his plate of rice and vegetables and doused it with tamari. Ray was pouring a mountain of yellow powder over his. "What is that?" Alex asked him, hesitant in speech, afraid to say a word that might be misconstrued. "Yeast," said Ray. "It's good for your brains." Alex nodded in agreement.

Fortunately, the food was quite good, as one might expect it to be with two cooks for a dozen people. There Vern's notions were fairly advanced, although Alex wasn't sure how he was working out the economics of the thing. He smiled at Cookie and complimented her, and she smiled back although she didn't say much. Virginia seemed less friendly, but she, of course, was hearing about it all from Vern. Alex sat on a log in the corner, and ate in silence. Catherine sat down next to the two young men and talked to Virginia, standing nearby, about cooking rice. After they finished eating, the two young men began rolling joints and passing them around. Alex got up with his plate and took it down to the river to wash. The water was numbing cold and he reflected that sooner or later he would have to bathe in it. Up the valley, the mountain caught the last sun from across the arm behind the western range and glowed in a startled pink. A blush? Sunburn? Afterglow? Alex watched it for a long time, until it began to turn grey.

In his absence, the cookshack atmosphere seemed to have lightened. Snatches of at least three different conversations greeted him. Catherine and the two young men were talking about a movie; Vern, Cookie, and Stoner about a band they'd heard on the Island; Ray and Virginia about tofu. Nick was reading a book in a corner and Alex asked him for a cigarette. They smoked together and began talking about planting trees. "We refer to it as the anarchy system," Alex explained, "but, in fact, there's nothing anarchic about it, except that everyone does what they please. See, if I learn to recognize your trees, and you mine, we can plant curlicues up and down the mountain as long as we fill the space. Straight lines aren't really relevant either because mountains aren't composed of straight lines, everything is curves and angles. A good planter plants differently every day because, well, because every day is different, in every conceivable way. First contract I was on, there was this guy who was the star planter and I asked how many rows he planted at a time. And he said 'rows?' Then he said 'two, four, ten, fourteen, it's all numbers.'"

"What are you guys talking about?" Vern wanted to know.

"Planting trees," said Alex.

"Well cut it out!"

"Pardon me," marveled Alex.

"Cut it out. No talking trees in the cookshack."

"What?" Alex couldn't believe it.

"The slopes are for trees," Vern told him. "This is home. We don't bring it home."

"No," protested Alex, "I'm a treeplanter, I have to talk about it! How can we not talk about it?"

Vern regarded him with lips pursed in a grimace. He spoke slowly and forcefully. "Everyone was talking just fine until you came in here."

Vern was bigger than Alex. That was one reason not to hit him. Another was that there were people crowded everywhere. A fight would knock over their tea, pitch someone against the airtite stove, could conceivably tear down the cookshack if it got rough enough. No one would take Alex's side if he did strike out at Vern. He was afraid, he realized, not only of a pounding, but of the destruction hitting Vern would involve, the self-destruction. If he did let go he might explode into a million pieces and float away in the mountain night. Instead, he reached fumbling for another of Nick's cigarettes, and stood, measuring each action and monitoring each nerve in his body, reached for a match, lit it deliberately by placing it against the hot body of the airtite stove, watched it flare, moved it toward his face, inhaled deeply and waited for more of something or other, not forthcoming.

"I thought you quit smoking," said Catherine in their tent.

"Jesus, Cathy! It's not as if I don't have a reason to smoke."

"Well, it's weakness to use tobacco to cope with your problems."

"I'm sure it is," he admitted. "But that's no reason not to."

"Has it occurred to you that you create your own problems?" she challenged him. "Vern was right, you know.

Everyone was talking just fine until you came in there. When you left it was like the sun had come out, and then you came back in and there was an argument."

Alex lay disconsolate in his sleeping bag. What she was saying was absolutely undeniable. She continued with her remorseless logic. "I'll grant you that they could be better organized. But treeplanting is always kind of crazy and disorganized. You're just used to a different set of crazinesses. You think Frans and his macho let's-go-plant-three-thousand-trees-today trip isn't crazy? You think a crew where even the women are macho isn't crazy?"

"I don't particularly care for Frans' contracts either," he reminded her.

"Well see, that's your problem, you aren't happy anywhere," she told him flatly.

"Yes, but not being able to talk about planting?"

"So you like to talk about planting. And Vern doesn't want to hear about it. It's just a case of different mores," she informed him. "Since when do you have to talk about trees? Frankly, I get sick of hearing treeplanters talk about planting as though it was the most important thing in the world."

"Yes," protested Alex, "but while you're doing it, it's the only thing in the world."

"I don't think that's true at all," she disagreed. "It's just another job."

They lay side by side in silence. The running river, only a few feet away, reached out with fingers of sound and gradually soothed him. "Did Vern take totals while I was outside?" he finally asked her.

"No," she said. "I guess we better remind him of that tomorrow night."

He awoke the next morning to the sound of rain drilling the tent. Rain always sounded harder than it actually was against the light fly, but for whatever reasons this seemed even heavier than usual. Their rain gear was stashed under plastic held down by rocks outside the tent and Alex got wet just rummaging for it there. Crows circled in the wind and rain over the shack, which he entered to encounter what in other circumstances might have been pleasant odors – wood smoke, frying eggs, dirt and evergreen, hashish. He made coffee in a large open kettle, boiling water on the camp stove, placing the kettle on the airtite, stirring in the coffee, and waiting for the grounds to settle. Then he drank a cup, huddled in a corner of the sofa, tying to avoid the leak in the roof that dropped water in a steady plop plop into a puddle on the ground. Already, little streams were flowing along the cookshack floor, downhill toward the river. One by one, planters straggled in, grimly clutching raingear, loathing in their eyes. Alex was almost relieved by the scene. This, he felt dumbly, could not be blamed on him. Catherine appeared last and barely ate. "This is the part I hate worst," she said. "It's about time for the rock detail," muttered Vern, lighting his pipe.

They loaded the back of the truck again, went up the hill again, filled their bags, went into the slash, everything like the day before, except encumbered by raingear everything slower, more difficult, Alex not wanting to move at all and not daring to stop since the wet was everywhere and the wind chilling. Water ran down his sleeves as he planted, wet sand filled his gloves, mud spattered his face, and his extremities grew soaked and chilled as the rest of his body grew hot under the heavy gear. Eventually, he was thoroughly drenched, and it was impossible to tell whether mostly from rain and mud or from his own sweat. The day passed like a long bad dream with a backache on a bed soaked with fever. Each time it seemed the rain might break, even for a few moments, the wind slammed back up the valley carrying enormous clouds and piling them thicker and thicker against the mountain until finally they rested heavy and solid like a mountain themselves, low over the planting site. Everyone worked seriously and with desperation in their motions. The crows circling over them looked a little distressingly like vultures.

Still, the day ended, almost surprising in its promptness. Alex was coming down the mountain perhaps a dozen or two trees shy of eight hundred, a figure with which he was well pleased, when the nine-ton's horn blew through the valley. Far below, he saw Ray leaning into the cab pounding on the steering column. Ray's crew lay huddled on the bed of the truck, and Vern stood hands on hips looking up toward Alex. Catherine and Pierre had already emptied their bags and Alex could see their figures bobbing in and out of the vagaries of the slashscape, now out of sight behind a boulder, now coming over a ridge, Pierre breaking into a long-legged lope at the sound of the horn, Catherine, her solid body close to the ground, scurrying like a bird on short legs. "Quitting time," Alex called to Nick, who was already barreling toward him waving an empty bag. "I'll be there in a flash," he added as Nick careened past. He planted his last trees feverishly, calling forth a final burst from his tired self. When he had only a half dozen or so left, the nine-ton summoned him again, insisting, relentless, and the horn did not stop blowing until he too was bounding through the slash toward the road. The rain had nearly stopped, and there was a narrow aperture of white light against the last slope of the mountains opposite, across the arm.

Ray's staccato nasal voice took up where the truck's mechanical command had left off. "Everybody's waiting, we want to get going." Vern was already in the cab, revving the engine. "I had a bundle to finish," explained Alex.

"So heel them in for tomorrow." Ray shook his head in exasperation. "We're all supposed to wait here in the rain while you finish the bundle?"

"I don't mind walking back," Alex told him. "Listen," Ray shot back. "We're all in this together. We come up together, we go down together."

On the ride down, Alex counted his money. He'd broken a hundred dollars already, fifty-six of it that day, and now he'd be able to increase it steadily. Soon he'd get to a thousand trees a day and stay there, that was seventy dollars. By the end of the week, he would have enough for his ticket.

"I'm going to take a bath," he told Catherine when the truck arrived at the cookshack. "How about you?"

"It's way too cold," she replied.

With clean camp clothes wrapped in a self-contained bundle under one arm, and towel, soap, wash cloth, and shampoo under the other, Alex contemplated the river. Not far from their tent was an open pool fed by a small stream. There, on a stretch of sandy beach, he laid his bundles down and began to pull dreary, mud-bespattered garment after garment from his body. Finally he stood, naked to the chilly wind, before the pool. He touched the water and, as could be expected from spring meltoff, it was the bare necessary degree warmer than freezing. He reached the washcloth into the water and soaped it. When it was frothing, he applied it to his body, beginning at his face and working downward in pursuit of the black icy rivulets that traced their way across the dirt-mottled goose-dotted pink surface of his flesh. The wind caught the wetness and chilled him. Even after his body was clean there was still the matter of washing his hair. He spread the dirty washcloth on the bank and knelt there, and with a quick decisive motion plunged his head under the water in the pool. The shock to his skull was incredible – a tightening tingling sensation suggesting instant headache – and he pulled back with a gasp and a yip. Shampooing was now an act of significant courage because his head would have to go back under for a rinse, but he summoned such courage, lathered his hair and beard, and scratched at the grit caked to his skull. He took an existential belly flop into the pool, screeched at the breathless cold, tried to stand but found himself so dizzy he fell to all fours. He submerged himself in that position, and grasped the pebbled floor with hands and feet and dunked his head and shook it hard. Clinging to balance he ventured a hand to his skull and massaged in a frenzy. He erupted howling from the pool, and found the beach, and stood there panting for breath. He felt sensational.

An overpowering warmth tingled through every part of his naked self. He lay the towel over a boulder, sat upon it, and lit a cigarette from the pack of Players that Nick had given him. The tobacco whacked at his hungry lungs in one more wonderful shock of bodily recognition. He knew again why he planted trees. Gradually, he grew chilly and so he layered on his camp clothing, the clean, dry, loose-fitting garments exquisite in their contrast to the grimy apparel he had been wearing for, how many? . . . four days now. After finishing the cigarette, he flipped it into the pool. A fish struck it with a sucking sound and a loud thwock of its tail.

"There's fish in the river," he announced to the dirty grim faces in the cookshack. That news was met with a series of resentful grunts and deliberate ignorances. Vern finally spoke. "What's the matter with you? Weren't you wet enough all day? What do we care about fish?" The two young men giggled.

Alex persisted. "What about fish for supper?"

"What fish?" said Vern.

"Supper's already cooking," said Virginia.

Only Cookie seemed the least bit interested. She smiled.

"I go a' fishing," Alex announced.

Catherine was in the tent when he went to his pack for fishing gear. "See, I told you there'd be use for it," he said triumphantly. "Christ, Alex, slow down," she told him.

It is said that for every hour a man spends fishing another is added to his life. Alex contravened this principle by smoking several cigarettes as he sat on the boulder and cast salmon eggs into the pool. There were fish, coastal cutthroat, and they were hungry. He caught six without really even trying. But what there was more than fish was time to think, and Alex used it to assess his situation. That took nearly as much courage as jumping into the pool had, but ended up being nearly as exhilarating. He was more in control of his situation than it might seem, he decided, and as long as he kept planting trees everything would be fine. So what if they were all crazy? For seventy dollars a day he could put up with nearly anything. The layered cloud had blown off the face of the mountain; horizontal shafts of evening light cut through the sky overhead and played in shifting patterns against its face. It was still a fairly ordinary mountain but it seemed to be smiling at him. Alex lit a final cigarette before packing up his fishing gear.

In the cookshack, supper was nearly over, but there was soup and bread left for him.

"Have you taken totals yet?" he asked Vern.

"I'm not into totals," said Vern.

Alex stopped in his tracks, tracks palpable on the muddy floor. Ray sat on a wooden crate hunched over a bowl of soup with a thick film of yeast covering it, and slowly raised his hard thin face to look at Alex. Arty and Jerry stopped giggling on the couch. Stoner stubbed out a cigarette. Alex looked finally to Catherine. She stared back, no surprise in her eyes.

"You're what?" Alex asked without moving.

"I'm not into totals," Vern repeated.

"But," Alex asked him, "how are we going to get paid?"

"He told you," said Ray, "Everybody gets a thousand dollars."

"He didn't tell me that!" protested Alex.

"Yes I did," said Vern.

"You told me seven cents a tree!"

"I said it would work out to about seven cents a tree for the crew." Vern emphasized the word about. "I told you we would all get a thousand dollars."

"And none of you are keeping track of how many trees you plant?" asked Alex, sweeping around the shack with his hand.

"Why should we?" said Ray. "We're all going to get paid the same."

"No one even knows how many trees we've all planted . . . as a whole . . . so far?" Alex was incredulous.

"No, why should we?" answered Vern.

"Did you count the trees before you signed for them down at the dock?"

"Whatever for? What's it to you?"

"What's it to me? The Forestry makes mistakes!"

"Nah," Ray dismissed the idea.

"I can't believe it," Alex continued, moving his feet for the first time. "We don't have any idea where we stand . . ."

"So what's the big deal with all these numbers?"

"Yea," said Ray, "I got so sick of that at MacMillan Blowjob. Always had to get our five hundred in. What a downer."

"But this isn't there!" Alex all but whispered. "The whole point of independent contracting is paying by the tree. People plant harder if they're getting paid by the tree."

Vern turned at him with a gesture of faint menace. "Leave it to you to bring up something like that," he snarled. "We're not good enough for you, are we? It's not enough for you that we're all in this together, that we're working as a group."

"That's not what I meant," Alex attempted, almost pleading for belief. "It's a system. It works."

"Well we do it different," Ray told him.

The ensuing silence was underscored by two sounds – the crackle in the airtite stove and the rush of the river. Alex looked across the shack at Catherine. She was smoking, and staring into a corner.

"Are you going to have enough to pay everyone a thousand dollars each?" Alex finally asked Vern.

"What kind of a question is that?" Vern shot back angrily.

"I'm wondering if you care enough about numbers to have added, subtracted, multiplied, and divided a few before coming up here," Alex told him, a little surprised at the clarity of his own voice. "I worked for someone who never intended to pay me last year. I'm not going to do that again."

"Listen here." Vern pointed a finger at him. "Don't give me any shit about leaving. We need your trees."

Alex pointed back. "Then you better be able to pay me for them."

"We've got enough!" shouted Vern. "We've got three cents a tree left for expenses. We've budgeted that, sixty dollars a day for the cooks . . ."

"What?" A sharp cry sounded from behind the stove. "For the cooks?" It was Virginia. The lantern's white light threw an angry red violet reflection off her face. Her voice echoed out of the shack and down the valley. A soft wind murmured in reply. She asked again. "For the cooks?"

Now it was Vern standing immobile on the muddy floor.

"What?" was all he said.

"You told me sixty dollars each!" she insisted.

"I did not," he breathed softly.

"All along, Vern, I was there when we planned, wasn't I, Ray? All along, you said sixty dollars each for the cooks."

Vern looked at her as though quite astonished. "I said sixty dollars for the cooks." He paused long. "To split."

A tiny, frightened voice from deep in the stove corner, Cookie's, "You told me sixty dollars, Vern."

"You big dumb bastard!" Virginia advanced on him. He hit her hard, across the face, with his open hand.

"See what you've done," Ray told Alex.

"His own wife," Catherine recalled it in the tent. They lay in their bags on their stomachs, looking out into the night, both smoking. "His own wife doesn't know what he's paying."

"Well, now we know what they mean by being in it together," said Alex. "This is no joke."

"Still," said Catherine, after a long pause, "a thousand dollars would be enough."

"But how long will it take?" Alex wondered. "See, we don't even know how many trees we're planting. We could be here all summer."

"Well, the bozos have to keep it moving. We can't take all summer."

"How does that work?" Alex pondered aloud. "Their timetable goes by area, not trees. So how have the plots been? We don't even know that. We don't know anything."

"One thing's sure," she realized. "If everybody gets paid a thousand dollars, you and I aren't getting seven cents a tree."

"What it works out to is Arty and Jerry getting paid for our trees," he said glumly. "No – it's impossible."

"Still," she persisted, "a thousand dollars would be enough."

"If we get it," said Alex. "And isn't there a principle involved? He told me seven cents a tree. There's just no question."

Sleep was long coming and, when it did, was fretted with peculiar and disturbing dreams. The last, and only one he remembered, had him trying to teach Arty and Jerry to plant trees. But all they did was follow him up the mountain pulling out each of his as soon as he had planted it. He would threaten them with his hoedad, and at one point chased them all the way down to the road. Then he was looking back up above him and there they were, planting together, literally together. Arty would put a tree down and Jerry would pound it into the ground like a nail with a hammer. Then, with an exchange of formal bows, they would trade hoedad for tree bag and reverse roles. Alex started up the mountain after them, and then looked at his feet to realize that he was following a line planted a foot apart in a weird zigzag. The trees were also upside down, with their crowns in the soil and the roots sticking into the air. It was raining hard again when he awoke. He left the tent without waking Catherine.

The atmosphere in the cookshack was impossibly thick, despite the conspicuous absence of both Virginia and Cookie. Vern was slicing bread. He growled at Alex, and Alex came right to the point. "You told me seven cents a tree, Vern. You'll have to pay it or we aren't working anymore. We're on our way out otherwise."

Vern scowled at him. "All right," he said. "You two keep track of your trees. I'll settle with you after the contract. I just hope you realize you're costing the rest of these people money. And I don't want to hear another word about totals. How many have you planted so far?"

"Eighteen-hundred-fifty," said Alex.

Vern looked as if he were multiplying by point aught seven. "And Catherine?" he said.

"Sixteen," said Alex.

Ray sat silently on his crate. Even Arty and Jerry were subdued. Alex sat down next to Nick, but neither spoke. Vern walked out into the rain and motioned for Ray to follow. Catherine arrived before they returned. "Something's happening out there," she told Alex, "and I think it has to do with you and me. Boy did they clam up when I walked by, and you should have seen their looks."

"I told Vern we were leaving if we didn't get paid seven cents a tree," he told her.

She looked at him curiously. "And he said?"

"He agreed," said Alex.

"I'm not sure you should have done that," she told him, but since they were not alone he did not argue the point.

The customary half hour loading rocks onto the nine-ton in the rain seemed even longer and more futile than it usually did, perhaps because they got no help from Vern and Ray, who had stayed in the cookshack. Alex went back in for a cigarette and they were still sitting there, very serious expressions on their faces. To address Alex, they had to change their posture and the shift apparently did not come easily. Still, with a nervous motion of his hand, Vern talked to him. "We've, uh, had some bad plots," he began.

"Not where we've been planting," Alex told him matter-of-factly.

"No," Vern agreed. "The problem is probably Arty and Jerry. Your plots have been so good we guess you're doing something right and we thought a little of it might rub off on them."

Alex thought about his dream. "Do I have anything to say about this?"

Vern looked at him seriously. It was really quite a different Vern. "I wish you would do it," he said quietly.

"All right," said Alex. "What about Catherine?"

"Ray wants to plant with her," said Vern.

"Yes," said Ray, and it was impossible for Alex to gauge the hard thin face. "I've never planted with a girl before."

"We're going to change our approach a little today," Vern continued. "We figure we can finish A. There are three little sections. So we're going out with three crews of three. You, Arty and Jerry . . . Ray, Catherine, and Pierre . . . me, Stoner, and Nick."

"That makes sense," Alex agreed.

On the mountain, Alex's dream did not come true. Arty and Jerry packed their bags with trees and approached him on the road.

"Where we goin', Big A?" Jerry wanted to know.

"You're Big A and I'm Li'l A," Arty told him grinning. "Let's plant trees."

So they would talk to him. That was encouraging. "We're going straight to the top," said Alex. "And when we get there you'll see a sight to behold."

"It's raining," protested Arty.

"It is in fact raining," agreed Jerry.

Being with them made Alex feel silly. They were contagious. "We're going to chase the cloud off the mountain," he told them. They were walking toward the furthest section, a triangle-shaped section near the woods. "But first we make strategy."

"Council a'war," realized Arty.

"Assault on that mountain," agreed Jerry.

They were hilarious. And in six days Alex had not figured that out. He loved little revelations. He addressed them expansively before they addressed the slash. "Now first though," he began, "I have something to say. You know Vern?"

"Vern? We know Vern," said Jerry

"Vaguely," agreed Arty.

"Vern," Alex continued, "told me that he was getting bad plots because you guys can't plant."

"No!" Arty declared emphatically.

"Not true," protested Jerry. "Not true at all!"

"Personally," Alex told them, "I suspect the problem lies elsewhere."

"Elsewhere," they agreed in unison, "is where it lies."

"We will not ask where," said Alex. Talking to them was the most amusing thing he'd done in weeks. He looked at the cloud over the mountain and could swear that it was lifting, the rain slackening.

"But we have an idea," said Jerry.

"A strong suspicion," agreed Arty.

"Holding that question then in suspension . . ." It was incredible, they were controlling his speech, he never talked like that.

"Suspension!" they shouted gleefully.

"Yes, suspension, where we are holding it . . ." He was giggling himself. "I would like to see each of you plant a single tree." He walked into the slash. "One at a time, here, and here."

Slowly, deliberately, but with certain grace, Arty planted a perfect tree. Jerry watched and clapped his hands when Arty stood. Then he, with an absurdly similar stroke and rhythm, did the same, and was himself applauded.

Alex looked from one to the other. "Do you two always plant like this?" he inquired.

"As we warm up," said Jerry, "we plant faster."

"But not too fast," said Arty.

Alex found himself readjusting all his perception of the contract he was on. "Do you know this trick?" he asked. He took several of the crown needles atop Arty's tree between thumb and forefinger and tugged them off. "If the tree comes out, it's loose," he said.

Arty laughed "ho ho ho" and quickly tugged at Jerry's tree. Alex planted one and Jerry tugged at it.

"There is still the matter of strategy," Alex told them. "On which we will not linger. There is here," he pointed to his left, "somewhere, a very likely tangled line."

"Oh no," said Arty.

"No indeed," said Jerry.

"No?" asked Alex.

"No," said Jerry.

"We planted that line," said Arty.

"We have a system," they said in unison. In two voice counterpoint with remarkable detail and clarity, they explained the anarchy system to Alex.

He looked at them. "Well shit," he said, "you guys are treeplanters!"

"Yes!" they cried.

By the time they reached the top of the hill the rain had stopped; early on they each hung their rain gear on stumps in the slash. Shedding the heavy garments left Alex feeling pounds lighter, and he bounded up the mountain following the best line of trees he had seen all season. It wasn't straight, it was much better than straight, it was subtle and appropriate. It took account of the topography on which it was laid. Although it rambled in response to boulder, ridge, and stump it was utterly clear. The next tree was always exactly where it ought to be. One inevitably pointed to another. "I am truly impressed," he told them at the top, where the sky was blue. Far, far, below they could see the Arm, and the wakes and sails of weekend navigation upon it. "You two are magnificent."

"You are not bad either," they replied.

"Vern can't follow our line," said Arty.

"It isn't straight," said Jerry.

"And we can't follow Ray's," said Arty.

"With difficulty only," said Jerry.

"He zigs when he should zag."

"Where is our dope?"

"Dope?" wondered Alex, inhaling the first pure exhilarating drag of the second cigarette of the third pack he had from Nick, a pack that was going to have to last him until Monday, when the bozos were bringing in supplies, and he would be beered and tobaccoed to his heart's content, and Nick repaid.

"Vern always gives us dope at the top," they told him.

"But I don't have any dope," he confessed.

"No dope," they realized sadly.

"You'll have to get high on planting trees," Alex told them.

"High?" said Arty.

"On planting trees?" said Jerry.

And without waiting for Alex to finish his cigarette they cascaded whooping down the mountain, planting remarkably swiftly for slow planters. The smile on the face of the mountain was palpable.

When Alex broke for lunch he encountered Catherine. "Arty and Jerry are great planters," he enthused to her. "Well Ray isn't," she said after looking around to make sure no one was listening, in the voice of a woman with a lot on her mind. "It's not hard to figure his game," she went on. "He's trying to run me off the mountain."

That was serious, and Alex's happiness deflated. "How are you doing?" he asked her.

"Well I'm doing fine," she told him. "He goes jackrabbit up the mountain strewing trees right and left. I follow behind and straighten his line and talk to Pierre. He waits at the top smoking dope and yelling at us to hurry. I've been working steady and he leaves lots of little openings to pop in extra trees." She pulled a handful, half a bundle at least, limp and dried-out, from the bottom of her bag. "I had to yank them all. Too close, or on their side, or bare roots. I'll be damned if I'm replanting them for him."

"I'll take them," Alex told her. "I'm working near the woods. How many have you planted?"

She grinned at him. "Five hundred."

"No shit!" he whistled. "You're ahead of me."

She nodded. "I've been working hard." She nearly smiled.

"Well look," he asked before getting up. "Do you want me to do anything, about him, I mean?"

She laughed. "For all you can do! And don't forget you got me into this. I blame you as much as him. I can take care of myself."

While Alex sat stunned, trying to figure out which if any of those things to respond to, she got up and went for more trees. The exchange definitely took the charge out of him. On the one hand, he had to admire the fight in her, but unfortunately a certain amount of it seemed to be a fight with him. And, try as he might to wiggle loose, he was hung on each of her four charges. One (he reconstructed her outburst in his mind), that there was nothing he could do; two, that he had got her into it since Vern had been his contact and, obviously, in retrospect, a questionable one; three, that he was to blame for Ray's behavior (true in the sense that he had insisted on being paid by the tree, a thing that Ray was now taking out on her); and four, and this he had no doubt of, that she could take care of herself. Those were hard things to think on, and as he and Arty and Jerry gradually squeezed the unplanted triangle of slash toward the woods, the two young men, still riotous in good humor, planted a circle or three around him. Even the radiant sky and the white visage of the mountain were turning out to be energy sources that he was leaving unutilized. He was extremely weary by the time they finished the section.

"I didn't sleep too good last night," he told them. The fact of finishing a thing seemed to be quite a tonic for the two young men. All they wanted to do was run down to the road and help the others finish their sections. "Go ahead," he agreed. "I'm whipped. I think I'll probably just walk back to camp. If I'm not around at the end, tell them I've already left."

"Yessir, Big A," said Li'l A.

"A pleasure, sir," said Jerry.

Alex followed the treeline toward the road and found a hollow stump and stuffed the trees that Catherine had given him deep into it. He was still carrying most of a recently broken bundle of fifty himself, and was a little surprised at the ease with which they, almost impulsively, slid into the hollow stump as well. The deed done, there was little to think of it, except to take a backward glance at the stump, to make sure little tufts of green were not sticking out. It was a very ordinary looking stump.

He reached the road and walked along it through the site toward the bridge. Beneath him, Vern, Nick, and Stoner labored their way along the river. That would be their last run. The bozos had marked the eastern boundary of area A with blue plastic flag tape, and Arty and Jerry were working along it toward the bottom down by the river where the rest must be somewhere, unseen. So that too was under control. Alex tossed his bag and hoedad on the back of the nine-ton and crossed the bridge. As he ascended from there toward the main road he thought he heard shouting in the valley and looked across. An enormous black bear was traversing the area that the three of them had just planted, loping towards the wood in that wonderful half-humorous and incredibly effective bear fashion, hind legs swinging forward, planting, front legs shooting forward in their turn. Shortly after seeing that, Alex encountered Rick and Dick driving up in their red pickup. They paused briefly to talk and he told them the area was nearly finished. After taking final plots they would be going to Vancouver yet that evening, and returning on Monday. Alex reminded them of his order for beer and cigarettes, which they had not forgotten.

Around the next turn in the road, he came face to face with a coyote, who told him nothing, only sniffed the air and regarded him curiously. As long as Alex stood still so did the animal, but Alex tired of that, took a step forward and, by no means nervously, the coyote slid across the shoulder down into the woods, pausing once to look back through the trees. The encounter revived Alex. Assuming Catherine – who could after all take care of herself – was holding off Ray, things were probably OK.

"An animal got your fish," was the first thing Cookie told him when he entered the shack.

"A bear?" he asked. "I saw one at the site."

"I think it was something smaller."

"I shouldn't have left them . . . last night . . . I'm sorry, you know."

"It has nothing to do with you," she said matter-of-factly.

"Virginia lying low?" he asked confidentially.

Cookie looked at him. "She's been out."

They were doing dishes together when the truck rolled into camp. Alex could feel her tensing herself as the noise of arriving treeplanters drifted into the shack. Vern entered first. "Where were you? Didn't you hear me shouting?" he demanded angrily.

"I heard a shout, I saw a bear." Studiously, Alex wiped the old tin pot with his towel.

"You can't just go running off whenever you feel like it."

"We're in this together," said Alex.

"That's right, we go up together we come down together," chorused Ray.

"You guys are crazy," Alex said simply.

Ray turned at him with shocking intensity in his eyes. "Just watch who you call crazy," he hissed, and exited.

"I'm helping Cookie," Alex told Vern. "Didn't Arty and Jerry tell you I was leaving?"

"Well you know Arty and Jerry," said Vern. "They're not always so easy to understand."

"Vern," continued Alex, "listen to me a minute. It doesn't make a nickel's worth of difference whether I ride the truck down or walk. On the way up, yes, you need the weight, but in the afternoon if I'm tired, disgusted, whatever, it feels good to walk back. I saw a coyote, it stood and watched me on the road, it nearly talked to me. These things are important."

It seemed as though Vern might almost be listening. "But how can you walk four miles after planting?" he wondered.

"It's downhill," said Alex.

"Downhill," Vern echoed. "Downhill."

Catherine was there and she broke in at the pause. "You know though, Alex, he has a point. People do get hurt. We need to know everyone's OK before we leave."

"Arty and Jerry . . ." Alex began.

" . . . Can tend toward the obscure," she finished for him with words not his own.

"Ray . . ." said Vern. "I don't really care where you are, but Ray . . ." He went out the door.

"Glad someone's on my side," Alex said to Catherine.

"He has a point, Alex, that's all," she replied.

Vern was no sooner out the door than he was back, along with Rick and Dick, who looked eager to be down the mountain and off to town. "Well I have good news and bad news," said one of them, Alex had long since given up trying to keep track of which was which. The bozo smiled with the good news. "You made full payment on Area A. By this much." He held thumb and forefinger a millimeter separate. "You wouldn't have, but the last four plots we did up in the far corner were all perfect." Alex thought his jaw would break from trying not to grin too hard. That was where he and Arty and Jerry had been that day. "Someone, and you should definitely figure out who and straighten them out, is still planting trees four feet apart. It looks like it's only one person, but it hurts your percentages. It could sink you if you aren't careful. That's the good news."

"And the bad?" asked Vern.

"You've got a bear. We saw him from the road just up the hill. You'll want to be careful with your food. He was heading this way and the bears up here are pretty bold. Do you have a rifle?"

"No," said Vern. "I'm not into guns on contracts."

"Would you like us to bring one in on Monday?"

"Well, I'm not into guns. Look, just because there's a bear doesn't mean we have to start shooting at it, does it?"

Rick and Dick looked at him seriously. "With bears you never can tell," one of them said.

After they had left, Alex turned to Cookie. "You didn't see any bears today?"

"I heard noises," she said, "and figured it was just Virginia."

"Have you actually seen her today?" Alex lowered his voice, as Vern was still standing at the shack's doorway.

"No, just heard . . ."

"Her voice?"

"No."

"This gets complicated, doesn't it?"

"More than thirty dollars a day worth," she answered solemnly.

Nick came in. "We've got a bear," he announced.

"We know," said Vern.

"You've seen it?"

"No, the bo-. . . er checkers just told us. You've seen him?"

"Coming this way. We should guard the food."

"With our bare hands?" asked Alex.

"Do we have a gun?" asked Nick.

"I'm not into guns on contracts," repeated Vern.

The crack of a pistol shot, a second, a third, obviously high caliber and not a hundred feet away, rang through the valley. Vern looked briefly and prayerfully through the transparent roof. Then they ran hard out through the plastic door flap. Virginia stood at the door of the house, fear in her eyes. On the road stood Ray grinning angrily, a very large handgun in his fist. Alex could smell gunpowder. Ray spun three shell cases out of the cylinder, and reloaded from his pocket. Through the ringing echo of gunfire, still answering from high up the mountain, came the crashing noise of a large creature hurtling through the bush. Ray dropped to a knee and fired after it.

"Jesus Christ, Ray!" shouted Vern. "Cut that out. What if you hit him?"

Ray sniffed the smoke still wafting from the barrel and clicked out the empty shell, replacing it. "You think I can't shoot?" he demanded.

"Put it away, please," Vern pleaded. "Christ, I don't like guns."

French Pierre had ambled up from the river all but

naked. He stood beside Catherine and Alex. "Dat little fucker crazy," he said.

"Don't tell him so," Alex warned him.

Ray swept the woods with the pistol, squinting down the barrel, flexing and unflexing his fist around the handle and trigger. Then he twirled it cowboy movie fashion, starting gracefully enough but finishing awkwardly as the thing's bulk asserted itself.

"God, Ray, put it away," Vern persisted.

Ray turned and swept them with his eyes. "He won't be back," he said.

Barely daring not to look at Ray, Alex glanced at the mountain. It told him nothing.

"Jesus, I hate guns," said Vern.

"Well, if we're going to kill a bear let's get a rifle and shoot it in the heart, but a pistol?" protested Alex.

"This'll blow your head right off," Ray informed him, waving the weapon in fairly nervous fashion.

"But a bear!" Alex persisted.

"A bear's head's no bigger than yours," said Ray.

"But if you miss . . ."

"Don't you think I can shoot?" Ray asked smiling.

As dusk fell, Alex and Catherine stood on the bridge and watched the lights of the city emerge far beneath them. "To think that a person can go bush ten miles from Vancouver," Alex mused.

"It seems like a thousand, doesn't it?" she replied.

"Maybe we'll be back there in two days," he suggested. "The bozos come in on Monday. Their boat will head back."

"We can't leave, Alex," she informed him.

"I think we can," he disagreed.

"You've made some mistakes," she pointed out.

"Maybe, but, look, I may have to leave. That gun, Ray, I

don't think he's really thinking of killing anyone, but those things have ways of pointing themselves.

"You don't want to go to England do you, Alex?"

"Cathy! There's nothing I want more."

"You don't want me to go. You don't want me to see Byron." He didn't respond to that. She went on. "If I last it here, no matter how long it takes, I have enough money to go to England. Look, in four planting days we're already one quarter finished, and even made full payment. And Vern really tries. And Ray is threatening the rest of us as much as he is you. You just think it's all directed at you."

By now it was quite dark. Vancouver lay splayed twinkling at the end of the arm. "Alex," she went on, "that tax money is mine. I did the work for it last year. It's enough for a ticket. Whatever you decide, whatever we do here, I'm going to England. I just want you to know."

"All right," was all he could say.

He heard the bear all night long and hardly slept, while Catherine slumbered like a princess in a fairy tale as he lay trembling. Every time his consciousness neared fadeout the heavy footfalls and harrumphing would cut through and bring him back to a stunning cold clarity. At least once the thing circled their tent. Toward dawn, a wind came up and brought rain with it and either that noise obscured those the bear was making, or the elements drove it away. Alex slept hard then for perhaps an hour, and awoke to heavy rain. Catherine was already up and gone, and he had not noticed her leaving.

When he entered the cookshack he expected bear talk but all was dead silent instead. Everyone was circled around the airtite stove watching Catherine and Ray facing each other sitting on wooden crates, like characters in a play. Alex had them in profile, Ray's sneering chin stuck out toward her, and hers absolutely expressionless, waiting for the little man to speak. Ray had the pistol in a leather holster on his leg.

"You did not plant nine hundred trees yesterday" he told her. Catherine said nothing, continued to stare at him, almost blankly. As though taking silence for an advantage, Ray repeated himself. "You did not plant nine hundred trees yesterday. I don't know what you did with them, but you did not plant them."

"You little bastard!" Alex exploded. Ray looked up in genuine surprise. Alex was much too angry to make sense, any control he had managed to keep for a week evaporated and he knew he would be swallowed by fury if he did not continue to shout. "Enough! Enough!" he raged. "I've had enough, taking orders from this little tinhorn fascist."

"Ray's not a tinhorn fascist," said Vern.

"He's not? Wearing a pistol at breakfast? Shooting it at a bear? What if he hits that bear? Fucking up the plots? Planting four feet apart? You want to save this contract? Send the little bastard packing. That's what I say."

Ray regarded Alex calmly. Catherine's stony face broke in exasperation. Ray spoke: "The contract doesn't need saving. And if anyone packs it won't be me. I just think that if you two are going to count your trees, you ought to count them honestly. I mean, she says she planted nine hundred, and I know she didn't. That means we end up paying her for trees someone else planted. That's not fair, is it?"

Catherine spoke: "Who says I didn't plant nine hundred trees?"

The answer was sure and immediate. "I planted eight hundred fifty. I know you can't plant more than me."

Thanks to his outburst, Alex had calmed somewhat. "You little jerk," he said simply. "You're accusing her of stashing trees because she planted more than you? Where have you been planting? You're the worst planter I've ever seen. Your trees are bad, you've got no sense of form, and you think you're fast because you plant four feet apart. Listen, I know women you couldn't stay with for five minutes. They plant two thousand trees a day. And you don't think Cathy can plant nine? What a joke. You're a a crazy fool."

"That's enough of that!" Vern finally succeeded in shouting Alex down. "Nobody's accusing anyone of anything. Keep cool, for God's sake."

"Don't you forget it," Ray spit at Alex, and exited the cookshack.

"Boy, did you ever blow that," Catherine told him. "I was handling him."

"You don't treat Ray like that," Vern warned him.

Arty and Jerry were sitting on the couch. "The bear comed all over our tent," said Arty. "He thought it was a lady bear," said Jerry. "We were terrified," said Arty. "Bears sure make love weird," said Jerry.

Pierre said nothing, but cast liquid sad eyes deep into Alex's own. Alex said, "I'm sorry. I haven't slept," and lit a cigarette. It was all he could do.

"Well hurry up and eat," said Vern. "We're ready to go. And listen, in case you haven't figured it out, the idea is to be careful of Ray. Let's go get rocks," he said to the others.

"Someone should take that gun away from him," said Alex.

"Not you," said Catherine, and Vern nodded in agreement.

Ray wore the gun up to the site. For the first time in his planting life Alex wished there were bozos around. Anything to indicate that there was another world out there, and that there were some rules in this one. It was cold on the back of the truck in the rain, which was falling as thick wet snow by the time they got to the site. Oblivious to it, Ray got out of the truck and packed trees into his bag. "Everybody take two hundred and follow me," he barked. No one moved. He fingered the butt of the gun. "Everybody get two hundred."

"I don't think we're going to plant today, Ray," said Vern.

"Listen, I give the orders on the site. Everybody get two hundred and follow me. You," he pointed at Alex, with his finger. He had to remove the hand from the gun to point, which was something of a relief, although Alex realized how utterly uncomfortable it felt to be pointed at so. "You're such a hotshot," Ray sneered. "Don't tell me you're afraid of the snow."

Alex held his pose.

"You! Bitch!" Ray shouted. It was pretty clear who he was talking to. "Let's see how good you really are. C'mon cunt, you afraid?"

"Ray!" Vern tried.

"Assholes," said Ray, and planted a tree in the snow. Then he planted another, and another, and by the sixth had disappeared into the showering whiteness that obscured the land, sky, and everything in between.

"Jesus, I hate guns," complained Vern. "I told him not to bring that thing."

"What now?" someone asked.

"We wait," said Vern.

"Ever hear of hypothermia?" Alex asked him.

"Just shut up," sighed Vern.

"It's a really good day for it," Alex went on.

"Shut up, will you please?" said Vern, without authority.

"You feel cold, and then you get light-headed, and then you don't think so straight, and then you don't feel like moving either. And then you die. Best temperature, just above freezing. Best medium, wet snow. Myself, I have to admit I don't care too much what happens to Mr. Schikelgru-

ber up there, but I promised myself I'd survive this day. I'll
see you back in camp. Remember, he's moving and we're not.
  "We came up here together, we . . ." Vern stopped.
  "We freeze to death up here together, eh?" said Alex.
"You might be able to make it stick if you had the gun. Leave
him the keys and your hashish, Vern. He'll never know the
difference. Maybe he'll break his leg and we'll be rid of him."
  "Alex!" cried Catherine.
  "Oh stick it," he told her, and started walking.
  They followed, they all followed, even Vern, he knew
this because later at camp, one by one, they filtered back in,
Vern last. Alex smoked by the airtite until all but Ray were
accounted for. Then, without speaking to anyone, he went
to bed. It was extraordinary how comfortable the dry warm
bag was on the ground, how the earth met his tired body in
a love embrace and nursed him at her breast. He slept deeply
and beautifully, and awoke to the sound of the truck arriving. Knowing what had to be done, he dressed slowly. He
was indeed scared, but that was quite beside the point. He
put on fresh clean jeans, dry socks, his good hiking boots, a
cotton shirt, Canadian Army issue sweater, and wool toque.
Without rain gear, he walked to the cookshack in the mist.
The mountain of course was not there, but it didn't matter
anyway. The truck was parked at a screwy angle nearly flush
against the house. The cookshack had that full look to it,
slowly moving figures played against the transparent plastic
wall, the flap half open as though someone had just entered.
As Alex neared the door he could see Ray's legs on his crate,
and through the plastic the tall figure next to him. At the
threshold, he lifted the flap, entered, heard Ray say, "fifteen
hundred, what do you think of that, cunt?" He had the gun in
his hand. French Pierre turned without ever looking at Alex
and hit Ray hard across the back of the shoulders with his

extended forearm. The pistol hung for the briefest of instants in the hand as Ray stiffened and then started to pitch to the floor. The gun fell with a plop into the mud and Alex fell on it, holding his body loose enough to absorb as much of Ray's fall as he could. No explosion, no struggle, he could feel the hard angular object against his gut. He pushed up with one arm. Ray seemed to be almost without mass and absolutely limp, and Alex placed the palm of his hand over the pistol. Then, with a heave, he pitched Ray off his back and rose to one knee, noting with a little wave of nausea that the hammer of the thing was cocked. Without turning to look at Ray, or even moving away, he knelt in the mud and cracked the cylinder. He emptied the cartridges into a puddle and retrieved them. He realized vaguely that the shack was filled with screaming, which stopped when he stood.

"I figure you know what to do," Pierre nodded to him.

"I figured you knew what to do too," Alex replied.

"I hope I no kill him," said Pierre.

"Me too," said Alex.

The limp figure groaned. "He's dead," cried Virginia, rushing forward.

"No he's not," said Vern. "Shit. He's our first aid man," he added.

"You guys planned that?" Catherine marveled.

"After a manner of speaking," said Alex, still holding the cracked pistol. "What do we do about this thing?"

"Jesus, I hate guns," said Vern.

The two of them stood together an hour later on the bridge in the mist. Alex had smoked a great deal of hashish, mostly with nervous energy, and was hugely stoned, as well as exhilarated, which did not make him fit for the cookshack where what had happened had to be treated as something regrettable, something that ought not to have occurred.

"So what now?" she wondered.

"Well, I guess I have to talk to Vern," he answered. "Find out what the story is."

"Boy he hit him hard."

"Yea, he did. Hey, how did you like my fumble recovery?"

"Alex! This is life and death and you think about games!"

"I thought it was a pretty good play, Cathy."

"Alex!" She was genuinely scandalized.

"The thing is, I don't see how I can stay here if Ray does."

"I guess it's his choice then, eh?"

"Well, he has to choose by tomorrow because that's when the boat comes in . . ."

"He was pretty dingy last I was in there," she pointed out. "How's Pierre?"

"Acting like Ray got hurt but that he had nothing to do with it, unlike someone I know."

"Well, I guess he had less at stake than I did. The thing is, I'd like to stay now. The contract's not out of the woods, and there's still a bear to deal with. I guess they need us."

"Get a rifle and shoot it in the heart, eh? Wouldn't you like that? You can't run away from your troubles, Alex."

He turned and looked at her. "And if I stay, you stay, and if I go, you go?"

She turned away and looked down the mountain. "Yes," she said.

"I guess you're right then," he decided.

(for Paul Wilkinson)

Baker's England

... she's so fine she's in my mind ...

What is there to say about an affair with someone you don't love?

No that's not where I meant to start.

Although in certain ways it's not bad. For one thing it tells you that this is going to be about sex and if your mind is as filthy as the next reader's you are at least interested. Is he going to describe it? What it felt like? Readers are all alike. If you really cared about literature you wouldn't be reading this, you'd be reading something by Henry James, or Joyce, or Tom Robbins. And while we're on the subject of authors let's get one thing straight. Anyone who thinks this is about Frans Vander Grove can take a running jump. Some people think everything is about someone. Being a reader, that is not being very bright, you might even think that. Who knows? No, my name is Baker. Not first, not last, just Baker. [1]

[1.] Baker has of course blown my cover here. How he found out I don't know. I emphatically disassociate myself from any insult to readers. FVG. [2]

[2.] A Few Words About Frans Vander Grove. FVG = Frans Vander Grove, not F------ Very Good, as Dennis Lamb once suggested. Frans is both the founder and Poet Laureate of independently contracted (hippie

When I saw the Cumbrian Mountains for the first time I thought I didn't want to see another mountain as long as I lived. Had had enough of them. But that's another story. The really odd thing is that I was in a British crummy with three

capitalist) treeplanting in British Columbia. It is a tribute to him that virtually all treeplanting in that province is now conducted according to a system which he originated. (In the old days, as is still the case in England, it was slave labour. See my *Trees for Tomorrow*.) However, with the evolving triumph of his system, and no doubt in relation to his poetic powers, [3] Frans has developed a certain megalomania: he apparently believes that anything that has to do with treeplanting belongs to him. He is thus referred to as Dominee (Dutch Reformed for Lord).

    M. Derrida describes the author of a text as the person to whom that text belongs. This one belongs to ME. DDV.

[3.] Fer e.g.:

    Pro Log

April in rain gear
has drunk her last beer for March
Every vein is full of it.

Virtue engenders to the flower.
Zephyr's sweet breath
sweeps through every little dirt farm

to inspire the island planting, the new sun
is halfway through Aries
the birds are singing

your eyes are open all night long
(nature pokes your good sense)
and you want to go treeplanting.

British treeplanters. British crummys aren't much like Canadian crummys except they smell of dirt and dirty people. The Canadian ones smell stronger on the whole and as far as I'm concerned better. The same goes for Canadian treeplanters although the British would probably disagree. This one was a Land Rover made by the fine British Leyland people. Funny square things, both the crummys and the planters. Actually only two of them were planters, the other was a boss. Imagine, a boss who doesn't plant! "How many trees do you plant in a good day?" he asked me. "Two thousand," I said. He didn't believe me of course, didn't say so being British and polite to strangers, just looked at the two kids (that's all they were, schoolboys) and said "Hear that?"

"The ground must be terribly well prepared," he suggested.

I laughed as politely as I could and explained about logging slash. And about mountains, and bears, and cookshacks, and blackflies, and the bush in general. "Why?" I finally remembered to ask, "How many do you plant in a day?"

"About five hundred," one of the kids said foolishly. Did you know that British treeplanters plant plowed ground? On old logged-off country estates? They call that reforestation. And only plant five hundred trees a day?

"How much do you make?" I asked as they pulled over to let me out. We were already in the mountains. "One pound thirty an hour," said the boss. "See, we make ten cents a tree," I told them, "that can be two hundred dollars – a hundred pounds – a day." Jaws dropped. Best argument for free enterprise I ever heard. Damned socialist country. And I knew they didn't believe a word of it.

But here I am in the mountains and I've missed my chance to describe them. That was important too, especially since no one said anything to me about mountains. I didn't even know there were mountains in England. I thought I was going to the Lake District, but there they were as we came over a crest of moor in the British crummy, sticking straight up on the horizon, real honest-to-god big precipitous mountains. I was fairly surprised.

So when I got to Windermere I bought a topo map at a bookstore called the Rambler's Hut, and sure enough, there they were, the Lakes were full of mountains. I should have known this from reading Wordsworth but I always thought he was talking about hills. You remember where he steals the boat?

> I struck and struck again,
> And growing still in stature the grim shape
> Towered up between me and the stars, and still,
> For so it seemed, with purpose of its own
> And measured motion like a living thing
> Strode over me.

Well that shape was one big mountain and maybe you knew that but I didn't and it made a difference to see it for myself.

The Lakes were full of British babynooky, I could tell that just standing on the street in Windermere, cute little things in khaki shorts and hiking boots, rosy cheeks and curly hair, see I promised you some sex. They were too young for me though, not to drool over but to talk to. I have to talk to get anywhere with women.

She was nothing like that. She was from Los Angeles, California. Of all places. I was hoping for someone British, I mean it would have been different, I like the way the British talk. It also would have been symmetrical, balanced off my wife and her British boyfriend. She was riding around England in a Morris Minor with him and his wife and their gigantic overbred French dog. You can probably see why I didn't want much to do with that expedition.

I hardly slept with her in my tent. "We can't find a place to stay anywhere in town," she and her two friends told me. "And it looks like rain," I said. Wasn't it gallant of me to suggest that one of them could sleep with me? Having her there, a stranger, made me very nervous. British people don't camp out, and they leave the field open for North Americans and Germans and Turks. And there I was, in a green grove behind the Ellray, ancient hotel, ancient by me, probably Victorian. I don't think it's in Wordsworth, at first I thought that's where the bells came from. Every hour tolling the hour, every quarter one more mechanical phrase, resolved hourly and followed by dong! dong! dong! That was at three and she was asleep, snoring in fact. It must have been a church, hotels don't have bell-towers. Every hour tolling the hour, every quarter one more mechanical phrase, every time I might have managed to drift off reminding me again that I wasn't sleeping, that she was there.

She wore a bra. Although her breasts were small. See. I promised you some sex. She said so herself. Your breasts are beautiful, I told her and she said, they're small, and we made love. It was light, it was morning, I could hear her friends a few feet away. She awoke gradually and I must have slept although I was awake by then and I reached out and touched her black hair, her cheek, unbuttoned her shirt, unhooked the bra, which hooked at the front, and felt her breast. No, she said, don't do that, please, it turns me on. Good, I thought, I said, how nice, and she said no, it turns me on and I won't be able to stop. And she stopped me. That time.

We stood on the bridge at Ambleside, it must have been Ambleside, we had ridden the boat across Windermere, her friends were on ahead, or behind. We had eaten a beautiful lunch of bread and cheese and the pubs were closed, we were going for a walk. We stood on the bridge and watched a boy fish in a glimmering transparent pool. I could see no fish. "He won't catch anything," I said, and she said, "Yes he will," and the glimmering transparent pool shattered with a commotion of light and sound, sun flashed on silvery tissue, the memorable noise of trout. "How did you know that?" I asked her amazed. "I know things," she replied.

In Windermere at the pub I bought beer. England without beer would be like Canada without beavers, I thought, and realized it would be much worse. Being an American she drank Heineken, brewed in England for sale in England, and quite good. I was a bitter drinker that summer. "Your wife," she said. I was nothing but honest that summer, she knew about my wife. "Your wife, aren't you trying to get even with her?" This I strenuously denied. I took my change and, nearly broke as I was, fed it to a greedy slot machine. "Why do you do that?" she asked. "Because it amuses me," I replied. We drank and watched another man play the machine; except for whirring and clicking it was absolutely still. He played for a long time, how much money can a sane man waste on a machine that will pay no more than 40p at a time? He grew more and more angry as he played, not at the machine, not even at himself, at existence I suppose. That's what she said. Finally he slammed it with his hand and left through the back. She fished in her pocket for coins and came out with 10p, got up and approached the machine, fed it, pulled the handle and hit three bells and three holds. "No," I called as she pulled the handle again, "you have holds." I showed her the lights. She smiled and hit three oranges and three holds. This time she held them, three straight times.

We drank all night, all four of us, on the tokens. "Esther," said Rod, "you have to figure out a way to get coins instead of tokens."

"The jackpot always pays tokens," I said. "That way you

have to spend them here." Rod understood. "We'll just have to do that," he said. "How long have we been in England, Esther, and you've held out on us?"

We were very drunk. "Telekinesis?" I asked. "Telepathy," she said. "Telepathy?" I exclaimed. "With a machine?"

"Sometimes I wonder," she said.

I unbuttoned her shirt and unhooked the bra, which hooked in front. Your breasts are beautiful, I said and kissed one. They're small, she said, which was true. "What about me?" I asked. "You are closed to me," she replied. How convenient for me, I thought. We made love. We were both very drunk. The floor of the tent was a tangle of blue jeans and sleeping bags.

The tokens were heavy in our packs. There was no way we could spend them all in a week, not two of us. Sometimes a publican would cash them, we ate many a ploughman's lunch together, could have survived indefinitely in the Lakes on beer and ploughman's lunches. There were four different kinds of tokens there, at least four, maybe more. Four that she won and we used. The mountains would have been less steep without them in my pack. She wondered, why carry them anyway, I always win, and although I saw this fact to be true, I never made myself believe it, and ended up carrying them everywhere. "Maybe you'll leave me," I said. "Then what will I do for beer?"

"Who do you suppose I'm robbing?" she asked me.

"The slot machine companies, I guess," I told her, not knowing. "And the government, of course."

"Then it's all right," she decided. She had a conscience. The publicans didn't seem to mind. They found it amusing. They don't own the pubs mostly, the breweries do. Maybe we were robbing the breweries. I was somewhat less conscientious than she.

We awoke in a pasture behind Ambleside to find the tent surrounded by sheep. She laughed hard, strange since she hardly ever laughed, least of all in the morning when she was always dead serious. I laughed too and hugged her, scrunched my thighs against her and mounted, reached my hands beneath her shirt and ran them along her belly to her legs, aroused, and she became quiet and worked free. "Not now," she said, with a certain authority and I asked her why she was laughing and she said it reminded her of an American beer commercial, and I laughed too, not because we were surrounded by sheep but because she said that in the commercial the couple gets out of the tent and goes to a pub. "To drink American beer?" I asked. "Schlitz," she replied hilariously. We rolled out of the tent onto the mountain half-dressed and stampeded the sheep, which is very against code, but fortunately for the sheep we were only half-serious about it. They hit a two-legged ridge and went down alternate slopes baaing in confusion. A magnificent formal occasion.

Still, there was a sadness to her.

"There's someone else, of course," I said. "I'm not telepathic, I wouldn't know. You were alone." She said nothing. I read her one of my better lectures in moral philosophy.

And what Lake was he, and I mean Wordsworth, on? It is something I wonder about. I struck and struck again, And growing still in stature the grim shape Towered up between me and the stars . . . Which mountain was that? The Old Man? Helvellyn over Thirlmere? Skiddaw over Derwent Water or Bassenthwaite Lake, Grasmoor over Crummock Water or Buttermere? Fairfield (at 2863) high enough but some way from Grasmere. Estwaite Water by Hawkshead (boyhood school still there in its tiny stone eminence a shrine by a campground where British people camp, door casement even I had to duck going under, people smaller then if spirits greater) but no mountain there, in the south now, north of Grizedale Forest, a British forest with trees in it unlike many, although one can never tell about mountains, perspective being such a factor, those big ones in high caps on maps, the ones you see from the road coming over a crest of moor in a British crummy, the PEAKS, not the ones you necessarily see when you're actually in the mountains, always that last ridge to get over before you see The Mountain and then it only a little higher than you. Cattycam, Watson's Dad, Blencathra, Lingmell Crag, the names roll off the tongue like words from an ancient language, English but not English, the language of primal poets. There is nothing like those mountains, a beck is a creek, or is it brook, a tarn an alpine lake, the rocks roll down the mountain-side instead of trees, when you get into bracken you meet black face sheep and contest with them for the path. There is nothing like those mountains.

Under Helvellyn for example, except it couldn't have been, that is further north, must have been The Tongue, an English name to be sure, lately named perhaps or in translation, we reached the top of the pass near Grisedale Tarn, turned left down the Old Packhorse Trail between Seat Sandal and Great Tongue, a ridge north of Tongue Gill and before us over descending ridges The Irish Sea spread out all unexpected, in this summer of drought cut against the mountain blue nearly Western sky. I caught my breath and stopped there. "I feel him everywhere," I told her and she said "Who?" and I said "Wordsworth," and she said "Words Words" somewhat scornfully, since she kept no truck with the dead. But he was there for me, open to me. There are places whose every aspect is a story or a song.

We said goodbye to her friends at the rail station at

Windermere. They were going to Cambridge. "I wanted to go," she told me, "there's a festival, but they want to be alone." I didn't ask how she knew that. They were to meet in Paris, it had something to do with their rail passes. "Meet us in Paris," Rod said to me, but I was dead broke, every day in England was potentially my last.

On Scandale Beck is High Sweden Bridge, beneath it waterfalls, series of cold water pools set in rock, on the path side broad leaf trees, ash, or birch, it seems there were willow, meadow on the other. We swam in one of these, deep and several yards across, shielded from the path although we could hear ramblers just overhead, private, idyllic. She undressed awkwardly, embarrassed, those California women shameless in swimsuits, I a treeplanter of course only too eager to shed clothes and hit cold water, the freest feeling in the mountain world, swimming chatteringly as she stood on the rock, then sat with toes in the cold, thick walker's legs spread on the rock, skin goose-pimpled everywhere. I swam to her underwater, grabbed a foot and pulled her in, she shouting with cold, an excellent swimmer, punching down to drown me, she could have had she chosen. We were watched from the meadow side by sheep.

So what is there to say? A great deal actually, although in words it comes to very little. My story is already ending, even though there is more to tell. Her breasts were small. Your breasts are very beautiful, I said, and meant it, but you already know this, and there is more, although in words it comes to very little.

There is almost nothing to Patterdale. It is on the way from Ambleside to Grasmere only if you walk in the shadow of Fairfield (2863) and its V shaped, spread-legged ridges. A pub, a campground where British people camp, an old people's hotel where we ate breakfast because it was open and the stiffly-dressed waiters very kind. Morning seemed to be difficult for her, perhaps she just needed coffee, not a thing always available in England, but not bad at the old people's hotel. We could hardly pay with slot machine tokens and she bought breakfast. We camped in plain view of the road on a grassy hill across from the pub where we took our tokens. That night it actually was raining although the next day the sky turned mountain almost Western blue. "The drought," I asked the publican, "has it affected the beer?" He laughed. "Never expected such a question from a Yank!" I did not correct him. She was obviously one, although a California Yank, and they are somewhat different. But people liked us anyway, we knew how to be polite. "It could," he said, "it could if it got worse. Such a question from a Yank." He would have stood us, tried to, but there was no point to it because we had all those tokens. We didn't even bother to play the machine there, or anywhere after a while. The fun was going out of it. He hardly believed I drank bitter, but I was a bitter drinker that summer. He cashed a few tokens for us at closing time and she bought breakfast with them at the old people's hotel the next morning.

Grasmere was another story. There is too much of everything in Grasmere. Dove Cottage, more tiny stone eminence, was for a reason I do not know closed. Or did we even go there? She had no truck with the dead, it was all words to her. She held words in scorn, as do I, although I am always using them. You are closed to me, she told me, as though it were an act of betrayal, it meant I had to talk to her. "You don't even like me," I protested. "Words Words," she said, "I'm with you aren't I?"

"But unhappily," I protested.

"I've never been seduced before," she said simply. "New things take time." I could see why.

"There's someone else," I said. "Someone you love." She did not reply. I read her a lecture in moral philosophy. More words.

There is too much of everything in Grasmere. Too many pubs for tourists, too much British babynooky if you can imagine such a thing, I must have been getting old. Too many buses. Too much coming and going. We camped on a grassy hill under some trees, oak I believe, if not, oak will do, on National Trust land where it is illegal to camp and thus the British do not, leaving the field open for Canadians and Americans. We camped on a grassy hill overlooking Grasmere, both town and Lake, from the north. There was a beck down the hill. I believed that I had found the most beautiful place in England, and of course he was everywhere. I felt this with an intensity that made me believe then that it was not just words at all, that there was spirit life in the Lakes. Who knows, he thought so. The trees etched against the mountains and the mountains etched against Cumbrian sky appeared as things I had seen a hundred times – that mountain against that cloud, that grove in that cleft. The Lakes, by the way, a very sexy place with everything coming at you in V's.

We arrived at Coniston in more rain, intending to climb the Old Man. We began in the pub at the bottom of the steep road to the Fell, map in hand. The mist hung thick around us. We bought a bottle of brandy with slot machine tokens. We had camped by Church Beck on the Major's land. He was very kind. Imperial might be the word, although perhaps it only comes to mind because he was a Major. Someone else had already camped there so we put up my tent, and they said they had permission from the Major, so we went up the road to the great house and were greeted at the gate by a strutting peacock. He was very kind, imperial even in his dignity. "Ah you Yanks are hearty, camping in this weather," he said. I did not correct him. "We slept indoors last night," I confessed and she blushed. I saw and wondered if he did. "And how long will you be?" he asked as we stood on his doorstep, and I said, "One night or two?" "Of course," he said, "A pleasure, hmph, wouldn't want anyone living there all summer you know," as though Yanks still bore enough ill-breeding (prisoners and riffraff hmph originally, you know) to do such a thing. "Please be very careful of the walls and no fires, you know," he said. He was very kind.

Between Hawkshead Hall (Childhood and School-Time) and Coniston we lost our way in the rain and were drenched. Tiny stone immanence with low door and ceiling, old boards and old books, old people selling pamphlets, and a palpable sense of presence. She had become accustomed to my spirit seeking and was almost amused, cheerier in the afternoon. "We'll have to sleep indoors tonight," she said. "I want a bath." Although the swim in Scandale Beck had done for awhile. We lost our way across the meadows and styles and were drenched. To walk his walks, his rambles, to be present. I told her so in my mind, told her it was more than words with more than words. "You are closed to me," she reminded me. She paid for the room, or rather I paid with her money, quite properly. I would have camped that night, every day in England was potentially my last, but she paid for me too, it may have been her way of saying she wanted me. It felt good. I paid, for my wife and me, I told the old man, who was very kind, talked with us after we had bathed and put on dry clothes, showed us where we could hang our wet things, talked to us about the crags and fells, and becks and tarns, might have yarned us all night long if someone else had not arrived to take his last room.

We regarded the Old Man in the morning mist. Will it

lift, she wondered. No telling, I replied. She wore blue jeans, wool sweater over cotton shirt. Hiking boots. So did I, identically costumed save minor details of color and design. We should have rain gear, I suggested. "Rain gear?" she said. "Who has rain gear?" It was the first year of the California drought, second of the English. "I do," I said. But I had left it in the tent.

She stood naked by the huge wooden bureau, looking into the great high mirror, hand resting on the polished surface. There were scented candles and I had lit one there. She was looking at the mirror but not at herself, at me on the bed? No, our eyes would have met. At the room itself in the candlelight. Everything so large after the tent, the bed with room enough for four, pressed lightly starched sheets under a quilted comforter. Such comfort there was, raven hair falling gently over her narrow shoulders, small breasts lying soft against her chest in the mirror. Then she did look in the mirror at me. She may have smiled. I was thinking, she told me. What did it feel like? I remember that yet, will never forget I don't think. A perfect fit in a sense so far transcending the mechanics of the thing that you, filthy-minded reader whom I have not forgotten, would never understand because it had nothing to do with words.

We tried to climb the Old Man but he would have none of it. It is not a difficult climb. Hear the words of the guidebook: "Follow the path, distinct for the most part, to Goats Hause (266983) and then up onto the easy slopes of Coniston Old Man." But he would have none of us. We approached from the south and he threw us off his back with a wind and rain of such icy power that we could no more imagine a drought than a tropical island offshore in that sea whose salt we could taste through the storm. We looked up the trail to the whiteness guarding the pass and breathed the Old Man's cold angry breath. Her teeth chattered. I was all for going on anyway but she convinced me that I was crazy. She told me she was freezing. I held her to my breast and squeezed hard. Blue jeans, no damn good in the rain, I suggested. We must go, she insisted.

And that was all, I knew I was close to the end. The next day she was gone. We both were. We took the bus back to Windermere, the train to Kendal. She paid for it with token money cashed in Coniston. We said goodbye in the castle ruins there, not much to see really although the grounds seemed to go on forever along the highway where I stood with my thumb stuck out and she waiting until I was picked up. Her train to London left later. She was on her way to Paris. I was on my way home, wherever that was.

And damn it, very literally, that is all. And you don't feel, and neither do I, that it can be. Henry James, whom you would be reading if you really cared about literature, was against first person narration because he said things happen to people in such random fashion. Bloody Hell! Not anywhere near enough ever happens, and when it does it goes by before you even know it was there. Two people. May be another story. She was running, there's no doubt about that, and I haven't seen her since. Have you ever heard of San Benito, California? Doesn't it sound like one of those L.A. suburbs? It's a gas station on a pass by The Pinnacles, a most remarkable geological formation on a ridge of small California mountains maybe ninety miles from San Jose. I know, because I went there, quite soon after I got back to the so-called New World. No one in San Benito, California, what there is of it, has ever heard of Esther Easedale Church. Funny girl, she. And why the three names? Esther Church I might not have figured out any sooner, but it wouldn't be pretending to say quite as much. And what is it pretending to say? Something about words, to be sure. If I'd met her a day later she would have been Becky. Which I happen to know is not her first name. I was a . . . oh never mind. She wrote it on a piece of paper in Kendal and I was just happy to have it. It's a good name too.

So what is there to say about an affair with someone you don't love? Only this and maybe not even it: Love is a funny word. I've slung it a few times myself, and I'd as soon face some of the people I've slung it at as climb the Old Man in a storm like that. Which I would do in an instant, and more, for the chance to see Esther, which must have been at least one of her names, for thirty seconds. Just enough to say I remember you, I know you, I live with you.

The Gardener

*. . . I have seen you in the movies
and those magazines at night . . .*

When Case first arrived at the laundromat, lugging the
khaki duffle bag, there were two other people there and he
didn't pay much attention to them. He was mainly paying
attention to his laundry so that he didn't lose any more
socks. Each of the last three times, he'd gotten home to learn
he'd lost another one and with the way the price of socks
kept going up it was becoming an expensive proposition.
Toward the end of the week, he even had to resort to wearing unmatched pairs, and if anyone noticed it must make
him look ridiculous. The thing was, he had no real reason
to believe he was even losing the socks at the laundromat.
When he went back to search for them they were never there,
although others were. A week earlier, he'd broken down and
finally helped himself to one with a pattern of stripes at the
top that seemed to match a singleton of his, an impression he
found to be much less accurate in fact than in memory when
he actually compared them. Nevertheless, that was the pair
he was wearing that Thursday, his laundry day.

He threw his clothes into a machine and sat down in
one of the plastic chairs to read the current issue of *Organic*

Gardening. It was autumn, and most of the magazine was devoted to the use of wood fuel. He was an urban gardener, so that was not of much practical interest to him. He read the letters, an article about "Rocambole: The Gentle Garlic You'll Love," and another about using autumn leaves in compost, and then struggled to focus his attention on an editorial about the ecological implications of burning wood. At that point, two men standing beneath the sign proclaiming NO LOITERING!! POLICE WILL BE CALLED!! were joined by another carrying a quart of beer in a paper bag.

It was not of any particular significance to Case that the three men were black, although it was certainly of significance to the one who had just entered, because the first snatch of conversation to attract Cases's attention was that man saying "they say they be lookin' for a suspect be a tall skinny black dude, and I do fit that description." At that, Case could not help looking up from his magazine. The three men were talking intently, and not paying any attention to him. He quickly returned his gaze to the magazine but eavesdropped instead of reading. Only part of the conversation reached him, and it came in confusing bits of street language over the noise of the washing machine, but he heard enough to piece together a story.

"He stop and take my picture outside the Limelight," the tall man was saying. "He say it maybe rape, maybe only C.S.C., and that maybe they pick me up later. What the fuck this C.S.C.?

"Criminal sexual . . ." said one of his companions.

"Shit nigger, rape," said the other. "That nothin' t'fuck with."

"They say they show the bitch my picture," the tall man went on. "He say they maybe put me in the lineup, see she pick me out . . ."

"Shouldn't ought'a let him take that picture," said the one.

"What the fuck I'm supposed to do?" the tall man demanded to know. "I'm comin' out' the Limelight high and happy and the man stick it in my face. Then he start all that jive 'bout rape and C.S. fuckin' C."

"He say who the bitch be?" wondered the other.

"He say fuck'all 'cept this trash 'bout rape and C.S. fuckin' C."

"Well what y'been doin' man?" they questioned him. "You been messin' where you shouldn't ought'a be?"

It occurred to Case that he might be sharing the laundromat with some fairly desperate characters and that perhaps he ought to be afraid. Yet, the alleged crime had nothing to do with him, and they weren't paying him any heed. And, as the tall man talked about what he had been doing, which seemed to confuse even him, the story interested Case because it suggested that a person might not know what he'd been up to even though it was something likely to get him into pretty ugly trouble. The tall man seemed genuinely and seriously confused, and what Case heard constituted a mystery composed of the man, a crime, the patently and eternally sinister police, and somewhere a fact or two inaccessible.

It was not until later – an exact week later – when he saw the newspaper story, that Case made any connection between what he had heard in the laundromat and the underpants he found in the pile of leaves.

He had been busy, shockingly busy, with school all autumn long. The very fact of going back to school, and at his age, had been an attempt to re-orient himself after Ann's leaving – a return to both intellectually and geographically familiar ground. He had returned from the coast to the midwest of his youth, and traded a disorganized life of taxi-driving, beer-pumping, treeplanting, and unemployment for the structure and security of the university. The only connection between those two very different lives was his garden.

He rented the apartment on the first floor of the old house because out behind it was a patch of overgrown ground that may once have been a garden, and would certainly do for one now. With methodical intention he set to working it as soon as he moved in. In the last month and a half, it had been his single amusement besides his books, which were now once again his work.

He assumed that the soil – weed-infested and ashy grey on the surface – was all but dead and went to work to rebuild it. He spent money that should have gone for books on a spade, a leaf rake, and a bushel basket. He broke the soil and dug a compost pit with the spade, and collected leaves from around the neighborhood with the rake and basket. He spread the leaves in a thick blanket over the soil, where the winter snow would compact and rot them. After the spring melt, he would fold the mushy decomposed cushion into the soil and plant.

To his pleasant surprise, he found that although the soil was a little dry and rocky it was anything but dead, if the hundreds of earthworms there were any indication. Case sometimes felt an odd combination of foolishness and pride collecting the leaves; too shy actually to knock upon a door and ask for permission to rake someone's lawn, he merely raked the terraces between sidewalk and street, knowing that if anyone did approach him and ask just what he was doing he could explain his cleverness and industry. No one did.

Curiously, he found that sunny weather motivated him to study and thus kept him indoors at his desk, while grey skies, even light rain, sent him outdoors into the garden. There was an accidental logic to that because rain softened the soil for digging, and also weighted the dry leaves against the wind. More importantly, though, grey weather seemed to suit the reflective mood in which he worked in his garden.

He thought a great deal about Ann during those dense heavy afternoons and that was important to him, both because there was so much to think through and adjust his mind to, and because when he was thinking about her he couldn't concentrate very well on anything else. If he let her into his mind while he studied he made no progress until she had been pushed aside, and that was no easier a thing to do now than it had been during their life together. On the other hand, she did not interfere at all with his gardening, and it was then that he could deal with her. That such mental seeing-it-through was most suitably performed under a grey sky bearing the promise of winter was so obvious a thing to him that he hardly thought about it.

He was, of course, lonely. Her leaving had opened an emptiness whose vastness he had not yet fully explored, even though it was his ability to explore such a thing which seemed to have kept him going into a sort of new life. He was, she had led him to believe, graceless in intercourse social and – although she had never said it in so many words – sexual, whereas she was high-spirited and huge in her relations with others. It was a wonder, she had told him, that they succeeded together as long as they did, a success that did not change the fact that they were badly matched and that it was not working anymore. As proof of the correctness of her estimation, he found his friendships lapsing quickly after she left. It was almost as though their friendships had been mainly her friendships, and that was borne out by the fact that while her life expanded upon her leaving him, his shrank and imploded. There were people, scattered all around the continent, who had at one time or another seemed important to him, but he had not summoned the wherewithal to contact them – among other things there would be so much to attempt to explain – and he was not really close to doing so. He certainly had no women friends to whom he felt he could turn, and it seemed as though turning to a woman at this point would raise in that particular woman's mind a very particular expectation that would make her ill at ease if she did not care to fulfill it, and make him even more ill at ease if she did. He stayed, instead, within himself. Although he was meeting other people at school, he felt very little ability to reach out to them.

He was thinking such usual thoughts under a low sky when he raked the underpants from a pile of red and gold maple leaves. They were bikini style, of a garish synthetic purple material decorated with tiny red roses, and trimmed around the waist with imitation lace. Case picked them up with his rake and held them before him, laughing to himself in what seemed the only appropriate response. He nearly set them down again but hesitated instead, laughed to himself once more, and flipped them into the basket. When it was full he carried it back to his garden. He paused and hesitated again when the underpants fell out with the leaves. He considered tossing them into the alley for someone else's amusement but did not, rather retrieved them, looked at them briefly, and stuffed them into his jeans pocket. He wondered self-consciously, and still half-amused, if anyone had been watching the curious little autodrama he was enacting, and continued working until it was nearly dark, always conscious of the slight bulk in his pocket. His imagination played over the circumstances by which such a rare – in color and decoration if nothing else – item had found its way into a pile of leaves in his neighborhood, but his conjectures, he had to admit, were mostly cliché-ridden. If women lost their underwear around town the way he lost socks, there was nothing particularly unusual about finding some on the street.

That night, after a supper of stuffed winter squash and an hour or so less than he usually spent with his books, he retired to his bed and the slick skin magazines that had become his sole source of erotic comfort. The purple underpants found their obvious place in his ritual. Once, during a period of particularly creative carnality, Ann had insisted on his wearing her panties during lovemaking, sliding herself along his erection over the tight slippery fabric. The pressure he felt now inside the garment reminded him of that, but he did not particularly miss her. She had usually found a way to take the fun out of it anyway, and the smiling ladies on the page, and the purple rose-spotted fabric, did not demand, complain, or criticize him. He had pretty much made his peace with the solitary nature of his current sex life, and if it left him feeling a little silly afterward, it was satisfactory enough as it happened. For the next few days, his singular practice grew a little livelier than usual.

The newspaper story changed everything. He was walking home from the laundromat on a faded blue afternoon a week after the end of daylight savings time when the headline accosted him from the vending box:

Suspect Sought In
Mutilation Slaying

Apparently they had a pretty good idea which suspect they were seeking because directly beneath the headline was an out of focus photograph of a tall thin black man, caught as if by surprise by the camera, head turned over his shoulder as though someone had just called his name. He looked an awful lot like the man Case had seen in the laundromat the week before. Case caught his breath and fished in his pocket for a quarter.

The story was lurid. In a trash can behind one of the dormitories, someone had discovered the dissevered limbs and torso of a young woman. Thanks to a tattoo, the body had been positively identified despite the absence of a head. No weapon had been located. The suspect was that by virtue of the fact that, ten days earlier, the woman had lodged a complaint of aggravated sexual assault against him and picked him out of a police lineup. Vengeance (and what a vengeance, Case gasped to himself) was the ascribed motive for the crime. The paragraph about the alleged rape sent a rattling chill through Case's whole body.

> The victim claimed that on the evening of the fifteenth she left a tavern on Fourth Street in company with Henderson and entered his car. She told police he then drove to an industrial section of the city and forced her to disrobe and perform a variety of sexual acts. Afterward, Ms. Richards charged, the suspect drove around for more than an hour, periodically throwing articles of her clothing from the car.

Case's heart was pounding loudly enough to be heard around the neighborhood by the time he reached his apartment. He poured himself a very long and very straight drink.

The police were looking for evidence in the case. And he, it would seem, had some of that evidence. At least he had some from the prior crime. He thrust the underpants, stiff with his own dead sperm, deep into his trash and poured another drink. Without being terribly specific, the newspaper report cast oblique aspersions on the slain woman's character, as though that mattered anymore. She had been known to frequent black bars on the city's west side, as though that were a crime. It did not say anything about her own race, as though that mattered either. If it had mentioned her size, Case would have known more. The memory of the feeling of those underpants, tight against his own body, returned to him and he dug them out of the trash and contemplated their garishness in confusion. He addressed a manila envelope to the police, stuffed them inside, and sealed it. A moment later he realized how foolish that was and tore the envelope open. He shredded it into tiny pieces to obliterate the address, and flushed the tatters down the toilet. If the underpants went to the police he would have to go too, since by themselves they had little to say. But first they would have to be washed. He filled the sink with scalding water and soap, washed them by hand, and hung them over the spigot to dry. But they were too obvious there, so he hid them instead, hanging them from a coil behind the refrigerator. If he did go to the police, they would want to know . . . What? They would want to know everything. The vision of a beefy leering sergeant with a spotlight – "and what were you doing with these for two weeks, eh, boy?" Perhaps he should call a lawyer, but he didn't know any, and besides he didn't have that kind of money. He finally took a ten milligram Valium and fell into bed, awakening shaky and a little nauseous late the next morning. He had already missed his German class and, after making a pot of coffee, he called in sick on the section of Freshman Comp he taught. He did not look either at the newspaper or behind the refrigerator, but drank the coffee and dressed in work clothes. He went out into his garden.

He had already prepared – put to bed, as he called it – several square yards of soil for spring planting. Now he took his spade and began expanding the patch toward the house across the languishing back yard. A light rain started to fall, but he worked oblivious to it, only pausing when his back hurt too much to continue. He found a length of rope and his pack frame and walked to the lawn and garden store where he bought a twenty pound bag of manure that he carried home tied to the frame. He spread most of the manure over the soil he had turned and set off into the neighborhood to rake leaves. He collected several basketfuls. By the time he spread them all, it was mid-afternoon and his garden plot was double the size it had been. He decided he needed a second compost pit and set to work digging one, laboring until it was nearly dark and his cramped back was shooting honest-to-god pain up his neck and through his limbs and he had fashioned an enormous hole against the foundation of the house. He dumped his kitchen garbage there, dusted it with manure, collected another basket of leaves and dumped them in, filled his compost bucket with water and poured it in too, and covered the whole thing with a burlap sack. By that time it was pitch dark and his clothing soaked through, the light rinse of rain meeting his sweat somewhere in the middle layers. He walked over to the liquor store intending not to buy a newspaper, but Henry Henderson – this time in mute mug shot perplexity – was gazing at him from the box again, flanked by the face of his alleged victim, a vaguely Latin-looking woman with hair done up in the fashion of a few years before and wearing the smile of a homecoming queen. Case bought the paper only after buying whisky, and did not read it until he got home.

Henry Henderson had been picked up in a stolen car in Texas, and Elena Richards' head had been found in a gunny sack in a dumpster. The police were awaiting Henderson's return and still looking for evidence. Henderson, it was matter-of-factly alleged, was widely reputed to be a fairly successful merchant in the local trade in illicit drugs. He had a lawyer in town screaming frame-up at the top of his lungs. Case poured a second drink and reached behind the refrigerator for the purple underpants. He noticed then something he had not the night before, that the coil on which he hung them had something to do with the ancient machine's power supply, and was hot, and had burned a thin black strip in the fabric.

So there he was. Changed as it was, the evidence, if in fact it was or ever had been evidence, was now a red – make that purple, he thought to himself with the first smile he had managed in twenty-four hours – herring. How could he ever begin to explain his part in the whole grotesque affair to anyone, let alone to policemen? No, it was impossible, he decided. Fair was fair, but Henry Henderson – who no doubt had plenty of sins on his heart even if the mutilation murder of Elena Richards was not (and weren't the odds on that fairly huge?) one of them – would have to fend for himself. What he ought to do was throw the underpants in the compost. Except they weren't organic. They wouldn't decompose. Case threw down the drink and decided to wander over to the Arena and watch the hockey game. For a few hours, at least, he fought back his terror.

For a few hours, at least . . . later . . . he found himself pulling back the burlap sack over the cavernous pit, so much huger than he could possibly remember having dug it, gaping at him like the mouth of the earth and, between the teeth, well what did he expect, the perfect except disseetered olive brown limbs and torso, fine beckoning fingers reaching from slender arms, sturdy shoulders sloping to pale apricot breasts, tapering waist, triangle of curly black hair . . . but there was something wrong . . . the head, two feet away from the rest and in a plastic bag from which he had to pull it to make sure, blonde hair and white almost dead skin, blue angry eyes, a mouth trying to move, this was taking him longer to figure out than it seemed it should, but of course, he finally understood, it was Ann.

Case could never remember having screamed in his sleep before, but as he awoke he realized, and somehow this took a while to figure out too, that it was his own screaming that he heard, as in the distance, and it was awakening him as an alarm clock blaring from another room might.

Nor had he ever known a heart to pound like his own was pounding, or a bed, even after the most intense lovemaking on the hottest summer afternoon, as drenched in sweat as his was. His body rattled hard with a deep chill. It occurred to him that men his age actually did have heart attacks and he gobbled great gulps of air, clinging in desperation to what slender threads of sense he could find in the cold air around him. Finally, he stumbled from the chilly swamp of the bedroom into his shower and deluged himself with hot water. The shower loosened his board-stiff back somewhat and it was the consciousness of that stiffness more than anything else that began to act as a bridge toward more acceptable reality. Emerging into it, he wondered just how crazed his eyes must look and was relieved not to be able to see them in the steamed mirror. He gulped a couple of 222's, was about to pop another Valium besides, but decided that a bit of whisky over the codeine would turn the sedative trick as well. With a glass in hand, in semi-darkness, eyeball-to eyeball with an old Magilla Gorilla cartoon, the earlier dream – Henry Henderson pleading with him soundlessly in the laundromat – flickered across his consciousness, flared once in an explosive vision of the man's confused dumb face meeting his own, and disappeared.

It was raining, lightly, outside. His garden clothes from

the day before were still wet, so Case climbed into clean jeans and an old sweater, dug his calk boots and raingear out of a nearly forgotten box of stuff from his treeplanting days, and went into his garden. By noon, through rain and mist, it had doubled in size for the second day in a row. Case was not finished. He took a garlic bulb from the shelf and two cigar boxes of seed packets left over from half a year, two-thirds a continent, and a blonde-haired blue-eyed wife before. Methodically, over a whisky, he sorted out every variety he had ever planted in the autumn – spinach, swiss chard, snow peas, scallions, carrots, cabbage, cauliflower, chives, parsley, Brussels sprouts, celery, parsnips, and turnips. Many of the packets still contained seeds, a couple had never been opened. Some, which he had kept for reference, were empty, and these he stacked in a neat packet bound with string.

His back, anesthetized for the morning by the 222's, was stiffening on him again, but the real world, if a bit thickly perceived, was starting to look more habitable. He decided to work in pain. He went out into the garden, raked the leaves there back into beds and rows and, under the vigilant scrutiny of an enormous crow sitting on the roof of the house, planted every seed he had. There was still ground left when he finished, so he collected his empty packets for reference and walked to the garden store. The seed rack there had been shoved into an inconspicuous corner behind the cider mills and popcorn poppers but he found packets of several varieties that he needed. "Have an indoor garden, eh?" the girl behind the counter asked him, and when he shook his head absently and said "no," she gave him a very queer look. He ignored it and headed for home. It was late afternoon and his planting nearly finished when his landlord appeared through the rain. "What in God's name are you doing?" the man shouted at Case in the gathering darkness.

"Planting a winter garden," Case told him mildly.

"I didn't tell you you could dig up the whole fucking yard!" the man cried in anger and confusion.

For the briefest of moments reality fluttered its gossamer wings before Case's consciousness. "Here pretty bird," he heard his mind call to it. "Birdseed." To his landlord – with a remarkable burst of clarity as the bird stilled its agitation – he merely said, "It's no big deal. The lawn is dying anyway. When I'm gone you can seed my garden."

The landlord regarded him curiously; perhaps he saw the bird too. "Listen," the man said, glaring, attempting vainly to be as lucid as possible. "No more, do you hear? No more, this is enough."

"All right," Case agreed.

He had not eaten for two days and realized he was terribly hungry. He changed his shirt, put on hiking boots, and walked into town for supper. Over a Pilsner Urquel, waiting for his steak, he read the evening paper. Henry Henderson had confessed in Texas, but his lawyer was screaming bloody murder about the inadmissibility of a confession obtained down there where everyone knew what kind of justice they practiced. Case turned to the sports page. Vancouver and Toronto would be on TV that night. He was ravenous.

❉ ❉ ❉

A little over a month later, several things occurred on the same day. Perhaps of greatest importance, the year's first snow fell. As it drifted down, silent and comforting, Case sat and wrote his semester's last exam, pausing between paragraphs to look outside at the showering whiteness. He was writing well, and knew it. His earlier weekend orgy of gardening, which, he had to admit to himself, had been a bit nuts, had hardly hurt him at all as far as school went. It had left him with a very sore back, but had loosened a few mental kinks, and he'd studied hard and efficiently ever since. The weather remained uncannily warm and sunny, and many of his crops actually germinated. He had been eating tiny but marvelously tasty salads of miniature chard and spinach leaves and whole shoots of green onion. A woman he made friends with had been utterly romanced at being served one. She arrived at his apartment for supper, took one look in his kitchen where he was cleaning the little bits of greenery, squealed with delight and ran out for a bottle of French wine. "If I'd known," she told him returning breathless with it, "that you were serving real food . . ." The root crops – the garlic, carrots, turnips – could very well last the winter and grow in the spring. He would spend the Christmas break building glass-roofed boxes to protect the broccoli, Brussels sprouts, and cauliflower through the cold weather. Articles he read in *Organic Gardening* led him to believe that it might work.

Now, on this particular December day, after the exam, he went first to his garden, and stood for a few moments watching the snow fall on the plants, joyed by the exquisite composition of white on green on white. Then he went to the mailbox. There was a letter from Ann.

She was pissed as hell. Why hadn't he written? Did the fact they were divorced mean they shouldn't still communicate with each other? After all they'd shared. He couldn't, she informed him, just kill her like a character in a novel. Hm, thought Case. Why not?

The paper had news about Henry Henderson. His Texas confession was not, after all, admissible evidence, but the prosecutor was not particularly worried. There was plenty of evidence, he averred, although he didn't say what it was. Case clipped the story from the paper and filed it under Henderson. While he was in his files, he pulled out the second manila envelope where he had replaced the purple underpants after tearing up the first one. He hadn't looked at them since and now, somehow, they struck him as less garish than before. Even with that burned streak they seemed clean, almost pristine. He took a scissors and cut them into little pieces. He did the same thing to Ann's letter. He pushed the scraps of cloth and paper across the desk into the envelope, took it into the bathroom, and emptied it into the toilet. Which he flushed. None of it was organic, he reflected cheerfully as the water and debris corkscrewed out of his life clockwise, it being the northern hemisphere, so it could go into the town's compost heap instead of his. It occurred to him that a sewage plant and a compost heap were not exactly the same thing, but somehow, at that moment, the distinction did not seem meaningful.

Michigan Winter

. . . I'm a barrel of laughs with my carbine on . . .

I

The thing Dean noticed that winter back in Michigan was that every golf course, soccer field, and public park was dotted with cross-country skiers. Stiff-legged figures seemed to slide and stumble across the entire visible Michigan landscape. There was a lot of snow that winter and it was as though, in five years, the whole state had sprouted boards.

Dean applauded in principle, but was not entirely pleased. He had foolishly expected to have the place, the out of doors, more to himself. From his battered Bonnas, migratory companions of years, their finish cracked and blistered, the tip of one patched with epoxy where he had splintered it in a particularly fine tumble, he hoped for one more season. After spring planting he would buy a new pair.

He applauded in principle because the skiers supported a theory of his: that the human organism, at least in North America, was fighting back against its grave and almost certainly fatal disease. A disease ill-defined for him, but nonetheless real. It had to do with all the automobiles and gasoline, and with the nuclear stuff likely to replace the gasoline someday, if there were a someday. And (a theoretical question) wouldn't an awful lot of earth surface finally just collapse if they took too much more of the substance beneath it away and shot it into the air through the backs of petroleum-fueled vehicles? Wouldn't it? Dean didn't know for sure, but things like that worried him. The disease had in his mind the name greed and, although an unbeliever, he connected it with original sin. He had no illusions about the final success of the organism's counter-attack, but it pleased him that it might be occurring. Whole battalions of human beings were presently running, swimming, growing their own food in order to avoid the plasticine the keepers purveyed from their supermarkets and, perhaps most important, not smoking tobacco, a thing Dean hoped to accomplish himself. As a counterforce to the original sin, such actions possessed an almost spiritual character, even if, for example, the keepers also purveyed the running shoes, swimming pools, and paper for publishing *Organic Gardening*. This contradiction did not escape Dean. In its larger subtleties it confirmed his notion of humanity as an entity at war with itself, encancered, although, perhaps because he still used tobacco, he rarely spoke the word cancer.

This was grim stuff indeed, It would have been grimmer had he envisioned the deluge coming in his own time, but he did not. It seemed simply that things were going in that direction, and plenty of people agreed with him. For an unbeliever, though, coming back to Michigan was nearly an act of faith; the work of the keepers was plenty apparent in BC and Alberta, but Dean located its specific direction as East, specifically in the States, specifically in the American coastal megalopolis where whatever it was the keepers used for money changed hands, where their plans were laid, their decisions made. Michigan was about as close to that business as he cared to get, and he wouldn't have been as close as Michigan if his brother Jack didn't live there. Michigan occupied a particular place in Dean's rendering of the geography of The End because it was the birthplace of the automobile, a thing upon which he depended absolutely for his far-ranging travels, but that he hated about as much as any other thing in the world. It consumed the very substance of the planet, threw the waste into the atmosphere as poison, allowed people to go wherever they wished without breaking down their walls or challenging their assumptions (a word he translated fears) about the world that used to be out there but was going away. Dean often attempted to imagine a North America without automobiles. What a simultaneously vast and intimate place it would be. Everything would be different, spectacularly different.

His brother thought he was crazy.

Jack was a fairly successful small capitalist who drove a BMW. A slumlord, he called himself glibly, but by that winter he owned more than slums. Jack and Dean had gone to college in old GR, and Jack had never left except once a few years back when he had flipped out and lost his job as a school teacher and gone traveling with one of his students in the ancient VeeDub he'd since sold to Dean. Dean was still driving it.

When Jack returned to GR after his summer on the road he needed an apartment because his wife wasn't about to have him back just yet after what he'd done. Without so much as a business course he figured out that, doing the necessary work (he was good with his hands), he could live in the best apartment in the old house his landlord was trying to sell ("Just had enough of them niggers," the landlord confessed in one of his more gracious moments), rent out the other three, make the payments, and live for free. He and Dean, who was a college senior then (and soon afterward followed his older brother's example and took to the road with the substantial difference that he was gone for five years) engineered a dope deal for a down payment. Jack had been making legal money ever since. The town's slums started doing better about the time Jack started buying them, and Dean's share in the dope deal evolved into a small interest in his brother's business, which paid off in the form of cabled money whenever he ran good and stuck in whatever godforsaken place out west, and that winter as free room and board in the inlaw unit downstairs in Jack's suburban colonial. Jack diagnosed Dean's politics as communist and his mental disease as paranoia, neither of which, Dean admitted, were very far off, although he would no more have joined the party of Marx than that of the Bennetts, no more have left his spiritual burden in Vienna than in Galilee.

Jack's wife Carole had taken her straying husband back once he started to show a profit. She was not so concerned about Dean's politics (or mental health) as his soul, although it seemed to Dean that she wanted to save his soul more for her own sake than for his. It occurred to him that that perception might only be more paranoia, but her bouts of apparent depression when he declined to go to church with them seemed real enough. And theological controversy, into which his conversations with his brother had a tendency to stray, was strictly forbidden him in her home because his unbelief might taint the faith of her four-year-old; faith which, considering the boy's tender youth, seemed to be prodigious. The lad spent the better part of whole days banging on a toy drum and singing "Onward Christian Soldiers" at the top of his young lungs.

So Dean decided right after Thanksgiving not to tax Carole's hospitality any more heavily if he could help it. Heading back to BC was a possibility, although he did not relish crossing the prairies in December, especially not in the old VeeDub, whose heater hardly worked at all. Finding temporary work was another – that would both get him out of the house and account for his beer and cigarette money. But if he were going to work, he had to show some principle about it.

There was no clamor for treeplanters in Michigan that winter. Now that was a principled occupation. Treeplanters struck back at the keepers, undid even a tiny bit of their destruction. It was a small gesture, but a significant one. Dean would not pump gasoline, on principle. He would not work in a factory, on another principle, that he would go crazy cooped in such a place repeating an action eight hours a day. Besides, he knew as much as he cared to about industrial carcinogens. There were restaurants, and certainly fewer objections of principle to them than, say, gas stations, but he didn't particularly care for the idea of dealing chemically charged food to chemically charged Americans. He didn't have any really useful skills, such as those of a mechanic or carpenter; it was kind of scary when he thought about it how little he was good for. As snow accumulated in December he would escape the inlaw downstairs to ski at one of the State Game Areas or County Parks. He'd spend the occasional evening in the March Hare on Wealthy Street. Even at that, the combination of a sanctimonious Christmas and an anything but festive New Year's holiday sent him to the want ads. He looked under tree and found "Tree Pruner: Piecework" and a telephone number.

He had an only vaguely peculiar conversation with a small capitalist whose success it was not really possible ? to gauge over the telephone. This individual, one James, spoke of tree pruning, at least his corner of it, in the first person plural. The trees were apple. Dean could purchase a saw for six dollars at a farm supply store down the road from the orchard. They were paying two dollars a tree. James revealed no interest in Dean's work history or job qualifications, and may even have been pleased that he didn't seem to have many. "How many trees can a person prune in an hour?" Dean thought to ask before hanging up.

"Two, maybe three," came the reply. That did not sound like a great deal of money, but Dean really needed very little. "So when can you start?" asked the small capitalist on the other end.

"Tomorrow," Dean supposed.

"We'll see you then," James agreed.

In certain ways, in almost all ways in fact, pruning trees was not bad. There was the small matter of money, or was it the matter of small money? At the beginning, it took a long time to prune a tree. You climbed up into it and, working limb by limb with the curved coarse-toothed saw, cut off every single branch or twig that touched another, that looked dead and useless, or that stuck up off the bough, suckers they were called. Climbing apple trees reminded Dean of several summers past, the summers he caddied at the country club where, waiting for a loop, he would sit on a branch against a smooth trunk formed as though expressly for his body, and read. For some reason he remembered reading Dostoevsky in that tree. Spacious construction and friendly size made the apple the preeminent monkey-swinging tree, at least for a human being to swing in, and now Dean thought more than once about his animal ancestry as he gamboled from branch to branch. Work time was always for him thinking time, half about the work, half something approaching pure thought, speculation, going out on a limb, which was not an inappropriate pun. And there was an ineluctable something about being in a tree and off the ground and thinking that necessitated the extra, the free, play of mind, the ungrounded thought, an even worse pun than the first, but equally appropriate. The thought's other half, about the tree, about the work, was, unlike practically any thought about any work he had ever done before (including planting trees), a real pleasure as well. Pruning an apple tree was a creative act, a cutting away not unlike sculpture, in fact a form of sculpture, and very satisfying. The only problem being that it took an hour and a half to finish even one.

The first day, he made enough money to pay for his saw. The second for his pacs – rubber boots with cheap pile lining he bought at K-Mart. The third day for his gloves and heavy socks. Having paid for his gear in three days, Dean went skiing on the fourth.

Had it not been for the Michigan winter he might never have gone back to the orchard. He had failed, after all, to make a decent day's wage in three, even if the work was principled. But after being outdoors four days in a row, and intending to drink coffee and smoke cigarettes and work crossword puzzles and then watch the basketball games with Jack on Saturday, he found instead that Carole's radio gospel hours and his nephew's drumming and bawling conspired to bring the walls in on top of him. The day itself was of the matter, generally grey, except that at intervals the grey glowed with luminance and exploded into brilliance as marked shafts of sunlight hit the ground like in a Jehovah movie. This would fade back to luminance, in the fading the light quality different by reversal, and finally go grey once more, all grace-noted by flurries of snow ebbing into and out of showers, in no perceivable temporal relation to the appearance of the sunlight. Such a process had repeated itself four times when Dean realized he didn't want to be indoors, and that it being Saturday the ski trails would be crowded, and that he might as well go prune a tree.

The thing was that it had been happening every day, not the same thing, but this almost painful sense of beauty around him, each of his last four days as clearly marked by its own features as by what he had earned, lined up in memory like fondly remembered lovers with whom one has parted on good terms. Huge globs of snowflakes falling, muffling the orchard warmly, on the first; on the next, the sky an intense blue dome fading peninsularly to white at three horizons, the sun defined not by its own gold ball but by a fiery corona spread like angel's wings, drawing the spacious composition its way; the fine biting fall of light powder on the third day. Which had lured him to ski on the fourth, kissed by a wind that sang overhead while he frolicked through the gullies along the creek in the game preserve. There was to that winter a beauty he had never expected; before in Michigan he spent winter indoors, and out west had come to think that where there were no mountains or ocean there was nothing to look at or feel. He had been wrong. When he thought of the huge expanses of ugliness into which treeplanters gaped, ruined mountains shamefully naked, thought of them and looked from his apple tree on the ridge toward the river valley etched with skeleton of oak and maple, brilliantly alive in their stature and posture, and clearly naked in quite a different way, naked in power and grace of line along a river bank that their leaves would only disguise come summer, background for a great barn and looming silo, and a red brick farmhouse decorated at windows and doors with yellow moldings in a design nearly a century old, then it made sense to Dean that he wasn't making any money pruning apple trees. It was too good a thing to be paid for.

So, although late, he returned that Saturday. The usual number of other pruners, half a dozen or so, were working in the orchard. A row or two beneath the ridge, James, whom

Dean was beginning to realize didn't care when or even if people came to work, was explaining it all to a girl, more a woman really, a tall woman in an Icelandic wool sweater, down vest, Andean chullo, and knee-high buckskin moccasins. Dean smiled at her and nodded to James, who acted as though he were absorbed in the act of teaching. For her part, the woman looked a little bored.

His day away from the orchard had refreshed Dean considerably. His arms had got some of their snap back and, glancing up occasionally to watch cloud and sun fight their running battle for the southern sky going west, he pruned swiftly, so swiftly that he finished an entire tree in less than an hour. He raked the debris into a neat pile with the saw, and climbed the next. The day was the coldest yet, he could feel it in his fingers and toes, so he worked relentlessly; he had pruned a fairly remarkable number of apple trees by the time the sun won out on the sky's southwestern edge and painted the fleeing clouds an iridescent pink, their undersides shimmering electrically. He dropped to the ground and paused to admire the sight.

"January sky," said the girl in the chullo, stepping up beside him.

She had an apple bough in one hand and a wheel in the other. An automobile wheel, not a tire, not even a rim, but an actual wheel that had broken from an axle.

He must have looked puzzled to her, which he certainly was. She laughed and said, "Never know when you're going to need an old wheel. Somebody left it in the orchard. This is not the place for it."

Dean supposed it must be heavy, but he couldn't have told that from the way she carried it. Her face was chapped pink, cheekbones high and sharp, eyes steel-blue. She looked tough. For all that, he thought she might have smiled at, or it may have been through, him.

The next day, Sunday, he made it a point to get out of the house early to escape Carole's customary pointed suggestions that he really ought to go to church again just once, just to see how much things had changed. Early and all, the girl in the buckskin and chullo was already there, perched in the row along the ridge where he'd finished the day before, sawing away, smiling that same tough smile. Dean bounded into the orchard clapping his hands and highstepping for warmth. It seemed as though she might really be smiling at, and not necessarily through, him this time.

James was the only other person to show up that day, and he didn't stick around long. "Guess no one else is coming," James muttered vaguely. His fat red face had taken a turn for the pasty. "I guess we had a party last night . . ." As James drove away, she shouted something from her tree, but Dean didn't quite get it. "What?" he called back. She shook her head and called again, something with more words to it, but he didn't understand that either. "What?" he tried again. He climbed down, and walked over. This time the smile was for him and showed a tooth missing. "That guy gives me the creeps," was all she said.

"I answered a want ad," he told her

"Me too," she confessed. "Although it seems like I should know him. I don't live that far from here." She gestured to the southeast. Dean fished for his cigarettes, and thought to offer one up to her.

"I don't want to die," she told him. "At least not that way."

Her name was Les. Leslie actually, Les for short and for friends, which, perhaps only because he had had the sense to stand and admire the end of a January day, he seemed already to be one of. When they broke for lunch, she invited him into her jeep. For no good reason, except that she seemed interested in hearing about it, and that it was something he liked to talk about, Dean started telling treeplanting stories. After they finished eating she brought out a small soapstone pipe and chunk of black hashish, and smiled in offering. She shaved the hash with a hunting knife, while he described the first time he had planted trees stoned on cannabis, the point, which grew more convoluted as he smoked, being that, although he hadn't planted very fast, he had experienced a kind of revelation concerning the relationship between himself, mountain, and tree, and that this had effected a breakthrough in his treeplanting style and perception.

She chuckled. "I used to have perceptual breakthroughs when I got high," she told him. "Now I just get high."

Aside from the fact that at one point he thought he had a grip on a branch when he didn't and had to break his fall by jackknifing at his belly on another, Dean experienced no corresponding breakthrough relative to pruning apple trees, although, perhaps because of the added danger to life and limb, he did work with a renewed level of interest, if not speed. From time to time the two of them would shout back and forth at one another, and the noise of their voices would seem to carry down the valley through the cold air, but their actual words never really escaped either's individual tree in anything but fragments. When she finished her last tree before he did his, she climbed up to help him with it, working the final branch beyond the one he straddled.

"This takes me way back," he remembered, finally attempting to communicate in sentences. "When I was a kid I used to climb trees with the girl next door."

"In ancient Ireland," she told him, "you could be executed for chopping down an apple tree. Those people took their trees seriously."

Just the sort of thing the girl next door used to tell him.

"So do you ski?" she wondered as they admired their work from the orchard floor when they were through. Particularly that last one on which they had worked together – lean, elegant, a little eccentric in design, a new form pulled from a tired old one.

"Everybody skis," said Dean.

"Well, we should go skiing," Les decided.

"Tomorrow," suggested Dean.

"No, the trails will be all chewed up. Let's give it a day or two and wait for more snow."

"Well, it's a date," he agreed.

"A date!" She laughed at the very thought. "Haven't had one of those in a while."

She had, he told himself, asked him.

II

Dean thought of himself as a pretty good skier. Les left him slipping and sliding and panting for breath. "You'll like this one," she promised when he finally caught up to her peering down a steep run into the woods. "There's a clearing at the bottom and another trail crosses down there. Turn right, or you'll end up in the trees." She flashed that smile with the missing tooth, which should have warned him. "If you can," she added, and jumped at it.

It was slick. It was also perfect, the track well-banked and fairly wide. Still, Dean nearly lost it immediately on the straightaway, going faster than he expected. He managed one tight curve where the bank did the turning for him, and then he saw the clear space she had described. An easy uphill escape to the left, but no, she said right, so he hit the clearing favoring his left, managed to plant his ski, kicked right with the right, lifted the left and turned it, which pointed him barreling straight, fast, downhill, and very off balance at a running creek. She stood relaxed beside it, on parallel skis. Still smiling. Dean bailed hard into the bank and came up spitting snow. "I ought to throw you in," he cried. He could see by a scraped trail of thrown powder that she had taken the turn at dead center and simply slid to a stop, a neat trick on cross country skis, the attempt at which would have launched him on a flight whose second somersault would have dumped him in the creek.

"Try it," she offered.

"You're bigger than me," he decided.

"And meaner," she reminded him genially.

She was not only a great skier, she was a sexy skier. She had an uncanny sense of gliding balance located in hips well swung, and since Dean spent a whole outing behind her, he saw enough to expand his conception of attractive skiing.

By the time she finally paused again, he was breathless. Since she skied so trimly, it was amazing to see everything she was carrying in her day pack: a piece of wool blanket for sitting on a log, a bota, salami, cheese, chocolate, the little denim bag in which she kept her pipe and hashish, and another piece of blanket on which to spread the meal across the snow. Everything seemed planned, right down to the log she chose, just at the edge of the forest, tucked under a ridge protected from wind at the north and west, facing a sweeping vista of rolling Michigan countryside. Dean's eyes followed the forested contours of the creek all the way to the river, itself marked by twin ridges snaking toward the horizon. The landscape was shrouded from above by soft greyness, the sun marked in the sky only as an indistinct circle of silver and – except for one rusty green stand of planted pine on a hill, and one long narrow finger of blueness cutting across the southern sky – the colors of the scene were the grey, white, and black of naked forest, suggesting photographic qualities of light and shade.

"You should quit smoking," she told him as he dug panting through his clothing for his cigarettes, and he responded by tossing a fluff of snow at her face.

He ducked her punch more to keep the cigarette lit than from any great fear of her mittened fist. "Where did you learn to ski like that?" he wanted to know. The bota was filled with a crisp red wine suited somehow to the winter's chill.

"Right here," she told him. "Along this very creek."

"Ever been in the mountains?" He imagined how stylishly she might attack some of the more demanding runs he'd been on in the west.

"Never in the winter."

"You'd love it," he told her. "The Snowy Range in Wyoming, even the coast range in BC, Garibaldi, right outside Vancouver even, when the snow is right . . ."

"I don't doubt it's wonderful," she told him, "But I have an awful lot right here. A winter like this, with all this snow, I don't even think about mountains. In a bad year . . ." She paused. "Well, then you wait for the next."

"It is close to home," he admitted. "Your home, I mean." She cut him a slice of the coarse-textured salami. "Is that ever good," he marveled upon tasting it.

"Deer," she explained. "I made it myself."

"I bet you killed the deer too," he realized.

"Well, yes. Last winter. Time to get another. Want to come along?" A date of another sort entirely?

"Deer aren't in season!" he protested.

"Well, you don't think I go into that shooting gallery in November, do you? For one thing, you can't find any deer, and besides it's dangerous. I'd rather take my chances with the

DNR. I track them on snowshoes out behind where I live."

"And the DNR?"

"They've never bothered me yet."

That morning, he'd left the VeeDub at her place, a small frame house on a yet half-wild acreage that seemed to be trying to hold out the era pressing toward it along the rest of the road – brick tri-levels and ranches on cramped lots with the hands of not particularly brilliant landscape gardeners everywhere evident. When they got back, she invited him to have a look around.

But the sad fact was, Brother Jack had laid down a bit of an ultimatum. Show up for dinner at least once a week or other arrangements might get made, monetary arrangements if no other sort, and that week's deadline had arrived. It was only the first week such a deadline had been threatened, but the ground beneath it felt a little uncertain at that moment. Carole, did not care to serve her roasts late for stragglers. It occurred to him that Les, clearly no vegetarian, might be welcome, perhaps, if she liked, and if she was interested he could come in and wait if she wanted to change. It didn't sound like quite so great an idea to her, apparently. She may have had a suspicion or two of her own, he supposed.

He did have the presence of mind to mention that a treeplanter friend was in town on his way to Ontario, and that a bunch of people were getting together that night at the Hare, their old college hangout. "I've heard of that place," she said, meaning something he wasn't quite sure of. So they talked overlapping plans, none of which quite suited. Saying that yes, he would like to see her place, but more conveniently, he finally left her standing in the driveway, and maneuvered the VeeDub back out to the road, conscious of the light but noticeable warmth where her lips had touched his cheek.

A most remarkable thing occurred at the March Hare

that night. Perhaps there was something in the beer. Dean's friend Calvin had arrived in town as he often did with a pocketful of BC magic mushrooms, which, even though ingested over Carole's roast beef, did a few of their familiarly peculiar things to Dean's locomotion, perception, behavior, etc. Although this accounted for certain oddities in his and Calvin's experience, it could hardly explain the fact that at least half the human beings to walk in out of the Michigan winter night, once inside the Hare became seized with an uncontrollable desire to drop everything they were doing with their lives, get in a car, any car, although preferably Dean's VeeDub, and head, starting that very instant, for BC to, of all things, plant trees. There must have been some cause and effect involved in all this, but Dean would have been hard put to figure it out. On the cause side, such facts as that some people in the Hare still remembered him from the old days and had heard garbled reports of his adventures in the Great Pacific Northwest, as that Frans Vander Grove, legendary Dominee of BC planting, had once gone to school with them all and drunk in the Hare and was not forgotten, as that maybe Dean and Calvin were telling each other loud war stories as soon as they sat down while the place was still half-empty, stories that may have been something of attention grabbers; all of that, probably was causal. But such effects! People in Michigan seemed to know a remarkable amount about planting trees. Such as that:

Treeplanting is . . . fun!

Treeplanting is, is . . . spiritual!

Treeplanting sounds like . . . a good way to make a lot of money!

Treeplanting sounds like . . . a good way to get close to nature!

Treeplanting is . . . free!

Treeplanting is . . . a good way to get into shape, stop smoking, lose weight, etc.

To each of which propositions Dean and Calvin howled gleeful affirmation, telling the people that it was all true, but that it was every person for theirselves out there, and that no one was going anywhere with them. Somewhere in the middle of this, innumerable trips to the pisser, to the parking lot to try someone else's dope, the Budweiser Clydesdales jitterbugging around their globe, the Hamms bear softshoeing through a remarkably downtempo rendition of "Can't Get No Satisfaction" and then falling in his sky blue lake, a phone call from someone in Hollywood who used to drink in the Hare and had just sold a script for $300,000 and was buying drinks for everybody the rest of the night, somewhere in the middle of all this Les came in.

What Dean remembered about it the next day, and she had not stayed long, was that in an incredible morass of shouted conversation, flashing colored lights, comings and goings, utterly jumbled causes and effects, her solid face and form stood for a brief moment as a fixed point in a universe twirling toward nowhere. She was there, finding him, he long beyond looking for a specific person, least of all her, and he knowing it was her, not by sight, because that night without her parka and chullo she looked quite different, but by her hand on his shoulder, a thing he had not felt before, but recognized immediately.

"You sure have weird friends," she told him in the tree the next day. She was already on her fourth when he arrived late, and rather than face a whole one, he climbed up to help her. If he hadn't expected her to be there, he wouldn't have come out of doors at all. But now, it was as though equilibrium were returning, and the winter sky with battleship clouds drifting across it braced him. It was good to see her.

"You mean Calvin?" he asked, only a trifle defensively.

"No, no. He struck me as quite sane. He wasn't nearly as far gone as you. I mean all those people talking about planting trees. I've never seen so many people so unhappy about where they were."

"Nobody seems to have any sense of place anymore," she concluded in afterthought.

"Boy are you ever burned," she laughed at him later as he fumbled with a branch.

"You should take credit for all these," he offered. "I'm not doing a thing up here."

"Don't be silly," she replied.

Soon after that, they quit for the day. "Let's ask James when we get paid," Les decided.

"Friday," James told them.

"For last week?" wondered Dean.

"No . . ." James answered foggily. "Just tell me how many you've done up until then and I'll pay you."

"Cash on the barrel?" Les wanted to know.

"Well, I'll write you a check," he promised.

"That seems reasonable, doesn't it?" decided Dean as they stood on the road.

"Yea, well, we'll see about that." She didn't sound quite so sure. "You get some sleep, you hear," she told him. "Tomorrow you have to do your share." She grinned and pulled the jeep door shut. Dean thought that, yes, it was time for him to do his share. He tapped on the window. "Shall I pick you up tomorrow? It's on my way."

"If you spend tonight like you did the last . . ." she began, arching an unplucked eyebrow. He shook his head wearily. "See if I'm still there," she decided. He waved from the VeeDub as she drove away.

The next morning was bitterly cold. The jeep was still

parked by her house and Les stepped outside when he pulled up. "Tea!" she suggested. "Come in for a cup of tea."

"But I haven't done a thing all week," he protested. "Once I get into a warm place I won't leave it."

Les looked at the sky. "We should take my jeep," she offered.

He was determined to do his share. "No, that's OK," he insisted. "I've already got this thing running."

She seemed to consider the issue for a moment, and then climbed in. He had to lean low over the steering wheel to be able to see through the semi-circular peep hole defrosted there.

There must have been a number value in either Celsius or Fahrenheit that expressed how cold it was that day, but no number could describe how the gritty wind whistled at the ridge out of an ice-white sky. "I've been fooling myself," Dean shouted over it through the branches, "thinking I was tough in the cold. I'm not sure how long I can take this."

She looked at him with eyes as sharp as the wind and nodded yes. It wasn't long before his fingers had gone away and his toes were thinking about following. "I'm going to have to quit," he realized. "I can't hang on to the saw." As if to prove that point the tool fell from his hand to the snow below. Dean managed his way out of the tree, but walking was a problem with no toes. Les took his hand and led him back to the road, where James and three others sat in a Vega with the engine running.

Retrieving his keys from his pocket was no joke, and he only got to them by scraping a balled fist around inside until everything spilled out. The keys fell to the packed snow on the road as he tried to get his glove back over his fingers. Les picked them up and got into the driver's seat. The VeeDub's engine clicked and complained, but wouldn't turn over for her. "Shit," muttered Dean, falling into the passenger side. "It must need its master's touch." He stumbled back around to the wheel but couldn't even feel the key, let alone turn it. She could, and did, while he punched at the accelerator with a numb right foot. No luck. "I really do have to get warm soon," he realized.

"I know," she agreed. "We better go get in James' car."

He hobbled over to the Vega. James tried to ignore them, but Les beat on the window until the man opened it just a crack. "Let us in there," she demanded. "Dean's starting to freeze."

"No room," said James. "And we're leaving."

"Wait a minute," she cried, "then give us a ride."

"No room," repeated James and threw the car into gear, rolling up the window as he accelerated. All Les could do was kick a dent into the rear fender as the wheels spun on the packed snow before gaining traction.

Dean had no hands, hardly any feet, and the world was becoming a good deal whiter than snow itself might account for. The VeeDub, the only object of which he had much consciousness, was taking on a fuzzy cottony quality. Les's hand was back on his arm. "Can you hear me?" she asked loudly. Dean nodded dumbly. "Here's what you have to do," she told him above the wind. "We can turn that engine if we get it rolling. Can you help me get it to the downslope there?"

Dean had a faraway sensation of stumbling against the vehicle and trying to shove with his shoulder. She had the wheel with one hand and the frame with her other, and he never knew if he helped her at all. The car was moving and then he was falling. He lay on his belly in the road and watched the fuzzy bug roll lazily down the little hill, until, halfway to the bottom it shuddered all over and there was a moment of silence before the engine sputtered alive.

He tried to stand, but the car got back to him before he found his footing. He heard the engine being gunned to full choke, and then he was being picked up and thrown bodily into the car. "Jesus, I'm glad it didn't kill," came a dim familiar voice. "Now listen, we'll be home soon . . ." they were moving. "Can you take off your gloves?" He couldn't. She reached for his hands with one of hers, and yanked off first one, then the other. She pulled down his parka zipper. "Get those hands under your arms," she ordered him. As if dreaming he did as he was told, crossing his chest. His fingers burned at the warmth of his armpits. "Can you beat that?" she mused, almost to herself. "He would have left you there to freeze."

"Cigarette," mumbled Dean.

"No!" she objected. "Not until we get home. That nicotine constricts your blood vessels."

"But I want one," he pled. Things seemed to be growing a little clearer. "They're in the glove box."

She was disgusted. "Get them yourself." It was painful, but his fingers were working again. He fumbled for the pack and managed to pull out the cigarette, but couldn't light the match. "You dope," she mocked him.

His feet were still numb and his teeth rattling when they reached her house, and he leaned on her through the stinging wind. Once inside, she set him down on a wooden chair. It was always hard for Dean to remember, afterward, what that kitchen looked like that first time he was there. He remembered sitting by a black iron stove, seeing strings of garlic and dried black chili hanging in a window over a cupboard, seeing walls covered with cookware hanging on nails, remembered a cat examining him. Les's actions had something like logic and selfpossession to them, although he was quite beyond understanding the values expressed by their order.

Considerately, she lit one of his cigarettes and stuck it in his mouth. "Now you may smoke, stupid," she told him. Then she unlaced his pacs and pulled them off. She poured warm tap water into a basin and placed it between his feet. "This is going to hurt," she warned him, picked them up one by one and got them into it. It did hurt, but at least they were there. She threw kindling into the stove and lit it. As it flared, she poured him a glass of whisky. As he came to, he realized that all this was being done for him.

"Are you all right?" he finally had the presence of mind to ask her.

"Oh, I'm fine," she assured him. "I'm cold too, but not like you were there." She stuffed firewood into the stove, and as it burned the room began to warm. Dean's feet were throbbing, and he must have grimaced because she said, "Yea, hurts doesn't it? Good thing too. It means they're all right." Then she threw him a heavy white robe. "Take off your clothes." He heard water running a room over as he undressed. It was a tremendous relief to be rid of the stiff frozen fabric. She reappeared in a bath towel. "Come on, I've got a treat for you," she invited him.

The bathroom was as warm and steamy as a summer night's dream, the shower primitive and functional, three cheap metal walls, a plastic curtain, and room for two. She took the robe from him and guided him in. "Come on, you'll have to share," she said and pressed against him under the warm downpour. They embraced, squeezing hard, and he rested on her strength, the pain in his feet a thing long forgotten. "How are you now?" she asked through the steam.

"Just very tired," he heard himself reply with a heavy sigh.

"Well then," she said, herself breathing deeply in the thick warm air, "I'll just have to put you to bed." She smiled, girlish, hair plastered against her forehead. "And I'll join you." She kissed his chest. "To keep you warm."

Dean smiled, shook his head, and said, "Of course."

She took him without apparent concern for contraception, ghosts in the past, or any time but then. Lit in the half-light of what was by now a blizzard outside, his body found its difficult exhilarating way through the final passages of thawing. It had nothing to do with seduction, with force, or even a distinction between male and female, between do and done to. It was mutual.

"You slept for hours," she told him when he awoke. She was dressed, standing by the bed, a book in her hands. "You should see the weather. Listen." She fell still. The wind tore at the house, crystalline snow hissing against the frame. "I wouldn't be surprised if we lost power sometime tonight." She seemed utterly unconcerned. "There's a good movie on TV too." Dean looked dreamily around a small dark room seen for the first time. He had not come to expect such blessings from life. He almost said, "I love you," but realized how foolish that would sound.

She undressed and was back in the bed with him. "I've made some supper," she told him. "But first . . ." They lay together afterward listening solemnly to the blizzard.

Much later, still in bed, which was the only place he wanted to be, Dean sat with his back propped against a large pillow, wearing her white robe, watching the movie on a small black and white TV. Les slept quietly, all but a small part of her face buried in the wool blanket and down comforter. The cavelike room smelled of many good things, snow, candle wax, hashish, apple sawdust, sex. The white robe bore traces of a scent she must once have worn, and fit him tightly through the shoulders. The movie was the 1960s British production of *Sons and Lovers,* directed by Jack Cardiff. It seemed to Dean to be somewhat disjointed, almost incoherent, but frightening in its visual beauty. He smoked a cigarette as he watched. Somewhere near what must have been the end of the picture, Paul Morel's tearstained face in full closeup simply disappeared from the screen as the power did in fact go out. Dean sat in the darkness and finished his last cigarette, particularly conscious that one of his shoulders, bared by the robe's wide neck, was being brushed gently by his own long hair whenever he moved his head. The blizzard may have been slackening a little.

III

They were afterward to refer to those three days as the weekend they fucked away. Which was not strictly speaking true in either sense of the word. The comforts of her bed undeniable, Dean did finally after twenty-four hours climb out of it. By then, it was as though the heart of the storm had gone by, although it remained very cold, the wind blew, and the snow kept coming down. The VeeDub out in the driveway had been parked in just the position to catch the biggest drift in sight. "Hell of a place for a driveway, isn't it?" Les laughed. "That's why I use the other side. It's a good thing we like each other. You aren't going anywhere for a while."

"You parked it there on purpose," he accused her unseriously.

"I think I had other things in mind," she replied.

Her domestic economies were what intrigued him and they were everywhere evident. The most striking thing about the living room was the four guns, two rifles and two shotguns, displayed in a hardwood rack just above one of her bookcases. She had no qualms about killing. "Even when I was a kid," she told him, "I never bought that Bambi as adorable little sweetheart bullshit."

The upright freezer in the cellar was running low on venison, but there were rabbit carcasses, several birds, large plastic bags full of fish fillets, green vegetables, berries of different colors stacked in a pattern that might have been taken for a color code, and it all struck him as expressing a remarkable formal intelligence. She held a frozen bird in either hand. "Pheasant or grouse?" she offered. "I save them for special occasions."

Dean chose pheasant.

In the furthest corner from the furnace stood a wine rack stocked with bottles whose labels suggested some delicate compromise between closeout-bin cheap and potentially expensive. There were still price tags stuck unpretentiously to several and when he looked at one she laughed. "Never pay more than four dollars," she advised. "Anything more expensive was a gift. Sometimes I feel like I'm in a foreign country and wine is the only thing safe to drink. The ground water's full of chemicals, and did you read what they just found out about carcinogens in beer?" Next to the wine, there were fishnet bags of carrots, turnips, and potatoes, and above them winter squash lining a ledge. Row after row of jars of tomatoes and tomato sauces in several different textures and shades stood in an open cupboard, and next to them peppers, apples, applesauce, peaches and pears, one after another like toy soldiers in a cartoon store. Behind the cupboards, some- one, presumably her, had stretched animal pelts on wooden racks. "Wabbit," she explained. "Useful stuff." The cellar's most pronounced odor emanated from there, but it was not disagreeable to Dean. It smelled like her.

"There's a word for what you're doing," he told her over the pheasant, delectable in a tomato sauce, by candlelight, the power still off. He had spent most of the afternoon sitting in the wooden chair in the kitchen by the stove, reading *Mu: The Lost Continent,* while she baked bread. He had no idea there were so many Mu books. Her library fascinated him nearly as much as her cellar. It was arranged alphabetically by author and the bulk of it seemed to be in the K's and L's: Kafka, Kerouac, D. H. Lawrence, and Ursula Le Guin, including the *Dangerous Visions* number with "The Word for World is Forest." Also poetry, history, and speculation, all run through each other on the shelves.

"So what do you think about this Mu?" he wondered.

"Well, it's curious isn't it?" she answered. She began to explain about continental drift and Gondwanaland, and handed him a big white book by a poet named Olson with an illustrative map on the cover.

"There's a word for what you're doing here," he said again.

"Yes," she answered him this time. "Survival."

"That too," Dean agreed. "I was thinking of husbandry."

Late that night, the power came back on and they watched the news. The blizzard had paralyzed the eastern American megalopolis; a few brave souls skied beneath Manhattan's stark towers. "But the problem is," he said, "if it really does all come to a stop . . ." He paused, and laughed. "I'm sorry, this is ungrateful, but you'd just last a little longer, you'd be one of the last to go, that's all."

"At least," she returned, "I can shoot, I'd go down fighting."

"Yes, but fighting what?" he murmured.

The next day they skied and that involved getting into town to get his skis. The snowplows had finally made it out, and from the number of cars impacted in snow banks it looked as though normal life in the area had been pretty thoroughly disrupted. They drove her jeep, which, Dean suggested, had they taken on Thursday none of it would have happened. "Wanna bet?" she shot back.

"Well, we might still be working for old James," he pointed out. "What are we going to do about him? I'd just as soon have my money, however little it is."

"You know what the problem's going to be?" she shook her head. "I kicked seventy-eighty bucks damage into that fender. My foot still hurts."

"And he just left us there!"

"Well, I'll think of something," she concluded matter-of-factly. "I'll fix him."

Jack and Carole were at church, with a Sunday roast cooking in the oven. "Wow, you can smell the PBB," Les decided. Dean collected his skis and some clothing and left a note saying he was alive and well. It had not occurred to him until then, standing in their suburban kitchen, so incredibly unlike hers, that his brother and sister-in-law might be wondering where he was. On the way out of town, he made a conscious decision not to buy cigarettes.

The next day, they shot wabbits. Or rather, Les shot wabbits. The old Merry Melody, Elmer Fudd, fat self-satisfied face-on mug shot, finger before lips, "Be vewy vewy quiet. I'm . . . hunting . . . Wabbits!"

She did it perfectly. "Ole James," she chortled, "I knew he reminded me of something. Elmer Fudd!"

"Ever shot anything?" she asked him as he hefted the .410.

"Only a bear," Dean told her. It was his best story and he'd been saving it. People were always impressed.

She didn't bat an eye. "Wabbits are smaller. Anyone can hit a bear."

They went back to the end of her property, she on snow-shoes, he skiing and feeling quite strange to be doing so with a weapon strapped to his back. They climbed a wooded hill, and she led him to a cornfield. The stalks leaned erratically, nearly buried in all that new snow. "Lot's of dry corn under there," she explained quietly. "Wabbits love it . . ." She brought the rifle, a Winchester lever action .22 out of a cowboy movie, to her shoulder and fired. It was as though the shot itself created a rabbit there, dead, next to one of the stalks.

"Holy mackerel!" breathed Dean. "I didn't even see that." She grinned. "It takes practice. I aim for the head to save the pelt." During the next two hours, she wreaked a mighty slaughter, plopping through the field on the snowshoes. Dean fired a couple of times himself but didn't hit a thing. It didn't matter, she killed enough for them both. And the shotgun would have ruined the pelts.

"The thing is, it's all well and good to kill rabbits," she told him as she stood over the bench beneath the bare light bulb and ran the knife along the furry belly, "but it doesn't end there. There's no point to killing them if you aren't going to utilize. I'd let you dress one, but I have to be careful about the pelt." She said it as though of course one would covet the pleasure of gutting a rabbit. He watched how she used the knife for leverage as she pulled the skin from the flesh. They ate two of them in a fricassee for supper. When they went to bed that night, Dean realized that the smell on her hands was blood.

IV

True to her word, Les fixed Ole James, or Elmer, as she had come to call him. Dean was reading about Gondwanaland and smelling the rabbit he was roasting in the woodburning oven when she came in grinning hugely, smugger than anyone he'd ever seen.

"Well, I went to see the farmer," she beamed through

that space where a tooth had once been.

"The farmer?" Dean replied blankly.

"Whose trees we were pruning for James. I told him about last week. Boy was he pissed. And he doesn't like their work anyway. He said there were only two good rows in the whole orchard so far. Guess whose?"

Dean could.

"Well, there's no legal contract on any of this, it's all word of honor. Ours."

"Ours?"

"Yours and mine, sweety, at five dollars a tree."

"James is getting five dollars a tree?"

"Not any more he's not. I doubt he ever was. I talked Farmer Brown into it by convincing him our trees would be good."

"You're incredible," was all Dean could say. "So how many are there? I've only got a few weeks left."

"About five hundred."

He did some quick mental math. "We'll have to work everyday and hope for no more blizzards."

"Don't worry, we'll make it." A car roared in the driveway. "I'll bet that's Elmer now. Boy, is he gonna be pissed."

He was, and Dean almost felt sorry for him. He had to keep telling himself that this was a person who had been quite willing to let him freeze his fingers and toes off a short week earlier. Les was just plain cruel, she mocked him, told him he was a fool, that she ought to bust his ugly face. Most of it James just took, he didn't seem to want a fistfight with Les any more than Dean might have, but he acted like something else was wrong besides and kept looking past her at the rifle rack. Dean didn't like it, he just wasn't sure about all those guns, although he had to admit he liked eating what they killed.

There was another hunting scene, and it left them with fresh venison. One morning, Les noticed tracks in the orchard. The next day she brought a rifle, and they arrived before dawn to find the whitetail buck lying on its side under one of their trees. When it arose and cast a deep, almost personal, gaze upon them she shot it through the heart.

He was by that time no longer amazed at her skill in such things, although he was growing to admire it more and more as his time with her ebbed away. But on this occasion his admiration was laced with an almost empty regret that their lives required another creature's death, and when he attempted to express this he did so clumsily, somehow phrasing it in terms of the legality of what they had done.

She looked up from her butchering on the work bench in the cellar. "Those laws are for people who kill for sport," she told him simply. "I abide by older laws."

Dean thought he understood. He was, he realized, coming to see things from her point of view. "Like not cutting down an apple tree?"

"That's right," she agreed. "Unless there's a good reason to."

It occurred to him that what set her apart from all the dirty old treeplanters and treeplanting old dirt farmers he knew in BC was her predation, and at that word he stopped. The next thing he knew he'd be putting her at the top of the evolutionary ladder because she was at the top of the food chain. Sometimes Dean wished he'd never been to school. He was glad he wasn't a small capitalist. He wanted to take her back to BC with him and she was as adamant about having none of it as a person could possibly be. Somehow, she connected it with that crazy night in the March Hare, even though, as he attempted to explain, that had nothing to do with anything since the people talking so foolishly had no idea about treeplanting, they weren't treeplanters. He could just see her as a hotshot on one of Frans' crews. She'd plant circles around most of them.

She would reply, with a logic demanding attention, that anything with that much bullshit attached to it at twenty-five hundred miles had to have a fair amount on location. "And besides," she said, "my life is here. I've built one. I'm not interested in romance and adventure. I'm interested in living my life."

"What's the most you ever made in a month planting trees?" she finally asked him over venison.

"Fifteen hundred dollars," he replied. It was true, for all the talk of hundred dollar days, they were matched one on one by traveling, frustrated waiting for one thing or another, and what an old not-fondly-remembered contractor he had worked for once used to call downtime. "Well look!" she told him. "We're making twelve-fifty each for this month's pruning. And we get to live at home."

"Yes, but we can't keep this up forever," he shot back prematurely.

She had him then. "Hey kid. Let me tell you something you may not have figured out, you can't keep that treeplanting up forever either. Aside from the fact that your strong youthful body won't be that way forever, one of these days that little VeeDub is going to break down, or the price of gasoline will go so high that you won't be able to drive twenty-five, or even five, hundred miles whenever you want. There's going to be a whole lot more world again, and what's going to count is what you've got and how you've treated it, how much hasn't been wasted. And you've wasted everything you've ever had as far as I can tell."

That angered him. "Listen goddammit," he began, "I love you," and stopped dead because that was the first time that either of them had said it.

Were those tears? On her tough cheeks? "It's been a long time since I've heard that word," she confessed.

He was confusedly eloquent. "Well it's not what I meant to say, but it's true. And Jesus, Les, you'd smother me, given half a chance, with all this prosperity, this readiness. I know it's an old silly story, but in a week I have to hit that continental trail. There's nothing to be said for it."

"Well, first of all," she was rubbing her cheeks, "I love you too. That's hard for me to say. It's a funny word. Second, I've got everything here. Prosperity, readiness, that's the whole point. If the end comes, if it all stops, we can go down fighting. Together. That's worth something to me."

"I think," he said, cocking his head at a curious angle, "that I just heard myself proposed to."

"Not marriage, silly," she corrected him, and those tears started again. Then she giggled. "Whoever heard of a marriage with two husbands?" She stood. "I have something for you. I was going to give it to you the day you left." She went to the cellar and returned with a light lever action Winchester in a style much like her .22. "Actually," she continued, "it's our back wages from Elmer. My half is a gift to you." Carved on the stock was a small gothic letter D. It was evident, though not obvious, that a J was embedded there.

"And that's why he was looking at the rifle rack that night."

"That's right."

"You pulled a B & E? You truly are incredible!"

"Whatever."

"If it weren't our back pay, you know, I'd have a tough time accepting it."

"It's a 30-30. I wouldn't be shooting it at bears if I were you."

There had to be a question about accepting it anyway, and Dean thought hard. To do so would be to accept the smell of blood on his own hands. Nothing was simple, and it was a beautiful piece.

"If you come back," she promised, and then corrected herself, "when you come back, we'll do some shooting."

V

A week later, the orchard finished, Farmer Brown handed them a fat check that they took to the bank and divided, cash on the barrel. Dean had never headed out to plant trees with a pocketful of money before. Or with a pair or rabbit moccasins, or with a pair of rabbit mittens. He thought twice about it, he thought more often than twice. But Calvin called, and they needed him in Vancouver. "When you come back," she promised, "I'll dress you in buckskin."

The last, rather silly, thing he said to her was, "well, at least I quit smoking." She stood in the road and watched the VeeDub puttfart away, heading northwest. The rifle, racked crookedly in the back window – the only way they had been able to get it to fit – and the bumper sticker reading **Support Your Right To Arm Bears,** were going to be a paradox to the motorists on Canada One, but Dean understood. So, he knew, did she. She had given them both to him. She had given him a great deal, and soon it would be time for him to start giving back.

What would he give? he wondered, and as though she were there with him telling him, he knew. He would write long letters back to Michigan. He would learn how to shoot.

In the Hall of the Mountain King

... the world on a string doesn't mean a thing...

My friend Jake was into strength that summer. Although I wouldn't have said it in so many words, I was into weakness, so we made quite a pair.

There was never any problem with Jake putting things into words. It was one of two things he did really well and the other was fix cars. Both his conversation and his auto mechanics were of the balewire variety; you never knew which connections were going to be made next, but somehow at the end it always came out right, eccentric in design, but fixed and running. I have to add that I am a mechanical failure. When I hear an engine making funny noises all I hear are funny noises, and they don't speak to me. I can't even change oil without losing the bolt from the pan, and whenever I have been so bold as to try a simple tuneup I have crossed the sparkplug wires, put the little point apparatus (I don't even know its name) on too loosely, and bought the wrong plugs at the parts store. Jake suggested that I read *Zen and the Art of Motorcycle Maintenance.* I understood the part about classical philosophy leading to schizophrenia, and realized vaguely that I was among the foolish who couldn't fix machines, but somehow it was no help to realize this, it just made me feel foolish.

At Mile 37 on the dirt road north from Mackenzie to Finlay Forks we came upon a sign fashioned from a Trees for Tomorrow box, FVG printed in big letters, and an arrow pointing down a sideroad toward Williston Lake. "I know this road," Jake cried happily, turning into it. "Frans and I had a slashing contract right here."

That was in 1968. The gears were building Bennett Dam and about to create Williston. Mackenzie barely existed in those days and I still don't know how Jake and Frans ended up there. I've probably heard every one of Jake's stories about that winter, and they are good stories, but there does not seem to be a first story, an originary story. All I gather is that they were there, with their chain saws, just when it came time for Bennett the First's government to log out a hundred miles of valley in three different directions from the confluence of the Peace, Parsnip, and Finlay Rivers, finish that dam, and name it in Bennett the First's honor. When we saw the dead crummy along the road Jake just said, "Well Frans will be happy to see me."

He was right.

I had never seen so many naked people of both sexes all together in my life. That was my first year planting trees, and I knew treeplanters were casual about clothing, but on the coast earlier in the year the weather was cold and rainy. There were a lot of people on Frans' contract and not many of them dressed; at least twenty went in and out of the sauna, lounged on Williston's sandy beach, a tall man and short woman washed each other's hair in the lake, a stocky man split wood, two women juggled war clubs on the landing. They were beautifully proportioned and the war clubs weren't all that was juggling. It was an amazing sight.

"Have a sauna. I'm on my way down there," was the first

thing Frans said. The two jugglers approached Jake. "This is Jake," said Frans. "This is Marty."

"Well well, so this is Marty," said Jake. "I've heard all about you.

He gave her a big hug, naked and all.

"Glad you brought the canoe," said Frans when we were inside the little plastic dome, steam hissing off the hot rocks. "There's a cabin across the lake. Someone lives there. We can see the smoke at night. I think it's Roland Skoggs."

"How do you like that!" said Jake.

He had been telling me about Roland Skoggs. As we reached further and further north Jake warmed to yarning about Mackenzie in the old days, when he and Frans were cutting the way for Bennett the First's lake. Roland Skoggs was an old, a very old, trapper who used to pass through their camp as he worked his lines, and always stopped for a coffee and a chat if they were around. The night before we had located one of his contemporaries, a prospector, who still lived where Jake remembered him, near Summit Lake, right by the ranger station. We had stopped anyway for Jake to balewire the engine, and when he finished we went down to a cabin by the lake and the old guy still lived there.

We were going prospecting for gold ourselves, but the old guy wasn't much help because he was losing his memory. What he did say, several times, was that if he were looking for gold he'd go to the Nation River, and that Roland Skoggs had disappeared about the time they put the dam in.

"Too bad about Skoggs," Jake said when we were back on the road. "Although he's probably better off."

"Why do you think it's him?" he asked Frans now in the sauna.

"I heard a story he was living on the lake. There's no road over there. If it's not him . . ." Frans' voice trailed off over the sound of splattered water hissing on the stones.

"Aaaah," said Marty.

Frans' cookshack was larger than I imagined one could be. I had been toiling in treeplanting's bush leagues. Five cents a tree and no benefits. Our shack for three straight contracts was always at least a third too small, both for the size of the crew, and for the weather. Planning, experience, and a sense of scale had obviously gone into Frans'. The camp stood on a large flat landing overlooking the lake and the shack frame was built of wooden poles twelve feet long, all unnaturally straight and uniform, stripped of their bark to a polished blonde color. The peaked roof reached high, like the ceiling of a church, but shaped like an L instead of a cross. The kitchen was situated at the foot of the L, to the far end from the entrance. The striking thing was the way the roof beams turned elegantly toward the kitchen, cutting over in a double angle:

And how neatly the support beams fanned away from the angle, and how the clear plastic spread perfectly flat along the poles. Someone obviously knew a great deal about building cookshacks, and there was also a feeling that the structure was designed not only for the comfort of the crew but as a temporary monument befitting the legend Frans already was.

Most people have probably heard about Frans Vander

Grove by now. The story goes that after he and Jake finished cutting out the timber for Bennett the First's lake, Jake headed back to Ontario, but Frans stayed in B.C. to found treeplanting as we know it. There has, of course, been tree-planting in B.C. forever, but before Frans arrived it was always done by crews hired and paid an hourly wage by the Forestry. Frans only had to plant trees for a year to realize there was money to be made, but not the way the Forestry did it. He, the story goes, told them that he could plant the trees, paid by the tree, for a great deal less than it was costing them, provided they left him to his own devices. Not the least of which was living in the bush rather than in town while the work was being done, towns tending to be some distance from most treeplanting sites in British Columbia. Paying planters by the tree put the work on an incentive basis and Vander Grove crews were tough, fast, and highly motivated. When the Forestry agreed to his scheme Frans made hay fast, and never looked back. By the mid-nineteen-seventies you couldn't find a Forestry crew to plant on, and his method was being imitated by a hundred contractors all around the province, although none of them planted as many trees or made as much money as Frans did.

I should have known that I was out of my league as soon as I saw all those naked bodies. The thing was that just to look at them I wasn't overwhelmed by an impression of particular strength, not even in the case of Frans, who is of husky peasant stock. Many of the people there were down-right wiry. Maybe the tipoff should have been all the noise, of people splashing in the lake, the steady whack-whack-whack of wood being split, the number of people shouting unintelligibly along the landing and beach. It was early summer and the camp was a circus. The thing I didn't understand until the next day was that they had all been up since four and five that morning and had planted a full day's worth of trees. I suppose I was too taken with the juggling act to think about that.

"Well," Frans said to Jake after we had saunaed, surveying Williston Lake as though he owned it, "we have to fix that crummy."

"I saw that one," said Jake. "You know what's wrong with it?"

"It was hitting on five, then four, then it stopped hitting at all," replied Frans. "Abram! Jesse!" he called at two guys trying to drown each other in the lake. "Find Teddy and go get the truck."

"Go with them, Jonathan," Jake ordered me. There was something funny about the way he said it, but I didn't know what.

The two men trying to drown each other came out of the water and headed up the bank. "Yes, big brother, anything you say," one shouted back. "Where's that Teddy?" wondered the other, big grin on his face.

"Probably smoking dope in his tent," the first replied. Then they laughed out loud.

"Who are you?" they turned to me.

"Uh, Jake's friend, Jonathan," I answered. "Who are you?"

"I'm Jesse, this is Abram," said the smaller of the two.

When we got to the cookshack they pulled on their jeans. I had left mine down by the sauna. When Jake saw me coming back he repeated his orders. "Jonathan, I thought I told you to help them get that truck."

Jake has a long face and his eyes can get very far away when he's not talking or working on cars. Those were the two expressions I was used to from him, delighted animation when something was really happening, and a sort of faraway boredom when it wasn't. But he wore a different look now, exasperation, I suppose, that something was supposed to be happening but wasn't. I must have looked back at him fairly strangely myself. "I am," I said. "I forgot my clothes."

"Oh," he muttered, and waved his hand with a quick downward flip and went back to talking to Frans.

Back at the landing, Abram and Jesse were already headed up the road followed by a strange sort of pear-shaped person. It was a hundred yards or so before I caught up to them.

"Hello," said the pear-shaped person, when I fell into step beside him. "Who are you?"

"Jonathan," I told him too.

"I'm Teddy," he informed me, and a wan smile played across his pink cheeks.

"Why don't they just take Jake's tools and work on the crummy where it already is?" I suggested.

"Uh, big brother does things his way," Teddy replied.

So we found the crummy and, with Abram steering, Teddy, Jesse, and I pushed it the whole mile back to camp. That probably sounds like harder work than it was; the road was mostly downhill toward the lake, and the crummy seemed to roll along on its own. The last few hundred yards sloped straight at the landing. When we got the wretched little truck over the last rise it took off by itself. Jesse scrambled up a steel ladder bolted to the back and ran straight to the front of the roof where he stood waving his arms for balance like a surfer. Abram never touched the brakes until the thing had careened past Jake's van and was bearing down hard on Frans' fabulous cookshack and then he slammed them hard. The crummy swerved to a stop in the sand and gravel, and Jesse let the sudden change in momentum throw him forward. He sailed into the air, somersaulted perfectly, and landed on his feet in front of Jake and Frans. Jake clapped his hands. Frans said, "You'll kill yourself someday."

Jake went under the hood with as much alacrity as Jesse had somersaulted over it. I started for the cookshack, curious for a look around, but Jake called me back: "Stay here, Jonathan, I need you to help."

Jake and Frans talked about trucks while I cleaned and gapped sparkplugs. I knew how to do that because our trouble with the van involved decaying valves, and every morning before we hit the road I would pull those plugs and clean them with a wire brush. That's what I did now. "That's not your problem," Jake told Frans when I had finished. He blew through a piece of curved metal tubing. "This isn't your problem either."

"Try and start it, Jonathan," he told me, so I climbed in and did. All I got was starter noise and funny clicking. Jake waved at me to stop. "Whadaya bet?" he said to Frans. "Got any gasoline?"

He unscrewed the wing nut over the air filter. I climbed out of the cab to watch him take it off.

"No, get back in there," he ordered me. He picked up a big red can and poured gasoline all over the engine. "Hit it," he ordered again and I jumped back in and did. The engine coughed and fire played around it and I turned the key off quick. "Fuel pump," Jake announced and tore the thing from its berth against the wheel well.

What Jake did next gets into areas as mysterious to me as the occult. Supper was close to happening, people were beginning to eat salad with chopsticks out of wooden bowls, but he sat down at the end of the table by the cookshack with the pump, a wire cutter, some electrical wire, his jackknife, and a couple of paper clips, and proceeded to fix it. It took him maybe half an hour. Frans, Marty, and the other juggler sat by him and watched. I sat next to her, the other juggler. She wore baggy cotton trousers and a sleeveless buttonless open-fronted shirt, and I attempted to talk to her. About all I learned was that her name was Lefty. "You juggle very well," I tried, but she hardly smiled. "Want to get high?" I suggested and she shook her head no, rather stiffly. When I lit a cigarette she waved the air pointedly. "Can't you do that somewhere else?" she said. I tossed the butt between the cookshack poles where the plastic had been rolled all the way up the frame.

That supper marked my first experience with tofu. For anyone who does not have the pleasure of its acquaintance, tofu is notable for two things. The first is the nutritional claims made for it. The other is its almost total lack of taste, a thing I have learned of since that night.

This tofu, for its part, had a very distinct flavor, best described as rotten, as in spoiled. I took one bite and went looking for the garbage.

The cook, a small woman wearing nothing but maroon and gold gym shorts gave me a look like she should know me but didn't, and directed me to the compost. The purpose of keeping compost on a treeplanting contract I never did get straight, but I went where I was told and found a moldering heap of organic matter under a burlap sack outside the kitchen.

When I got back to the table Jesse was telling a joke. "You dig a big hole," he began, "and then you put in a layer of horseshit. Then a layer of tofu, then more horseshit, then tofu, until the hole is full. Then you build a fire over it and let it bake all day. Then . . ." he paused for what attention he had. "You dig it up and eat the horseshit."

Nobody laughed. I started to and stopped. Jake may have cracked a smile. If Frans heard, he sure didn't let on. Marty and Lefty both shoveled it in. Work hard, eat hard. I followed Jake into the kitchen to watch him tease the cook: "So Jesse doesn't like your cooking?" She answered quietly. "Well, you know, Jake, I don't like my cooking. I was going to do the grain and vegetable trip and I get here and all he's got is these buckets of tofu and a book about it. He must have thought it was a cookbook, but there's no recipes. It's just about how great tofu is."

Jake eyed her all up and down. "Ann!" he told her. "You've just got a bad attitude."

She looked back into his deepset eyes. "I think I've got a pretty good attitude. I'm making seventy-five dollars a day. That will get me some places when I'm done here. I'm going to Afghanistan with that English guy."

I hesitated to interrupt anyone's travel plans, but at the pause I edged forward. "Uh, is there anything else to eat?" I wondered.

"More tofu," Ann told me.

"Eat what's put in front of you, Jonathan," Jake ordered me.

"Uh, besides tofu," I suggested.

"Nuts and raisins, granola?" Ann suggested. "Bread and cashew butter?"

The salad, I noticed from the oily wooden bowl, was gone.

"Is there any cheese?" I kept trying.

"Cheese?" She jumped at the word. "On this contract?"

Marty came up behind us. "Frans wants the cayenne," she announced.

"You know where it is," Ann told her.

"And where's the garlic?"

"Where it always is."

Marty picked up the biggest tin of cayenne pepper I had ever seen in my life. It occurred to me that the tofu might be palatable if I dressed it in enough of that.

"Hey! Who's throwing away good food?" a shrill voice protested outside the cookshack. Jake and Ann both looked at me. I took a small portion of tofu and followed Marty and the cayenne to the table. I had to wait a long time to get some of it, because Marty improvised a funnel from a piece of paper, and spooned cayenne through it into pharmaceutical casings the size of moose turds. She must have filled twenty, and they went as fast as she could manufacture them. Frans gulped five in one swallow.

"What's that for?" I asked her, not so much appalled as simply amazed. The poet Keats, the story goes, used to put a dash of cayenne on his tongue and swirl claret wine around his mouth, ever the sensualist. I myself am rather fond of hot food. But these people were sneaking gigantic quantities of nothing but cayenne pepper past their tongues encased in nothing but whatever those gigantic capsules were made of.

"Purification," said Marty.

And while she did that, Lefty broke up the garlic bulb, peeled the cloves and chewed them down raw. I had wondered about the smell at that end of the table.

The tofu was no better with cayenne. I remembered then that Jake and I had an emergency ration of pork and beans in the van. This, I decided, was an emergency if ever there was one.

I was firing up our camp stove out the back of the van when Jesse peered around the corner. "Whatcha' got there?" he wanted to know.

I was almost ashamed to tell him but he spied the can. "Pork and beans!" he cried. "Mucus! Harry! Calvin!" He'd have jumped out of his pants if he had any on. "Mucus!"

"Mucus!" answered a throaty brogue from halfway down the beach. "Dat's not allowed!"

A dark brown man almost totally bald and slender to the point of apparent fragility came running at full speed. Close up, his eyes burned with anger, mischief, or desire. "Hoo boy!" he looked at me hard. "Give me some of dat!"

Behind him, at a much less anxious pace, followed a strange short bearded elf who actually talked to me. "Calvin," he introduced himself.

"Jonathan," I told him.

I opened another can and found the pan I'd been meaning to fry tortillas in all along. I kept cooking and they kept telling me about mucus.

"See there's mucus in practically everything," Jesse explained. "Meat, dairy, eggs, pork and beans, everything that tastes good. Mucus is bad for you. It clogs you up and slows you down."

"Says who?" I asked.

"Frans!" they all told me.

"And how does he know this?" I wondered.

"He read it in a book!" cried Jesse.

"Well," I murmured. "That's almost enough to put you off books."

To judge by the way the three of them scarfed those beans and tortillas they were fairly tired of tofu, cayenne, and garlic.

"Well, anyone here get high?" I asked tentatively. "Does that have mucus in it too?"

"Getting high's bad energy," said Jesse. "But if you got dope, we'll get high.

"Ja, we get high," Harry agreed.

"Yes," echoed Calvin.

Behind us, the only recently dead crummy roared to life.

"Dat Jake, I hear he good wit' d' cars," said Harry. I nodded.

Calvin contemplated the lake. "There's the smoke again." He gestured over the surface and there it was, white plume against the huge northern sky. I noticed the steady plip-plop of fish breaking the water. "Can we fish around here?" I asked them all. Calvin's eyes lit up. "Nobody has," he said. "But he hasn't told us we couldn't. And you have a boat," he realized.

Jake did, was the thing, a very large imperfectly crafted freight canoe, tied to the top of the van. We'd just hoisted it down from there when Jake came out of the cookshack. "Yea, let's haul that down to the lake," he said. "What's going on here?"

"We just had some beans," I explained.

He went back inside.

"Can we fish three in that canoe?" wondered Calvin.

Jake came back out and picked up one end of the ungainly vessel. I took the other, and we lugged it down to the water. "Get that motor," he told me. He went back to the shack. By the time I was done, Jesse, Harry, and Calvin had finished the beans.

Jake and Frans came out together now and got into the canoe. "Give us a shove, Jonathan," Jake told me. I did, and started splashing after them to get aboard. Jake made one long stroke with a paddle and they were gone. I was up to my thighs in Williston, and confused.

It was hard to have anything against the legendary Frans Vander Grove, especially since he had not said so much as a word to me. And as Jake and I had enjoyed our leisurely tour of British Columbia, headed toward north and gold, but really, more than anything, just out for a couple of weeks' lark, I heard enough of Jake's stories about Frans and Mackenzie to realize that this stop in our trip was important to him. His stories seemed to glow more lustrous, set against the very mountains and forests in which they occurred. And now, I was in one of them. If I wasn't that excited about my bit role, I was at least stranded in a reasonably remote place with a bunch of fairly weird strangers, always a memorable, if sometimes peculiar, experience.

Calvin and I tried to fish from the shore but that didn't work at all. The fish were jumping but they weren't feeding, not on what we had to offer.

Williston Lake is a long way north and June days hang on tenaciously there. My interest was taken gradually by a setting sun that rather than simply sinking as it does in more central latitudes sailed slowly northward along the horizon, turning redder and redder as it cruised. Sometime during our fishless vigil a couple of women discovered the tape deck in Jake's van and, about the time Jake and Frans came back into sight on the lake, treeplanters started dancing on the landing.

I broke down my rod as they docked. "A couple of things, Jonathan," Jake told me as soon as he was out of the boat. "Don't do that again."

"Pardon me?" I eyed him.

"Don't throw any more taco parties. Frans has his own food trip together here. He's never had a crew plant more trees. He doesn't want outsiders messing with it."

I digested that, but before I could make a reply he went on. "And did you do anything to help out while I was gone? Wash some dishes? Haul some water? Chop some wood?"

I had to confess that I had not. "Well, Jonathan," he reminded me. "You're their guest. They're feeding you. You have to help."

And then he told me I could plant the next day. "But listen," he added, "your trees better be good. You can't be screwing up their plots."

"Listen," Frans told him when he was through with me. "You have to do something about that music. This just isn't the place for it."

Jake nodded his agreement, went right up the hill to the van, reached through the open passenger-side window, and yanked a wire. The music died in midchord. Half the dancers simply stopped moving and looked around curiously, all of them except for a tall and extremely handsome dark-haired woman who accosted Jake. "Why you do that?" she demanded to know.

"Frans doesn't want music," Jake replied.

"Frans a big fart!" she cried, and turned toward Frans in front of the cookshack. "Frans Vander Grove! You a big fart!"

Frans started laughing. I think it was the first, it may have been the only, time I ever saw his blonde eminence laugh. He shook his head and moved toward the cookshack door, but she chased him like a baseball player after an umpire who's turned his back. "Frans, you a big fucker!" she cried, following him to the door. He turned calmly on her. "Gretel, if you don't like it here, find somewhere else to work. Go to bed. It's late."

"Bastid!" she hissed, but did as she was told, exiting with an unhappy look on her face.

I followed her as far as the van, leaving Frans, Jake, Marty, and Lefty talking at the cookshack table. It was not yet dark but the sun had set and it couldn't have been long before midnight. I vaguely remember Jake reaching into the van for his sleeping bag yet, and imagine he slept under the sky that night.

The thin bald guy Harry, it turned out, was the fastest treeplanter in the whole world. I haven't seen them all, and that doesn't matter. He was it. Mucus and bad energy and all. Boy, could he ever plant trees.

Jesse Vander Grove was right behind him too. You can't imagine how fast those two were moving, arms and legs just swirling. The thing about Harry was that he didn't look like a big strong guy. But, Jesus, he planted fast. I guess I've said that already, but I still can't get over it.

There are no shouted orders at the site on a Vander Grove contract. Everybody already knows what to do. People just dive out of the crummy and tear into the slash. Jake and I ended up at the tail end of this arrangement, on a flat expanse of hardpacked clay. I walked across it to get to softer soil. "Where are you going, Jonathan?" Jake called after me.

"You don't plant this," I answered back. Jake was hammering away with his mattock. "Of course we do," he told me. "We plant everywhere."

"How can you plant good trees in this?" I wondered aloud. I swung with all the strength I had and dented the ground maybe three inches.

"Jonathan," said Jake. "Don't ask questions, just plant the trees."

Coastal and interior planting, I learned that day, are very different matters. On the coast, you work up and down slopes, the ground tends to be soft from spring rains and meltoff, and summer's growth of weeds and ground cover has not yet asserted itself. I know that it probably sounds easier to plant a flat plain than a mountainside, but I'm not sure it is. It wasn't easier for me.

Frans and Marty had been talking by the crummy so they were the last people into the slash. Frans blew past me in a cloud of dust. All I heard was a series of thunderous thwacks on the hardpack and when I looked back the whole thing was covered with trees.

"Wow!" I said to Jake, who seemed to be having as much trouble as I was. "How did he do that?"

Jake stood and wiped his long sweaty brow. "Frans didn't get where he is by being a weakling, Jonathan," he informed me.

Marty was on Frans' heels, planting solidly herself, classic breasts juggling rhythmically to her mattock strokes. She stopped to watch me. I had finally cleared the hardpack and was moving into a sandy area overgrown with weeds. "You put that right by one of Frans'," she told me matter-of-factly. I couldn't see where, so she pointed with her mattock, and sure enough, there it was, a little green tree in all those green weeds, about eighteen inches from where I had planted. I pulled mine out and moved eight feet over. After I replanted it she tugged the crown. "Guess that's OK," she said, not unkindly. I moved over to plant another. "Why don't you just go single line," she said. "You won't confuse anyone that way."

She laid in a triple row right in front of me and passed Jake with a smile.

Another difference between coastal planting and interior planting is the weather, and this particular June was dry and hot. It must only have been about seven in the morning by then but the sun was well along its wide looping northern summer arc. I had last worked three weeks earlier, concluding my season sore but strong and managing a steady thousand a day on mountainside. But on this day, the heat, the unfamiliar terrain, and my three week layoff conspired to make treeplanting very hard work indeed. It seemed to be pretty hard for Jake too – his motions a few trees ahead of me were jerky and strained. I could have caught up to him with a quick energy burst, but I was finding a regular, if ponderous, rhythm, and decided to just plod along one tree at a time not thinking too hard about treeplanting or anything else. After an hour or so, and a bare hundred trees in, I was maybe halfway across the flat plain.

Something happened then that returned my attention to trees. Who should come barreling toward me, planting at least a quadruple row, but Harry, with Jesse right behind.

"Ja! Tanks for last night," Harry called grinning, never breaking stride, as he sailed past.

"Wow!" I said to Jesse as he followed Harry. "That guy's incredible."

"Yea, but his trees are sloppy," Jesse replied, and moved me over another twenty feet with a triple row. He was sweating rivers, but did not seem unhappy.

The midmorning sun was high and toward the south by the time I reached the far end of the plain where, mercifully, there was a stream for soaking my hot tired head and sipping at some brown water. Harry and Jesse lapped me again as I paused. Jake barely stopped to rest, took a quick drink and started back. He looked fairly frustrated, annoyed at some inadequacy, and he had nothing but a grunt for me.

For my part, I had decided not to be too hard on my own self. The most frustrating thing was being passed continually by people planting eccentric two-three-and-four-tree rows, and every time I got passed I had to move over several feet and learn to follow a different planter's line. I was beginning to adjust to this disruptive mode when a woman about my size with the body of the Venus de Milo and the face of the Wicked Witch of the West chewed me out for not keeping the line straight. I recognized her voice from outside the cookshack about the tofu. "These trees, all through here, they're terrible," she accused me.

"But I haven't been in there," I said. "And I'm only planting single row."

"Everybody else keeps this straight!" she cried shrilly. "Everybody but you."

I must confess that I laughed.

"It's not funny," she stormed, waving her mattock in my face. "I'm going to tell Frans."

Ahead of me, she stopped Jake, pointed back at me, and screamed at him. He nodded weakly. He did not look good.

By the time I reached the road I was miserable with heat and sweat. I found the water tank and drank deeply, which certainly helped. Lousy as I felt, it had to be better than Jake looked. He was turning somewhat green. Nonetheless, he did an extraordinary thing. First of all, hardly able to put words together, he reprimanded me for an offense he didn't exactly seem to understand but that my witchy Venus had assured him I was guilty of.

"Jake," I replied, "I don't know what her problem is, but she's full of shit."

He asked how many trees I'd planted. I said five hundred and he stumbled over to the box, took a single bundle, untied it, put the trees into his bag, and went back into the slash. I went to the lunch stash and had a grapefruit. About the time I was feeling a little better and ready to go back in, Harry and Jesse came walking toward me with empty bags and mattocks over their shoulders.

"How many d'ya plant, Jonathan?" asked Jesse.

"Five hundred so far," I told him.

"So far?" he smiled. "It's all over, we're done. Just so they're good trees."

"Jesse?" I marveled. "All over? How many have you planted?"

"Two," he told me.

"Two thousand!?" I cried startled.

"Yea," he said. "Too much mucus in me, I guess."

"And Harry?" No one could plant two thousand trees in one morning.

"Twenty-five."

"Twenty-five hundred!?"

"Ach ja," said Harry. "Too much mucus."

They both started laughing.

"Time to go swimming," said Jesse.

On the way to the swimming hole Jake hung over the crummy door and barfed his guts out. Everybody left him very alone, as though he weren't really being sick.

"Dehydration," I suggested. "I didn't feel so great out there myself. We're not used to this."

He looked at me unhappily, I couldn't tell from sickness or disgust. He shook his head no. "Drank some bad water," he insisted.

When we got back to camp Frans told Jake he should go sit in the pyramid. This structure was made of poles and plastic like the cookshack, and was where Frans and Marty slept, down on the beach. The idea was that anyone who needed their batteries recharged spent an hour or two in it. Jake was gone until suppertime and I have no doubt that the pyramid did him a world of good. I spent my time alone on the beach reading a book.

There was more tofu for supper. I made it a point to get a very large portion of salad. Although it contained two or three things I didn't recognize and that were peculiar to my palate, it was edible. Ann had baked bread and, except for its being full of weird little seeds, that was pretty good too. After being on contracts where the only cooking happened over gas camping stoves, the luxury of having a wood-burner complete with oven was not lost on me, and a steady diet of tofu, aside from the obvious problem with it, somehow seemed like a waste of a resource. But I kept my mouth shut. Jake and I had some cheese in our emergency provisions, and after my salad I snuck out to the van for some mucus. Then I remembered what Jake had said about being their guests, so I went and split some wood. I felt pretty good actually, although a little discouraged about only planting five hundred trees. Still, Frans paid something like eleven cents a tree, so I'd earned fifty-five dollars, whenever I got paid. I whack-whack-whacked away with the axe until Calvin approached me. "Let's take the canoe and go fishing," he suggested.

I suppose there is mucus in fish too, and the idea of a trout sounded really good. We went to tell Jake we were taking the boat. He looked a little peaked but claimed to feel fine. "Well, do you know how to run that motor, Jonathan?" he asked me.

"I think so," I said. "There's a choke, a throttle, and a cord starter. I realize you won't be there to fix it if we break down."

"Take the paddles," he reminded me. "And when are you going to haul some water?"

"Later," I replied.

He went back to his conversation with Frans and Marty and Lefty.

"You know," I said tentatively to Calvin as the canoe broke Williston's light waves. "This is a pretty weird contract."

He just shook his head and laughed. "It's a Vander Grove contract is all. Every winter Frans sits there on Kootenay Lake and has revelations. This winter, tofu and pyramids were revealed to him."

"But it's not just that."

"You mean your friend?"

"I guess I do."

"Frans has that effect on some people," Calvin told me simply.

"The thing is," I continued, somewhat reassured, "when Jake talks about when he and Frans were in the bush here, Frans is always the klutz, the guy who's forever fucking up."

Calvin regarded me intently. "And we wouldn't know about that, you see. Frans never tells stories. People tell stories about him." He turned to face the far shore. Then he resumed speaking, just loudly enough so that I could hear him over the boat's little motor. "Frans is full of it. He's always been full of it, he always will be. We all know he is."

"And you put up with it," I interrupted.

"Of course we do. Wouldn't you? I'm making a thousand dollars a week working for Frans. Harry's making more. Where else can we make money like that? I make enough money in three months to do as I please the rest of the year. The rest of the year, I'm a free man. And look where we are," he gestured around Williston's impressively forested rim. A fish practically plopped into the boat. "He's got these Williston contracts sewed up for years to come. They love our work. They know we'll come in, plant more trees than they can believe, and get out ahead of schedule without leaving a mess. It's perfect."

Without exactly thinking about it, I had the canoe pointed at the plume of smoke from the cabin on the cliff. Calvin said something about finding a hole there and we found a beauty, a swirling pool with a bit of shore ledge on one side, the rest rock wall with a small waterfall pouring under a smooth circular natural stone bridge. Above which stood a very tall, very splendid, white-haired man.

"I thought you were those other two boys," he told us solemnly. "My name is Roland Skoggs."

Just as Frans had thought, although Jake hadn't bothered to tell me about it. Was I hurt over that? I suppose I was, although a fairly important lesson was sinking in, that I would have to be more than Jake's sidekick to make it in the hall of the mountain king. But, by another slow-developing token, I wasn't so sure that I wanted to make that scene after all, anyway.

"We're very pleased to meet you," we told Roland Skoggs formally.

He was reputed to be very old, but appeared to be ageless. Straight of posture, tanned face, powerful burning eyes. An absolutely steady hand and firm grip when he shook mine. Standing there by his waterfall, he was awesome.

"It's a pleasure to see you folk," he said in careful exact diction. "Since they put the lake in I don't see many people anymore. Not that I want to see most of the folks around here. Drunken wasteful people, they are appalling."

Calvin and I nodded respectfully. From what I'd heard in Jake's stories about Mackenzie I thought I knew what Roland Skoggs might be talking about.

"Do you mind if we fish here?" Calvin asked.

"It would pleasure me if you did," said Roland Skoggs. "I've been watching your camp. I look forward to being your guest on Saturday night. Those other two boys invited me to supper."

"Well they certainly can't feed him rotten tofu," I protested to Calvin, four Dolly Varden trout and two Arctic grayling later.

"I think we better save these fish, and catch some more tomorrow," he decided.

Calvin cleaned the fish, most of them bigger than I usually caught, over the lake as we cruised gently back. A range of low mountains, the last extension of the Rockies, rambled along the eastern shore, beyond Frans' fabulous cookshack and the green northern forest. Despite the destructive power that had formed it, Williston seemed a hallowed place with the sun arcing along its coastline. There is something almost druglike about those long northern days, about the continuing energy that looping parabolic solar circuit supplies.

"I'll talk to Ann," Calvin plotted. "She'd probably like to cook something else for a change."

"We met Roland Skoggs," I told Jake before crawling into the van to sleep.

"Well that's nice," was all he replied.

The next day the treeplanting went a little better for both me and Jake. I only planted six hundred but that was a hundred more than the day before and I didn't feel quite so absolutely rotten when work was through early in the afternoon. As for Jake, he managed to get into the middle of the pack and stayed close to Lefty all the way. He didn't plant nearly as many as she did, but he kept up with her, probably getting in one for her two. In the distance I could sometimes see him, talking at her all the way, his motions quite a lot smoother than they had been the day before. We were on the way back to the camp after swimming in the river when the crummy broke down, a couple of miles north of Mile 37.

Jake and Frans went under the hood, Jesse and Abram shadow-boxed on the road, Marty and Lefty juggled oranges. I stood watching all this until Teddy came by and said, "Let's get out of here. We'll just have to push it back."

He wore his saddest smile.

"You mean walk?" I wondered.

"Sure," he agreed. He gestured at a sideroad a few yards behind us. "That must go to the lake. We can walk along the beach."

Jake was muttering something about the fuel pump and how he couldn't fix it there. I realized that Teddy might have a point. We hightailed it down that sideroad, past a sign decreeing the drainage closed to fishing until July.

So Teddy Vander Grove and I went out and got lost in the bush. I didn't mind it too much, we weren't all that lost, and I would have minded it even less had I been properly dressed. I hadn't pulled my jeans back on after swimming so I was only wearing jockey shorts and boots, but since we thought we were going to walk down a road and up a beach it didn't seem like I'd need to wear any more than that. For a while I didn't. Instead of taking us to Williston, however, the road took us into a swamp.

We were being mercifully spared mosquitoes and black-flies and no-see-ums so far that June, which was dry and breezy, and Frans' camp being situated as it was on a sand hill, bugs weren't really a problem. They were a problem in that swamp though, and my body was not what you would call adequately covered. Of course we had no repellent with us.

Teddy, who seemed never to be heard from in the camp, who in fact didn't seem to be around much at all, was real talkative as long as the road made for easy walking. "Doesn't treeplanting ever suck?" he began.

I didn't feel quite that way about it yet, but I had to agree that it was hard miserable work. "At least the money's good," I said.

"Money? What money?" scoffed Teddy.

"You don't get paid?" I asked, appalled. The road turned, and the river began to flatten into marsh.

"I borrowed three thousand dollars from Frans this winter," he explained. "To buy a truck. The truck broke down but I still owe him the money. I have to work one more week and then I get to go home. Boy, I'm sure not going to do that again! I can't wait to get on that bus!"

He was awfully sick of treeplanting. He didn't like tofu, garlic, or cayenne. He didn't juggle or do Tai Kwan Do. He liked to fish and drink beer. "Can I go into town with you tomorrow?" he wondered.

I hadn't known I was going into town. "I heard them talking," he told me. Not too hard to figure out who they were. "Frans goes into town at least twice a week. Pays himself a hundred fifty bucks a day for it. Says somebody has to do it, and that he'd rather plant trees. I told him I'd do it for fifty, and he could plant, but he tells me I'd just fuck up. How can you fuck up if they never let you do anything?"

I had to agree that Teddy had a point, but by then we were walking along the outer edge of the swamp, and my attention was caught by a fairly depressing sight. If I thought it would do any good to get angry about that swamp I would. I'd write with blood, but it wouldn't help. The damage is already done, and my describing it isn't going to knock down Bennett the First's dam.

You could tell the swamp hadn't always been there. Because the river that ran into it had been clean and sweet and gurgling not a thousand yards back. Because the road we walked on was an old one that simply disappeared into muck. Because the trees that tottered now half dead before us were still making leaves and needles and trying to stay alive. But mostly because smack dab in the center of a small lake of stagnant water stood a circle of wooden cabins with peeling tarpaper roofs. "It's the Indian village," said Teddy. "Frans said it was around here somewhere."

I'd heard about that village. Jake claimed to have slept there and fought off a couple of squaws a couple of times. He said Frans and he learned to live in the bush from those Indians. Then Bennett the First's government gave the Indians the choice of moving a hundred fifty miles up the new lake to the Ingenika River, or into the Mackenzie Hotel Beer Parlour where they could drink themselves to death on the Province's money. I don't think Bennett the First's government cared which they did, and about half chose one, half the other. That part *is* written in blood, although admittedly not mine.

"Doesn't seem right, does it?" was all Teddy said. There wasn't much else to say.

An osprey had a nest in one of the dying trees. I'd never seen an osprey that close, and we watched it fish while the mosquitoes bit us. You move out an Indian village and create a habitat for mosquitoes and osprey. That's what's known as ecology.

"So what now?" I asked Teddy. "I thought you said this led to the lake."

We could see open space through the dying trees, so Williston must have been over there somewhere, but we didn't feel like wading in. Instead we headed toward higher ground and that's when I wished I had my jeans because the bush got fairly thick and my legs got good and thrashed. We whacked through it for an hour or more. We saw a moose. It looked at us with that peculiar confused moose look and then did a one-eighty and piled into the bush. Moose have a fairly hilarious way of doing that and we laughed, but the swamped village and being lost had brought us both a bit down. Eventually we hit the winding road into camp, where we encountered treeplanters wandering home like refugees. None of them spoke to us, or we to them.

Frans and Jake were already in camp, Jake playing with the fuel pump on the cookshack table again. Frans was talking to Ann in her maroon and gold gym shorts. At night she'd pull on a shirt sometimes, but mostly she just wore those shorts. She was kind of cute actually. I figured out what they were talking about because the first thing I heard her say was, "But Calvin's right, we can't feed him rotten tofu."

"There's nothing wrong with that tofu," Frans insisted.

"Frans," she said, "good tofu doesn't have any taste. This does. It's rotten. It's been sitting here for two weeks."

"Tofu doesn't spoil," he informed her.

"Well listen," she answered back, "if you're going to make the old guy eat rotten tofu you're going to have to cook it yourself. Because I'm not."

"But we can't get tofu in Mackenzie," he protested.

"We're just going to have to think of something else."

"Like what?"

"Well," she began and then she looked my way and asked, "didn't you and Calvin catch some fish last night?"

I nodded yes.

Frans regarded me scornfully. "Fish are full of mucus," he proclaimed. Then he sneezed dryly. He reached for a garlic bulb on the cutting board.

"Mucus this, mucus that," grumbled Ann. "You don't have to eat it."

"I'll bet he gets to eat fish all the time," Frans complained.

"And I'll bet he prefers it to rotten tofu," she retorted. "Look, Frans, if you like, I can do a pot roast."

His jaw dropped aghast at the very idea.

"Well," he finally conceded. "The next day is Sunday. Give Jonathan here a shopping list before we leave tomorrow."

Ann smiled at me, which was unusual for her.

That night, after more of the same for supper, Jesse organized the biggest fishing expedition in the history of tree-planting. I had two rods, he had one, Calvin, of course, had his, Teddy had one, a couple of others appeared from sources unidentified to me. "What do we do for bait?" I asked Calvin. "Go dig grubs?"

"I've got a better idea," he said, but he didn't say what it was. We had rigs for seven people and there seemed to be at least that many vaguely interested parties hanging around where we were organizing on the landing. "We can't take all these people to that hole in the boat," I suggested.

"We'll go to a river," Calvin decided.

"The rivers are closed until July," I remembered from the sign.

Calvin laughed. "So?"

"Well maybe the fish are spawning," I objected. "We shouldn't abuse the resource."

Calvin, Teddy, and Jesse all started laughing and talking at once. Jesse gestured over Williston. "What do you call that?"

"For all the abuse we'll be!" cried Calvin.

Teddy spoke the crispest sentence I ever heard him attempt. "If they can drown Indian villages," he said, "I don't see why we can't kill a few fish."

"Go ask Jake if we can take the van," Jesse suggested to me.

"Uh, would you?" I suggested back.

He paused. "Of course," he agreed.

"He said we could use it if you cleaned the plugs first," Jesse reported on his return. We got out the spark plug wrench and I pulled them and Teddy cleaned them. "This engine's a mess," Teddy informed me. Calvin left and came back with a plastic bucket of rotten tofu. "To bait fish withal," he indicated with a reader's conspiratorial grin.

It was quite a sight, treeplanters with fishing poles lining the banks of that northern river, despoiling a resource. For the record, Dolly Varden running in the Arctic drainage in a dry June are more than happy to hit on rotten tofu. We caught a bushel full in a couple of hours. "Look at all that mucus," exalted Jesse when we lay them out on the bank.

The next morning, Saturday, aware that I did not have to arise with the thick grey dawn to go plant trees I lay half awake and half noticed the rest of the crew preparing for work. Jake must have balewired that fuel pump one last time because I dimly heard the engine cough to life, and then sat up to see the crummy roll by, Jesse at the wheel, maniacal grin flashing through the window. He waved as he passed.

I decided to cop some mucus in Mackenzie and didn't bother with breakfast, Jake looked happy and ready to go at the wheel of our van, but Frans was snuffing at the nose and sneezing rather frequently. I had my shopping list from Ann and we were about to leave when Teddy appeared, dressed rather nattily for a treeplanter. He regarded me imploringly through the van's side door, and I admitted him. "What's the deal?" Frans asked between sneezes. "How come you're not working?"

Teddy just shrugged. "You, hachoo, still owe me six hundred dollars," Frans reminded him. "I know," said Teddy. "You'll get it."

Frans turned to Jake. "Let's go, hachoo."

The trip to Mackenzie was marked by quiet conversation and sneezes in the front seat. Strain as I might, I heard none of it, besides the hachoos. Teddy stretched out on my mattress and went back to sleep. I would estimate that Frans sneezed a hundred and eleven times before we got to Mackenzie. Jake and Frans dropped me and Teddy off at the shopping center. "We're going to go to the parts store," Jake informed me. "And then we're going to talk to Asa Buning."

"About gold," he added rather pointedly.

Asa Buning I'd heard of too. More of Jake's stories. Another guy who was always screwing up in the bush. It was a relief to find that gold was still on Jake's mind. Even if I was picking up beer money and catching Dolly Varden, I didn't particularly care to hang around the hall of the mountain king for that much longer.

The beer parlour wasn't open yet after breakfast, so Teddy and I went to the Super Valu. Ann's shopping list was full of mucus. Pasta, tomato paste, and Parmesan cheese, mushrooms and butter, what? could this be? white flour? cream cheese and eggs? I still wonder if Frans would have given me money had he known what was on that list. Perhaps he was sneezing too hard to think straight.

"Do you suppose Roland Skoggs drinks whisky?" I asked Teddy as we walked past the liquor store in the tiled mall.

"Who's Roland Skoggs?" he wanted to know.

"The old trapper who's coming to dinner," I told him. "That's who all this mucus is for."

Teddy shrugged. "Nobody ever tells me anything. Frans wouldn't like it," he added.

"So?" I said. We went in and bought a bottle, with Frans' money.

The Mackenzie Hotel beer parlour has nothing in particular to recommend itself, except that it serves beer. Really quite new, it was already coming apart at the seams, plaster cracking on the walls, indoor-outdoor carpeting on the floor tattered and frayed. Teddy and I opened it up and killed the better part of the day there. It is very large, being the only beer parlour for miles around, and at first it was just me and Teddy, a couple of old timers, and a few Indians. Teddy and I drank beer, played pool, and told stories. He was really homesick for Ontario and kept talking about getting on that bus. He hoped he could find a job in a garage. He vowed never to borrow money from Frans, let alone plant trees, again. As the day wore on the most curious additions to the swelling beer parlour crowd were the players from half a dozen softball teams in like-new doubleknit uniforms. Mackenzie must have changed a lot since 1968 when Jake and Frans lived with the Indians. One team was called the W.A.C. Bennett Damns. Another the Finlay Forks.

We were reasonably full of beer when Jake and Frans found us. Frans sneezed two hundred and twenty-two times on the way back to camp. They were dry hacking irritated sneezes, and he didn't look good. Jake did most of the talking in the front seat, Frans grunting and sneezing in answer. When we got to camp Jake went under the hood of the crummy and I went down to the beach for a nap.

The four of them, Jake, Frans, Marty, and Lefty were sitting at their corner of the table when I returned, perhaps an hour later. Jake was talking and gesturing with one black-from-engine-grease hand, playing absently with the old fuel pump in the other. "Yes, I communicate with machines," he was saying. "It's a really important thing to do. That's Jonathan's problem."

I was becoming vaguely conscious that I had a problem, maybe two or three. I wasn't so sure that not communicating with machines was one of them, though.

Jake hadn't seen me enter but Lefty had, and our eyes met. She looked a little embarrassed and Jake must have sensed this because then he turned and recognized me. He looked back at the table and stopped talking. I didn't say anything, but I was thinking a few. Frans Vander Grove sneezed. "Hey Frans, better go sit in the pyramid," Jesse called down the table.

I went over to the kitchen and volunteered to help Ann with what I deduced brilliantly to be a trout and spaghetti dinner. With cheesecake for dessert. She already had white bread rising in the oven. Although she did not seem to have much by way of native friendliness to her, few people on that contract did, and I tried to de-ice her a little as we worked. Unfortunately, she seemed to be the type who cooks silently. I suppose it is possible that she had nothing to talk about, at least not to me. I don't think my help, chopping onions and mushrooms, went unappreciated, and it certainly couldn't have been expected, since no one else ever seemed to help her, but it was most definitely taken for granted. I was pondering what a truly peculiar place a Vander Grove contract was, when Jake came into the kitchen. "Well, Jonathan," he said, "I found gold."

In his hand he carried a little plastic pill bottle containing three tiny gleaming yellow metallic pebbles. My eyes must have bugged right out of my head because I saw a satisfied grin cross his face. "Where?" I gasped.

"Just up the beach," he replied. "Mountains of gold. We're rich. We're all going to stop planting trees and stay right here and mine gold. I'm going to stake a claim on Monday. You're going to drive the van back to Vancouver to get Sandy and Maggie.

Sandy and Maggie were our wives. They don't really figure in this story, except that they were going to pan for gold with us later in the summer. If we ever found a place to pan it. I believed Jake's story about the mountain of gold just the instant long enough for him to score. Lefty snickered.

"Jake," I said, "we need some water in here. Would you go get some please?"

"I'm going to get Roland Skoggs," he said, and Lefty followed him out of the cookshack toward the beach.

Roland Skoggs, it turned out, was very fond of mucus, and of whisky as well, although not as the Mackenzie drunkards whom he despised are fond of it. He sat at the table in that majestic cookshack, tall and regal, bottle and coffee mug before him, and told stories until, during, and after a most appealing dinner of broiled trout and spaghetti with mushrooms. He praised Ann's cooking solemnly and by the end of the evening she was ensconced at his side, suitably clothed in maroon and gold gym shorts and open white shirt. Eyes twinkling, he made plans to take her home to cook for him, and told her she would have his house and traplines in thirty-five years when he went to the spirit world. "Until then it will be you and me and my wolves," he explained, and she sat there as though she were seriously considering the offer.

"There's still some life in me too," he teased, and she blushed without smiling.

I asked him about those wolves and learned that there were a dozen that he looked after each winter. "We are quite good friends," he said. "They like to talk to me, and I like to talk to them. And they are so much wiser than the fools in Mackenzie. This was so much a better place ten years ago."

Roland Skoggs yarned late into the translucent night. There was a great deal of jockeying for position around him, and I guess I probably heard no more than an hour or so of his talk. When I think about it now, in memory, I suppose his stories weren't all that unusual. Partly they weren't screw-up in the bush stories like Jake's so they weren't funny or ironic, or even, a lot of them, real stories in the technical sense. A wolf that he knew for ten years. The Indian who first guided him along the Parsnip River, where it was now Williston's Parsnip Reach. Trapped animals gnawing their own feet off to escape. The time he had to kill a grizzly bear with a revolver. That kind of thing. The trance that settled on me, and to judge by their expressions, on the rest of those around him, probably had most to do with the steady dignity of his voice, the precise perfect Canadian English that he spoke, the air of authority and understanding to his reminiscence. The story goes that Roland Skoggs was such a hit with the Vander Grove crew that as soon as Frans was feeling better he went to Mackenzie and bought a canoe, just so people could go across the lake. Apparently, the old trapper became a frequent supper guest in the fabulous cookshack at Mile 37; the story goes that he learned to like tofu, and that Frans arranged for a health food store in Vancouver to ship him a winter's supply. The story also goes that Ann would canoe him across the lake after dinner and stay late into the night, sometimes arriving back barely in time to make breakfast, after which she would sleep all day. The story goes that after ten years of militant hermitage Frans Vander Grove's tree-planting crew restored to Roland Skoggs a small measure of faith in the human race.

The next day was Sunday, and Sunday is a day of rest on a Vander Grove contract. Of all Frans' notions, I think that is the one of which I approve. Personally, I believe in the Hebrew myth that has the Lord and his creation taking a Sabbath. Every contract I've ever been on where the idea that such a thing as a week exists has been denied, and where people are expected to work every day, has run into trouble of the sort that costs both time and money. People get hurt, they get sick, they get ornery, and I don't think they plant as many trees in seven days as they would in six. I slept late that morning, awakening to the startling sound of two people in white robes whaling away with bamboo swords at a hanging straw-stuffed dummy. Tiring of this, they began to whale at each other, crying so as to curdle the very blood. There was juggling. One woman had strung a rope between two trees and stalked it back and forth, costumed as you might imagine. A half dozen people booted a soccer ball around the landing with great zeal. I decided to play a Sunday round of golf.

I realize that I probably strain credulity by claiming to have had golf clubs on a treeplanting contract. I can only say that this a true story and mine really were in the van. I had introduced Jake to golf two summers before in Ontario, and he thought it was the silliest thing he ever heard of. He also thought it was great fun. And no one will believe this either, but it was his idea to take those clubs along, in case we wound up goofing around somewhere and there was a golf course nearby. I went to the cookshack with our secret stash of coffee (you can believe there was none of that in Frans' kitchen), made myself a cup (Sunday was also the cook's day off), smoked a cigarette and then a joint (I was enough by myself that no one seemed to mind, and bad energy might even have been alright on Sunday), and went to the van and hauled out those clubs. There by the shore of Williston Lake, where the damage had already been done anyway, I designed an impromptu golf course. Neither Robert Trent Jones, Sr. nor Jr., have anything on me. I teed up on the landing, just past the soccer players, and envisioned a red flag at the top of the hill where the winding road turned toward the main one, about three hundred and eighty yards away. I called fore to the warriors in the white robes, took a practice swing, addressed the ball, paused, and then stroked, full extension on the backswing, left side firm. The ball clicked solidly on the club head, soared more than halfway up the hill, and landed right in the middle of the road.

I shot something like an eighty-six that day, which for me is a pretty good score. I had the advantage that once I reached where I had decided a green was, I could pick a spot to putt at like a cup, and I may have been generous with myself about how close those cups were to where my ball had come to rest. I also didn't take any penalty strokes for lost balls unless I sliced or hooked a shot deep into the bush. On the other hand, it was a forest course and most of the fairways were extremely narrow. The par 3s were the four best landings I spied after finishing other holes. The ball bounced hard over the first of those, but on the rest I punched shots three-quarters of the way to the target and ended up in good shape. At the twelfth tee, just off the main road, Jake and Lefty drove up in the van.

"Jonathan!" cried Jake. "What on earth are you doing?"

"Playing golf," I explained. "I'm having a really good round. What are you doing?"

"Playing golf?!" he marveled. He shook his head in wonder. Lefty hardly smiled, and Jake drove away still shaking his head.

I heard other vehicles from there, but didn't see them, so they must either have been turning around, or into the camp. When I started back down the road in that direction, one did pass me, a late model Chevrolet sedan containing two puzzled-looking middle-aged couples. As I set up to hit my second shot on my seventeenth hole I saw that several solid-citizen autos were parked at the top of the hill overlooking the beach.

I also recognized my final hole. Frans' pyramid stood in the middle of a terraced patch of grass, the only real grass for miles around. I don't know or care how it got there. Maybe somebody planted it. It was about three hundred and fifty yards away, an obvious tricky lakeside finishing par 4. I teed off from the landing with the automotive gallery watching; drove directly out toward the lake, and let the breeze and my natural fade drift the ball spectacularly, and safely, over a hazardous finger of driftwood. The next shot was an eight iron, and I hit a beauty – the ball dropped smack through the opening that Frans had left at the top of his pyramid so it wouldn't blow away in heavy wind.

"Jesse, hac hac, cut it, hac hac . . . what on earth, hac hac . . . a golf ball!?" cried a mournful raspy voice from within.

Considering how perfect the shot had been, I could have taken an eagle, but decided a gimme putt for birdie 3 was fairer. I wandered over to Calvin, sunning himself on the beach, and gestured back at the cars. He laughed. "Happens every Sunday," he explained. "People just can't get over all the naked hippies."

I shook my head, took off my own clothes, and ventured into the chilly shallows of Lake Williston. I didn't see Jake the rest of the day. For the record, the four and half days I spent on that contract, I never did haul any water.

Part 2.

Considering the turn the karmic worm took next, it is nearly unkind to report Jake's conversation as we rolled out of the camp at Mile 37, and headed toward the Nation River on Monday morning. I am aware that a great deal of what follows may seem to be told at his expense, and can only say that if that is all you read here, then you are not reading very hard.

First of all, he was duly amazed at what Frans had wrought. "I just never expected things to be so together," he marveled. "Do you know that they're planting between thirty and forty thousand trees a day? That's more than some whole contracts. In two months they'll have planted almost three hundred thousand dollars worth of trees. It averages to six and seven thousand dollars a planter after expenses. I don't know why we're even thinking about gold."

Strength. Strength and self-sufficiency. That's what you needed to make a show like that go. Strong and self-sufficient people.

"Most people are so weak, Jonathan," he explained to me. "Put them out here in the bush and they wouldn't know what to do. They wouldn't know how to build shelter. They wouldn't be able to fix things when they break down. And they get so intimidated by the bush they do stupid things. They make bad mistakes."

I listened to this most of the way to Mackenzie. For my part, every mile from Frans' camp brought an increasing feeling of freedom and relief. "Everything you say is true, I'm sure," I finally answered back. "But you know, I liked working on Smiff's contracts a lot better than that back there."

"What?" Jake was shocked. How could anyone not like working for Frans?

"Smiff's people were a bunch of old derelicts," I attempted to explain. "But they weren't all trying to make a point, and really, I still don't know what the point is. I had room to breathe, people were different from each other. They talked. They smiled. They smoked dope. Frans is so trippy."

"I don't know what you mean, Jonathan," he said, sounding puzzled, and then he remained silent for a long time.

We passed through Mackenzie and reached the main highway toward Prince George before he spoke again, and when he did his voice had to it a lilt that I recognized from a mere five days before, that old familiar genial yarn-spinning traveling voice. "Did you know that Lefty's name is Leftitia?" he chuckled, emphasizing the tit.

I have said that our wives, back in Vancouver, don't figure in this story, but I guess that isn't entirely true. Jake, by his tone of voice, had just let a little cat out of a big bag, where, in any event, it wouldn't have stayed forever. Sometimes I think people, at least married people, have affairs just so they can gloat over them afterward. I mean, most of the time while it's going on they act so serious and downright miserable. Then, safely out of it, it's all knowing grins and self-satisfied giggles.

"Curious name," I said noncommittally.

"Did you see her left breast?" He grinned slyly.

Well, I saw them both, several times, but hadn't noticed anything more special about the left than the right. I told

Jake that and he shook his head. Then he wouldn't tell me what the joke was. He did say, "I don't want you telling Maggie or Sandy about Lefty."

"Until a couple of minutes ago, I didn't know there was anything to tell," I replied truthfully.

"Well, let's keep it that way," he instructed me. "She's really a good shot," he added. "We were popping bottles with the twenty-two yesterday."

That twenty-two was one of Jake's prize toys. A real wooden-stocked Winchester lever action. Early in the trip, we hit our high point for frivolity by taking turns banging away at signs along the dirt road north from Kootenay Lake. Disrespectful and juvenile as hell, and something we had both always wanted to do. This before Jake's serious phase set in.

There was one shot I couldn't resist. "Jake," I asked, "how could you get that close to all that garlic?"

He laughed happily and, almost miraculously, our camaraderie, if not totally restored, flickered once more in his eyes. "I grew up on a farm, Jonathan," he said. "It's a good natural smell."

And I laughed too.

To get to the Nation River, which feeds Williston on the side of the Parsnip Reach opposite Frans' camp, we had to go back to Prince George, then west on the Yellowhead Highway to Vanderhoof, and then north to Fort Saint James, a trip of some two hundred miles in all. Don't ask why we didn't just take the canoe across the lake and up the river, it had something to do with upstream and downstream, and, no, I remember, Roland Skoggs had told Jake that there was heavy water where the Nation fed Williston, that was it. So we ended up in Fort Saint James that night, where we went to the circus.

If I were trying to keep this thematically tight, I suppose I'd skip that circus, but I'm determined to get it in. Formally, it was the interlude, the instant of narrative nonsense between two events displaced from each other by moment and geography, but spiritual brother and sister, or perhaps mother and son.

The trip went slowly because we had to stop periodically for Jake to balewire the van's engine, which was, in fact, not running so good. We had a big lunch of mucus and bought supplies in Prince George. It was nearing six o'clock by the time we reached Fort Saint James, and just as an indication of how our travels were returning to their old equilibrium, the first place we went was the pool hall. We were playing our usual incompetent game when I spied the poster over Jake's shoulder. The circus was in town, that very night, starting in about ten minutes. We dropped our cues and went running for the town park, only a couple of blocks away.

Fort Saint James is not much of a town, and this was not much of a circus, but I'll bet every parent and child for miles around was in those stands. After months of nothing but staring at nothing but Stuart Lake and trees and maybe an occasional movie, the corporeality of that single ring with its ringmaster who also did a tumbling act with a lady who also walked a tightrope over a clown who also juggled and played catch with the trained seal while a chimp rode a bicycle, all that real live stuff happening must have been a great change for the town of Fort Saint James. Even I, jaded by Vancouver's concerts, and theater, and hockey, have to say that it was a limited but very fine show. The lady rode bareback on one foot, the clown had a goose who could add and subtract by honking, the ringmaster threw knives at balloons held by the lady, they kept this up for two solid hours, the long northern daylight illuminating the show through gaps in the canvas.

I suppose there must have been stagelamps and spotlights, but somehow what I remember is a sense of bright natural light, like in Frans' cookshack. I had a ball.

So did Jake, and when it was over and the ringmaster said, "Thank you, you've been a wonderful audience, and if any of the town's young men would like to make a little pocket money by helping take down our tent they should come to the front of the ring," Jake returned my big grin and shook his head yes.

We made five dollars each for that, forty-five Frans trees worth, and we had the more than likely once in a life-time pleasure of taking down a circus. They didn't really need us for much. We helped collapse a few portable bleachers, steadied a pole here, held a rope there, rolled the heavy canvas onto a long metal cylinder, which, heaving together, several of us lifted grunting into a long truck bed.

Then we went to the hotel with the ringmaster, the clown/animal trainer, and a couple of young men who did most of the lifting and carrying, and returned them their ten dollars in the form of Uncle Ben's, the local beer. The ring-master owned the circus, which played the Western Canadian north in the summer and wintered in Texas or Arizona. Every year was going to be their last, and every year they went north one more time, hardly making expenses, but doing it because it was what they did. As the wine-red sun set over silver Stuart Lake glowing through beer parlour windows, members of three of the world's more curious professions – circus performers, treeplanters, and prospectors – exchanged toasts. For myself, that night, I most hoped the circus would survive, partly because its chances were the slimmest, partly because I realized already then that its purpose was more worthwhile than either prospecting for gold or planting trees.

For reasons having to do with the van's hitting on five cylinders and blowing an awful lot of oil, we didn't pack the canoe and get it into the Nation River – actually, into a still, swampy little pool that opened onto the Nation River – until the next afternoon. Realizing that Jake had the expedition's corner on strength and self-sufficiency, I let him handle that detail while I cooked up some mucus on our camp stove. I was happily frying sausage when I heard the crisp pop of a twenty-two rifle. The bullet plicked the ground at my feet. I turned, startled, but not half so startled as Jake looked, big hand surrounding the lever mechanism of that pretty little rifle.

"Jesus Christ, Jake, watch it!" I hollered.

"Well who left this thing cocked?" he shouted back.

"Well it wasn't me," I replied, I guess fairly indignantly.

"Well who else could it have been?" he returned in kind.

I could tell by his face as soon as he said it that he wished he hadn't. Jake does not like to be shown up, but I pressed my advantage. "So who was shooting at bottles on Sunday?" I demanded to know.

He shook his head. "We shouldn't have done that," he said. "Damn women."

Whatever that meant. A look passed over his face like he was tired of the whole thing. He shook his head solemnly. "We have to get our shit together, Jonathan."

There was no disputing that. I felt pretty tired myself. I believe that travel can be, in fact generally is, a spiritually broadening experience, but there is something about traveling around British Columbia, maybe only the size of the place, that always leaves me wishing at some point I were home in bed, wherever home might happen to be. That's how I felt then. And I also felt another peculiar sensation from deep in memory. When I was a child and my family went on a trip, my mother would always begin with a solemn prayer to the Lord Above, offered there in the car before my father started it. I confess to feeling the need for such a gesture then, although I neglected to act upon it. Jake finished packing the canoe, brumming under his breath the entire while. After eating, we set off down the Nation River, latterday voyageurs.

I should add that the rifle going off marked the low point of the trip, at least as far as our relations with each other went. For whatever reasons, flowing east on the breast of the Nation was a marvelous tonic. We positively zipped along, tugged by a determined current, as Jake steered with the little two-and-a-half horse motor.

I could write pages about that stretch of the Nation. Years later, the details of its geography are imprinted on my mind as though I were there even now. Hardwood and conifer mottling the forest that rolled away from marshland in graceful undulating line or stood above high sandy cliffs. Once we had cleared the first bend, there wasn't a trace of human activity other than our own. Not a one. All of space opened beyond the lacy clouds over the horizon. A deep pounding noise echoed above the drone of the motor. "Moose," said Jake, a hallowed look on his long face.

"Uh, I think those are blue grouse," I suggested. "There was this television program."

"Naw," said Jake. "You mean a little bird makes that noise?" It was as though a sound that big had to be made by a big animal. We saw one, a moose, a bull in a pool, feeding, raising his great head and shaking his shoulders, fine spray flying from him, glistening in the late afternoon sunlight.

I attempted to chart the river's turns on a topo map, but the country seemed more complex than the map representing it and it wasn't long before I couldn't really be sure where we were any more.

We camped where we did, just past a sand cliff at a bend, for the simple reason that it was the first suitable campsite we saw, and so suitable we couldn't pass it up, a wide flat grassy area, high and dry, rimmed with birch. We hauled our camping gear out of the canoe, and Jake went to work chopping firewood from a fallen tree. We made a marvelous campfire. At one point, a young moose ambled along the edge of our clearing, eyeing us curiously. "Veal," grinned Jake, and glanced toward his twenty-two.

But that was for later, for after we'd retrieved Sandy and Maggie from Vancouver. Jake was convinced that you could shoot young moose with a twenty-two. Never having tried it, for all I know, you can. But that night we dined on beefsteak purchased in Fort St. James. We went to sleep under an open sky glowing red at the north.

And the next morning we went out to prospect for gold.

The specific gravity of gold is greater than just about anything else's and that's why you pan for it. If you swirl dirt and gravel in water and there is gold in that dirt and gravel then the gold remains at the high edge of your pan glinting yellow. Asa Buning gave Jake those little yellow pellets in the pill bottle so we could practice the necessary swish, and recognize the gold when we saw it.

By the same token, a river is likely to swirl gold into the wide outward turn of its banks. Theoretically at least, that put what gold there was on the Nation River along the bottom of those sand cliffs. And there one was, just upstream from our camp.

Although I don't remember the weather being particularly chilly, Jake was wearing a big old sheepskin coat and looked like the prospector on the Yukon Jack bottle we had cracked open the night before. I guess I probably still looked like a treeplanter. He navigated the canoe along the bank against the current. When he got past the bend, he swung the vessel back around.

It's hard to believe he didn't see the snag. I sure did. The current must have been tricky and we broadsided a springy branch. You wouldn't think that a few twigs sticking out of the water would do much damage, maybe there was something beneath the surface that I didn't see, I seem to remember a thunk against the bottom of the canoe. At any rate, the canoe tipped, not all that much, but it definitely did tip, and, not entirely uninvited, in flowed the Nation River. "Aw fuck," said Jake, a really disappointed look on his face.

Canoes filling with water have a tendency to capsize. The first thing you notice upon being dumped in the Nation River is that it is wet and cold. Jake swam for shore in his sheepskin coat. It's a good thing he was strong. For my part, I was not yet ready to accept the indelible reality of what had just occurred. The canoe sailed by me upsidedown and I grabbed the rope tied to its bow and tried to swim ashore pulling it but I wasn't strong enough. In fact, I think it was pulling me. About the time our fifty gallon drum of gasoline came bobbing by I gave up on saving the canoe and grabbed the drum. It beached me halfway back to camp.

My boots squished as I bushwhacked along the shore returning to the gold bank, where Jake stood contemplating the Nation River, looking sadder than I have ever seen him or anyone else.

"Jonathan," he told me, "we should have chained that motor to the canoe."

"We!" I hooted, much as a crow hoots, with just a trace of mockery.

"This isn't funny, Jonathan," Jake replied and then he started to laugh as though it were, after all.

I hadn't taken my golf clubs up the river, and most of our cooking and camping gear was back in camp. But there were a few things still in that canoe when it went down. Like all of my fishing tackle. Like our rain gear. Like a sixpack of dark Heineken that I had been looking forward to and would not have minded breaking open right then. Like all of our gold panning stuff, including the pill bottle of gold nuggets. Jake and I may have the distinction of being the only prospectors ever to put gold into a river without taking any out. Like two canoe paddles, the only ones we had. Like every last sucking one of Jake's tools.

"How did that happen?" he marveled, appalled, but I had no answer for him.

So we bushwhacked back to camp in our squishy boots, built a fire to dry out, and finished off the Yukon Jack. Jake took the axe to the fallen tree and broke it. The axe, that is. Right at the blade, handle splintered to bits. Either it was too weak or he was too strong. I don't guess it matters which. I had a good long look at the topo map.

If, as I imagined, we were five bends down the Nation, we were in luck, relatively speaking. Bushwhacking back from the gold cliff we had crossed a fairly substantial stream. I found a representation of such a thing on the map. It led straight out to the road, no more than three miles away and, more luck, relatively speaking, it led from a place where the river turned more or less due south to a place where the road turned more or less due north. It could all have been much worse than it was. I explained this to Jake as he contemplated the axe blade next to the fire. I was all for calling it a bad job and hiking out, right then. But Jake had a better idea.

He was determined that capsized canoes do not sink, and he turned out to be right. Ours was there, belly sticking up, not very far at all from our camp, snagged in a marsh. Finding the canoe was phase one, and it didn't take long, maybe an hour.

Phase two took longer, like the rest of the day, and wasn't quite so successful. Jake was sure he could see that outboard motor in the river about twenty feet from shore, off the bank. I guess there may have been something there, but I couldn't have sworn it was that. He could have and did. We had ten feet of rope from the boat, and he tied it to his waist. I waded as far into the river as I could and still keep my balance and hang onto that rope, and he went diving. Unfortunately, once he submerged, he couldn't see anything but rocks on the bottom and water swirling by. Nevertheless, he spent the rest of the morning trying.

His next, and only other, recovery idea was to build a rock bridge out into the Nation. In theory, this kind of thing is possible; ancient people built breakwaters that way. In our case, however, there were practical circumstances against us. Like the fact that it takes a lot of rocks to get twenty feet out into a fast river to a depth of, say, ten feet. Like that the bank above us was made of sand, not rock, even though there were a number of rocks around, every last one of which we did throw in the Nation River, without, I'm afraid, making much of a dent in it. The thing about throwing rocks in a fast moving river is that they don't just form a neat pile. They tend to be round and slippery and get moved about. Jake was determined, tenacious, strong, all the things you have to be to undertake such a project. But if circumstances and material are wrong, even that won't pull you through. It was some long time after I had realized the futilities involved, and let my labor slacken off to a token toss or two, that Jake succeeded in exhausting himself.

After that, much too tired to even think about walking out, we reached an understanding, with each other, with our situation, with whichever god it is that I choose to think of as the real mountain king. We cooked up all our best provisions and had a feast of mucus. Fortunately, our dope hadn't been in the canoe and we smoked it until we were giddy. We sat and watched the northern sky, the gorgeous swollen Nation River, we listened to the blue grouse thundering around us. We set up a target range and shot the twenty-two until our shells were gone. We didn't want to carry them out anyway. I think that, in memory, I regard that evening more fondly than any other on our trip. We didn't even discuss how we were going to get home.

We discussed that in the morning, and narrowed our tactical choices to three. We could float the canoe out to Williston Lake, some what? thirty or forty miles? east. There were good reasons not to do this: we didn't have the topo map for the last bit of the trip; Roland Skoggs had spoken of heavy water; and we didn't have paddles. The Nation didn't come out that far from Frans' camp, but we had no way of getting across the lake and would still have to bushwhack to Skoggs' house. Besides, how would we get across Williston once we found him? And we'd still have to come back for the van. With amazing good sense, we toted all that up and vetoed it.

Choice two was to hike out along the Nation. The positive side of that idea was that it wouldn't be too difficult to keep track of such a big river and we would end up back where we left the van. The negative was that the trip looked like six or eight miles on the map, and there would be swamps full of moose, and who knew what else, to either skirt, or slog through.

Which left choice three – to assume that the creek we had been crossing was the one I thought it was on the map, and to hike up it to the road. It only looked like a three mile hike, in a straight line, on the map, and straight lines are reputed to be the shortest distances between two points.

The only problem was that in the middle of the route, on the map, was that little symbol for marsh.

Just one of them.

But on the map there was also a high ridge paralleling the creek. It seemed to me that, if we stuck to high ground, the walking wouldn't be bad. Jake, for his part, bought this.

We had a slight disagreement about what gear to pack with us. We agreed that the styrofoam ice chest, camp stove, and most of our dishes could stay to await our return with our wives, whom we still fully intended to bring back from Vancouver for a summer's fun and frolic in the gold fields. So we stashed all that in the canoe and hid it in the marsh. I took my backpack with clothing and some books, and a day's provision of granola and mucus that did not require cooking. As far as I was concerned, aside from that pretty little twenty-two, everything else could stay right there on the river. Jake had other ideas, but we accommodated each other in a most reasonable fashion, we were learning to agree to disagree about some things. He had a fairly heavy four person popup style umbrella tent for which he had paid a lot of money. He rigged it in its canvas bag with the twenty-two and fashioned a makeshift pack with the canoe rope. He carried his cast iron skillet in his hand.

Cast iron is not light, but Jake was inordinately fond of that skillet. He had had it since the old days in Mackenzie before Williston, had plundered it from a derelict logging camp, and was determined not to be parted from it now. Of all the images from our hike out, it is Jake in his wet sheep-skin coat, whacking his way through the bush with that skillet in place of the axe he had broken, that I cherish most. He was strong as a bull.

Maps are like stories, reality charts. They tell you where you are and what to do. The problem with both is that sometimes they can shift and slide on reality. If you take them seriously, which from time to time you sort of have to do, you can find yourself at the mercy of someone else's vision of things. Most of us tend to think of landscapes, both of mind and of the outside world, as fixed and permanent. In fact, nothing could be less true. Find an old map of B.C. and follow the Nation River east and you'll understand what I mean. How long has Vancouver, so imposing on paper, been there? Where was it a hundred years ago? The map Jake and I had that day, subject as it had to be to our interpretation, was maybe as accurate a representation of that bit of British Columbia bush then and there as what you've got in your hands, and I'd defend the accuracy of this, my true story, about as vehemently as some government cartographer would defend his map, certainly not to the death, but with at least a superior smirk, a puff on the pipe, and an "Oh, but you had to be there." The biggest problem was that swamp.

We stuck with the high ground theory for a long while. Every time the ridge sloped toward low ground we would move up to higher. The walking wasn't bad, we were in good spirits, the forest got a little thick at times, but Jake strode through it with determination, attacking the branches with his skillet. I have always since been fond of that word *bushwhack* because I can't hear or use it without seeing Jake very literally whacking that particular bush with that particular skillet. We probably went through six or eight different sorts of forest, most of them fairly thick, although the trees were quite small. A forestry type could explain the different growths, climaxes, slopes, elevations, but I don't describe trees, I just plant them. We had been walking for a long time, it must have been midafternoon, and I guess we were getting a little nervous about not hitting the road when we came upon an open meadow with a wide opening of sky beyond the trees ringing it. Jake broke into a trot, heavy ungainly tent, rifle, cast iron skillet and all. But when he got across the meadow his shoulders sagged and he turned to face me sadly. "Aw fuck," was all he said. At our feet, beneath a steep cliff of sand, lay the Nation River. We were directly above the bend where we had capsized. We could see the beginning of our stone breakwater, and our campsite in the clearing. We had whacked our way to the highest point for a couple of miles around, and it wasn't remotely where we wanted to be. We found it on the map.

"Any more bright ideas, Jonathan?" Jake asked me. He didn't say it any more unkindly than it sounds on paper. I took off my pack and we sat on the cliff and ate some granola.

"Yea," I said. "We go down to that creek and don't let it get away."

"We'll end up in the swamp," said Jake.

"I know," I agreed. "We'll just have to get through it. It doesn't look so big on the map."

But I think we both had lost a little bit of faith in that piece of paper at that point.

The creek took us straight into the swamp quickly enough. "I sure don't want to go in there," said Jake. Neither did I, but we did. I don't even hate swamps out of hand, as some people do. I admit that they are full of mosquitoes, that they are wet and dirty, that the footing can be uncertain, that they smell. But that swamp was as natural a thing as the admirable Nation River, and in the final end, did us no more harm than the river had. I'm not even sure I buy the symbolic construct in which swamps represent the dark, less wholesome, recesses of human consciousness. Were Jake and I in that swamp because we had strayed too far into the dark night of our related souls? I'm not sure of that at all. Look at it this way, the real darkness and confusion that led us to that swamp had played their way into our lives in light and airy places, the admirable Nation River, broad Williston, Frans' fabulous cookshack. Our minds and spirits were never clearer on that trip than they were as we slogged through that swamp. We slogged with purpose and courage. We went at the heart of it because we knew that was where the main stream, straight as a rifle barrel on our map, lay, and if we went straight in we'd end up straight out. Because the shortest distance between two points is a straight line.

At least it is in Euclidean geometry, the kind we learned in high school, another of those reality charts, one we pretty much agree on. And what I learned that swampy evening is that geometry is just another form of poetry, and that the geometry of the bush is determinedly non-Euclidean. Which is just a fancy way of saying there's no straight way through a swamp, any more than there is through life. The problem with that geometry is that it doesn't account for material. Material behaves as it pleases. Reality has substance. Reality has form.

We slogged waist deep in scum. We whacked our way through thickets of thistle and vine. We waded across a broad pond of still black water that looked as though it just had to be full of snakes, although we didn't see any. We found bits of high ground with game trails, and they were a pleasant change, but we knew we couldn't wander off down them, whenever the walking got too easy we knew we had to head back into the swamp. Finally, late in the evening, we came upon a series of low parallel ridges like the toes of some monumental foot. If we'd had the stream by then we would have just kept walking, but we were still pretty lost. So we climbed one of those toes for a look around. We could see the glow of the setting sun through the trees.

"We can't be far from the road," Jake insisted, mainly to himself. "You know, what we need is a compass."

If there is a moral to this story it's probably this: if you ever go prospecting in British Columbia and are thinking about bringing your golf clubs, remember that in the long run you will have more use for a compass. Jake and I did a lot of dumb things on that trip. Forgetting to bring a compass wasn't the worst of them, but it has to be included in the list.

"Well, at least we can figure out which direction is north," I decided.

"Right," Jake agreed, setting himself on the hill and swinging ninety degrees right from the setting sun. "Right there."

We were wet, tired, miserable, and lost, but I realized that I had him, and I savored my triumph.

"Jake," I said, "You better learn to communicate with the big machine."

He looked at me sadly, as though he did not comprehend. "The big machine?" was all he replied.

I spread my arms to the sky in a gesture that I realize now was worshipful. I remember a sensation of great spiritual pleasure which finally had nothing to do with throwing Jake's words back at him, but exploded into the ecstasy a human being can feel when a great mystery comes clear. All that time watching those red sunsets, and there at that moment, for that moment, I understood. "The big machine," I repeated. "The universe."

"The universe," Jake repeated after me.

My ecstasy found its appropriate scale. For a moment, I had felt the full weight of that universe, but for purposes of getting out of the bush a primitive sense of the structure of the solar system would be sufficient. "The earth tilts on its axis," I began to explain.

"Of course," realized Jake, having been to school once himself.

I knelt to the ground, and drew a map of the solar system in the dirt. I omitted everything but what we needed to consider, that is, everything but the sun and the earth. It wasn't to scale, it was not strictly accurate. In fact it was just two circles, one with a slanted slash through it. Like this:

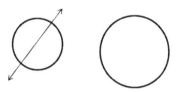

"What's our latitude?" I asked him. He pulled the by-now tattered map from his pocket. "Is that the ups and downs or the straight acrosses?" he pondered.

"The straight acrosses," I told him.

"Fifty-four degrees, thirty-eight whatever they are," he told me.

"Thirty-five degrees south of the pole," I calculated. "That puts us here."

I slashed an equator diagonal to our axis and marked where we were.

Jake and I grinned at each other. "Well, we're not lost after all," he decided. "We know right where we are."

I recollected the approximate times of the sunsets and rises on Frans' contract, and factored into the equation the variable that it was now two days closer to the solstice than it had been Sunday night. I arrived at a rough idea of how far along the horizon from where the sun was positioned north might be – somewhere in the neighborhood of ten degrees, if I recall correctly. I took off my pack and leaned it against a tree, and placed a large stone at the base of another aligned with my pack in that direction. If I was a little off due north, it wouldn't matter much. "Tomorrow, we're getting out of here," I promised.

It barely got dark at all that night. I remember awakening briefly in the tent and finding myself conscious of how utterly and perfectly grey the light filtering through the mesh window was. I heard a vehicle engine over the swamp's stillness, and knew it came from the north, because that's where the road was, although the sound seemed to echo from every corner of the landscape. I crawled out of the tent the next morning just in time to see Jake hurtling down the hill in the line I had determined.

Getting out of that swamp and to the road that day was probably the most balewired job of Jake's entire fixit career. He certainly should have waited for me, but he was determined to do the rest by himself. He was gone for an awful long time. For hours as a matter of fact. I sat on the ridge and waited, reading *How to Stay Alive in the Woods,* the chapter on being lost, and thought of something a friend once said. "If you haven't been lost, you haven't been anywhere." That chapter is full of good advice, none of which we had followed, but not a word about finding north by drawing a map of the solar system in the dirt. Finally, I heard him shouting my name from the swamp. I shouted back. "Jake! Jake!"

His voice seemed to move all through the swamp, and it was pretty obvious that he couldn't hear me. I climbed a tree, to call from overhead, but he was on low ground and I was on high. His calls carried up to me from those depths, but mine simply floated away on the breeze. Finally, I went looking for him.

I managed to do one thing right, and that was keep track of every ridge and swamp finger I went over, through, and along. It's a good thing I did because when he finally heard my voice and came charging through the bush toward me, Jake was a very lost son of a bitch. And here's what had happened to him while I was reading *How to Stay Alive in the Woods*.

I said that he took off running. Well, it worked. He couldn't maintain an absolutely straight line north, but he concentrated on staying pointed in that general direction at whatever cost and eventually came upon the stream bubbling its merry way through high dry forest, game trails for easy walking along its banks. So we were saved. We had figured that we were in the heart of the swamp. Jake figured that the creek led back into that heart and that if he walked along it he would get back to me.

Which may sound like good thinking but wasn't. If we couldn't follow the stream out from the south, and couldn't find it at all in the middle of the swamp, why did Jake think he could follow it back to me from the north? I don't know, and not only that, Jake mixed up upstream and downstream all together in his sick-of-being-lost brain and walked on out to the road. His first clue came when he saw a beer bottle. He looked up, and beheld the welcome strip of dirt and gravel.

Which was great, except he still had to find me again. He started back downstream and was soon again as lost as ever.

Except that one thing had changed. He knew for sure that there was a stream, that there was a road, that the government cartographer wasn't too far off.

"That's great, Jake," I congratulated him after we figured all that out. "Now all we have to do is do it again."

I led him to our camp. "Jonathan," he kept saying, "are you sure you know where you're going?"

I was and I did. Chasing his voice, I had taken the trouble to turn from time to time and examine where I had just been, remembering the world's property of looking different coming and going. It really is amazing how a landscape can shift and slide in the short space of an hour or two. But I managed to keep a hold on that one, and we got back to camp and tore down the tent. And then Jake, rigged with tent and rifle in the bag, his cast iron skillet, and his sheepskin coat, and I, wearing my backpack, went back to where we had lately met.

"So where do you think the creek is?" I asked him. He gestured vaguely to the north.

"How far?" I asked.

"Not far, I don't think," he replied.

It was the *I don't think,* that worried me. I gave him the plan. "You start circling out," I decided. "Every minute or so you shout. If you can't hear me shout back, you've gone too far. We've got to keep voice contact. If you cover the whole area that our voices will carry, and haven't found it, then we'll move north and do the same thing again."

"Why don't you just come with me?" he asked, puzzled.

"Because I know where I am!" I answered back. "It's a nice feeling for once."

He looked at me as though he were thinking. Then he said, "I see . . ." and bulled into the bush.

It worked. It took about sixty shouts each but it worked. "Jonathan!" I heard him cry. "I found the creek!"

Then I bulled through the bush myself, both of us shouting all the way, until I reached him. And then we walked out. It couldn't have been more than half a mile. It was one o'clock in the afternoon by the watch of the logger who picked us up almost immediately after we reached the road. We had covered that three miles of bush at the rather remarkable speed of point-aught-seven-six miles per hour.

The van stopped hitting on a second cylinder between the Nation River and Fort Saint James. It smoked, it smelled, it made awful dying noises. But it made it to Fort Saint James. I got drunk in the beer parlour while Jake bought a spark-plug wrench, a vice grip pliers, and a screw driver, and, as he explained to me later, I wasn't watching, I was getting drunk, simply disconnected the two pistons whose plugs were fouling, rather grievously, I believe, by then.

There is such a thing as a four cylinder engine, even I know that. There's such a thing as a one cylinder engine, but if yours is meant to run on six you can only disconnect so many pistons before it won't go anymore. We were down to three by the time we made Prince George and a few miles south of there the van declared an end to that day's travel. Jake managed to coast it to a sideroad off the highway and we slept in it, hardly caring at all. The next morning, he somehow coaxed the engine into firing one last time and, heroically, got the poor thing back on the highway pointed at Vancouver. We made it to the metropolis of Strathnaver where, convenient at least in its timing, cylinder number four went out with an awful unhappy rattle. "Jonathan," said Jake. "She just died on us."

"Goodbye, old friend," he added, patting the dash.

We headed for the general store. "When's the next bus south?" I asked.

"In five minutes," said the lady.

We stripped what we could carry from the van and just left it there. We did it fast because we didn't want to wait a whole day for the next bus. We took basically what we'd lugged off the Nation, and my golf clubs. If I looked as bedraggled as Jake, we must have made quite a pair. The bus driver nearly collapsed laughing when I handed him the golf clubs. "I never go on vacation without my clubs," I explained seriously.

"No sir," he agreed.

Jake carried the cast iron skillet on board. He told me a good long story, most of the way to Vancouver.

Have you noticed that I keep talking about Jake's stories, but that I never tell any of them? There's a reason for that. Jake can tell his own stories. Very well. Although by then I may have been growing a little tired of them. Part of the time I listened. Part of the time I read *Playboy.* Which will give you an idea where my head was at. *Playboy* had an interview with a famous American author. Whenever Jake's story dragged I read that. Two for the price of one through the Fraser Canyon. When we got back to Vancouver, neither of us could talk. Me from shouting at Jake in the bush, but he yarned me all the way to Hope. I know Sandy and Maggie would never believe this, but Jake had a voice yet in Hope, British Columbia. I swear to the mountain king. And you think Hope isn't a long way from Strathnaver? Get on a bus with a bag of golf clubs in Strathnaver sometime. You'll find out.

It was in Hope that Jake paused, and rasped, "Give me that magazine."

So I did. He read it until we got to Mission. He rasped laughter at the interview with the famous American author all the way, and since I'd just read it myself I mostly knew what he was laughing at. By Mission, he was to the part where the famous American author talks about success and failure.

"Aw, how great," Jake husked, his vocal chords tight as bowstrings. "'Which is best for you, success or failure? Failure. Which do you prefer?' "

All but voicelessly, we laughed together. "Success," we agreed.

Christmas Comes Late to California

for Carl Byker

*... Live music is better bumperstickers
should be issued*

Long after he left that state he kept his license. The next time he needed a new one, he told the necessary lie, that he had lost it. He raised his right hand and swore to it, paid for the wire back to California, endured a stiff lecture from a lady with glasses anchored to her sweater by the same kind of chain that connected the pen to the tile counter in the Michigan Secretary of State's office. It was worth the trouble.

The license pictured a young man of something less than thirty years and, although the slack jaw, the reddened cheeks, the dark shallows under the eyes, the bedraggled hair plastered in no particular order against a large skull and reflecting a light that Sam associated with sea salt, all transcended the usual harsh ugliness of state photography, it was the eyes that years later still interested him. They looked, quite simply, mad, but – he liked to think – with the madness of poetry and prophecy, the madness of a person who has just had a vision and after a period of substantial tribulation has acquired the leisure to be very sick.

"What amazing weather," cried his friend Calvin, leaping off the train at the Palo Alto Southern Pacific station.

To the west, the palm fronds, the heavily peeling bark of the campus eucalyptus groves, the grass on the mountainsides, even the leaves of the live oak in the foothills and the tanoak and redwood forest climbing toward the summit, were all brown – golden brown in the case of the grass, red-brown the palm fronds, silver-brown the eucalyptus, and green-brown the mountainside forest, but brown, brown, brown the base color. Even the early winter afternoon sky was tinged in golds instead of pinks. "I hear drought is general in California," said Calvin.

Calvin was the most sententious of Sam's friends. It seemed sometimes as though he went through life never forgetting a phrase he read or heard, and paying attention to the rest of the universe only in order to quote at it. He was a one-man guided tour of the world's literature and song and Sam (who had learned to recognize when Calvin was quoting by his tone of voice) habitually inquired after the references with a particular sideways glance they had arranged between them, because Calvin never footnoted unless he was asked to.

"The Dead," Calvin replied. Although Sam had owned nearly every Grateful Dead album at one time or another, he could not place that particular phrase, but if he inquired further Calvin would recite an entire song, and what Sam wanted to talk about was the drought.

Which was beginning to get on his nerves. Two years earlier in England, a snow drought last winter in Montana (from which Calvin was arriving), and now in California, everywhere these blue-golden skies, dropping water tables, conservation propaganda over toilets. Everywhere that Sam went. It was as though the drought were following him around. It was freaky.

"Kind of reflects your emotional life, doesn't it?" suggested Calvin.

"Unfair! Unfair!" cried Sam.

"I know," Calvin taunted him. "No ideas but in things."

"Whatever that means!" Sam fought back. "And it's not even true! You've been talking to Heather!"

"She was in town," admitted Calvin.

"Well she's a born liar!" Sam tromped the van's accelerator and it responded in the only fashion it knew, by killing out. Calvin laughed hilariously.

"Actually," Sam confided as he coaxed the engine back to life and headed up the dusty palm-lined drive, "my emotional life is not bad these days. You'll love Stella's people. Can her mother ever cook! They fast on Christmas Eve. Which seems to mean that you have to eat crab cioppino, fish lasagne, crab louie, two kinds of gnocchi, drink cases of champagne, and then there's four kinds of dessert. It's enough to make me think about settling down."

"No!"

"Well I can't live in this van forever."

"No! In California?"

It went that way until they got to a party in the hills thrown by a bunch of musicians from Texas.

"The Dead!" hooted one of the musicians. "You came all the way to California to hear the Dead?"

"The Dead are judged by their works," replied Calvin, unperturbed.

I

Sam and Calvin watched Denver beat the Steelers at a bar in Mountain View and celebrated early.

Stella eyed them suspiciously over the patio gate. "Are you guys drunk?" she wanted to know.

"He is!" they cried in unison. The dog heard it all and bounded across the back yard, barking either in welcome or threat, it was hard sometimes for Sam to tell. The back door slammed and out cascaded Stella's mother, Maria, a grey curly-haired Roman-nosed woman well over four feet tall. "Who's that?" she demanded of the dog and then saw her daughter in the arms of a strange man. "Oh, hi Calvin!" she greeted him.

Sam was more than a little confused. "She knows Calvin?" he marveled.

"Well of course I do," Maria assured him. "Stella said you were bringing a friend."

Over the insistent barking of the dog, and their own shouting there in the backyard, an even louder din emanated from the Orienti house. Although there always seemed to be a din of some sort emanating from there, this was more of one. The first time Sam had met Stella's people that summer he had wondered helplessly, "How can you take all this noise?" and she had replied, "What noise? This is normal."

Indoors was redolent of seafood in tomato sauce with oregano and garlic. Calvin sniffed the wind with grave satisfaction. "Cumbah!" a husky cousin saluted with an open palm.

"Pisan!" Sam returned. "Hey, meet Calvin."

"Anatale!" called Uncle Luigi from the living room. "What about these hippies? Now we have to give two haircuts!"

"It's not PiSAN, it's PIEsan," Stella corrected Sam, emphasizing the accent with her body.

Stella's father, Anatale, appeared from the living room. "Hey!" he wanted to know, "how come these guys aren't drinking?"

"Because," Stella began.

"Get them a drink," he ordered her. "Sam knows where it is. Make yourself at home, Cal."

Which the situation in that place generally seemed to lend itself to.

The doorbell rang and before anyone even went to answer in came Mrs. Ruse. The decibel level fell by half. "Who's that?" yelled Maria from the kitchen.

"I just came to wish you all a very blessed Christmas," said Mrs. Ruse. "Isn't this a wonderful time of year? Don't you think it's terrible that everyone doesn't know the Lord? If only that nice Mr. Reagan was President. He'd put the Christ back in Christmas."

The noise in the room dropped by another half. "Do you boys like Ronald Reagan?" Maria asked Sam and Calvin.

"No!" cried Sam.

"Watch out for the false, the wide ones, frauds . . ." quoted Calvin.

"He tried to take away my pension!" agreed Uncle Luigi.

"Yes, and he made us pay for Stella's college and we hardly had any money," Maria remembered.

"He wanted to cut down the redwood trees," chimed Stella.

"I'd rather have that Buddhist we got now than him," Anatale declared.

Mrs. Ruse retreated quickly in the direction she had come.

"Well, I'm glad she didn't get into the kitchen," Maria

sighed with relief.

"She gives the evil eye to the food," Stella explained.

"What?" Calvin inquired in amazement.

Maria stopped and turned back toward him. "That's right. I'm making pizza dough, and she comes in and ruins it."

"She wanted a look at you," Stella explained.

"When I bring Stella home at night she watches us through the window," added Sam.

"Where's Jimmy and Irene? We're not waiting for them, are we?" Luigi wanted to know.

"Hey, Ma!" Anatale shouted back to the kitchen. "What are we waiting for? Jimmy doesn't eat that fish. Not even Christmas Eve."

The Christmas Eve fast at the Orientis was as meager as Sam had been led to believe it would be. Anatale briefly asked a blessing for it, but his asking lacked the formal seriousness that Sam was used to hearing before meals in the Protestant home where he grew up. People stood politely wherever they happened to be while Stella's father addressed his God, less sharply and loudly than the members of the family addressed each other, and without the presumption with which Sam remembered hearing the Deity importuned at his own family's holiday gatherings. But there was a serious tone to Anatale's supplication and, aside from the request for the blessing of the meal, which he sounded fairly confident of receiving, he asked only for rain, not sounding nearly so certain about receiving that. Just then, Sam, who generally had trouble in the middle ground between believing and disbelieving, found himself envying, and perhaps even resenting, Calvin, who seemed so comfortable with the simple thingness of things.

"I suppose you boys miss having your white Christmas,"

said Maria as she draped them in great paper bibs.

Michigan winter gleamed in Sam's mind's eye. "It hardly feels like Christmas without snow," he admitted.

"So when did it ever snow in Bethlehem?" jeered Stella.

"Actually," Calvin pointed out, "the weather there is probably a lot like this." He motioned to indicate the palpably dry California air around him. "And besides, it does snow in the mountains there sometimes," he added, addressing his attention to a bowl of cioppino.

"That's right," Maria told Stella. "Just like it snows in the mountains here sometimes. But not this year." Then she turned her own attention to cioppino. "In restaurants they shell it for you," she explained, "but that's soup, that's not cioppino." With an apparently perfect understanding of such a distinction, Calvin engaged in an attack upon redly dripping clams, white-grained crab shell, opaque prawn casing, explored the recesses of each with a nutcracker, steel pick, and his hunting knife, relishing, Sam could see in his eyes, not only the flavor, as someone long stranded in Montana might, but the pursuit itself of the ocean-nurtured flesh. Maria watched him eat and gleamed in beatitude. "Do you like it Calvin?" she kept asking. "Do you want more?"

It seemed impossible that anyone might enjoy a meal as much as Calvin was enjoying that one, but Sam enjoyed his own quite a lot, despite the fact that coordination failed him at times and large chunks of uncracked crab leg would levitate from his grasp. "Block that kick, Sam!" a cousin hooted genially.

"Remember," Stella told him, "you have to be Santa Claus tonight."

It was the first Sam had heard of that. "I do?" he answered her dumbly.

"Adam Grizzly!" cried Stella's Aunt Irene as she bustled

in through the back door.

"Hey, he brought his bear this time!" chortled Stella's Uncle Jimmy right behind her.

Calvin beamed and ursinely unhinged a clam.

"Get your hamburger, hey?" cried Anatale from the living room. When he reached the kitchen, Sam was amazed to see there wasn't a drop of tomato sauce on him. Calvin and he were painted in the stuff – tentlike bibs and all – and had managed to spatter the entire table as well.

"Don't you know you're supposed to fast on Christmas Eve?" Maria chided Jimmy.

"I did," he defended himself. "I only ate one." He patted a belly that could obviously have held more.

"Well, I'm ashamed of you, Eye," Maria persisted to her sister.

"Oh, but I had a fishburger," said Irene.

"This is Calvin," Maria changed the subject.

"And you already know this other hippie," added Anatale.

"He's going to be Santa Claus," Maria informed them.

"I am? But what do I do?" marveled Sam, feeling increasingly befuddled either by champagne or his triple role as new family member, shaggy mountain man, and Christmas saint.

What he did was sneak out the back and around to the front where he was supposed to say "Merry Christmas, ho ho ho, have you all been good little boys and girls?" but on the not very long walk around the house the clear star-bespattered California night hit him full in the face. There was to it, besides the palpable dryness, a vague trace of magic that he was not totally successful in resisting. It had to be more than champagne that had him knocking on the door and, instead of "ho ho ho" howling, "It's Santa Claus! Watcha' got in yer bag, Santa! I got apples and oranges, I got plums and tomatoes, I got Masked Marvel comic books, I got an eight by ten color photograph of Bo Diddley suitable for framing!"

Maria opened the front door half an inch and cried, "Bye Santa! Bye Santa! Bye Santa!" and then slammed it in his face.

Across the street, Mrs. Ruse watched through a crack in the curtains.

When Sam came back around to the kitchen Stella took a punch at him. "You should have seen the kids," she berated him. "Jeffy kept saying 'Who's that?' and I said 'it's Santa Claus,' and he said, 'Nooo! It's Adam Grizzly!'"

"You destroyed the faith of a little child." Calvin shook his head sadly.

Maria came into the kitchen carrying an empty champagne bottle and raised it to hit him. "What will the neighbors think?" she demanded to know.

Sam turned to Stella. "Was I that loud?"

"Loud?" cried Maria. "To wake the dead!"

"Isn't she something, my new mother-in-law?" Sam turned proudly to Calvin.

Calvin's jaw dropped. Stella regarded Sam magnificently, informing him with a single look that his real triune role was crazy, drunk, and dangerous.

But Maria looked neither surprised, nor as though she had even heard the words. Instead, she opened another bottle of champagne, poured each of them a glass, and said, all goodnaturedly, "Well, Merry Christmas anyway, Santa."

II

In California that year, the weather on Christmas Day, as well as the day after that, was probably very like the weather around Bethlehem, or in any other mountainous desert country.

But the next day was different. Sam took the train to Palo Alto to work before anyone else was even up, hoping Calvin snoring in the van had not forgotten that he had come to California not just to eat home-cooked Italian seafood, but to see the Dead, that very night.

The thing that was different was that it was, all day long, cold, damp, and misty grey.

The few people who came into the cavernous library had faraway looks of anticipation in their eyes, and from his station at the check-out desk Sam could see them hurry their steps toward the great double doors when they left. They would look anxiously from side to side when they got there, and reach out their hands to feel the air upon exiting. He kept waiting for the first person to walk in shaking the droplets from their hair.

But it never happened, and was merely greyer, and that from coming dusk, when Calvin and Stella picked him up in the van. Before they drove off, Calvin poured him a glass of a brown substance from a blender. It tasted of black walnut with the shells ground in for good measure.

"You should have heard him explain to my mother why he needed her blender," Stella laughed to Sam. "Isn't that stuff foul?"

It grew darker as they drove, but at one point along the Junipero Serra, the self-congratulated most beautiful freeway in the world, they came out of the mist and actually beheld a narrow patch of pink-blue late afternoon sky.

A rainbow arced from the mountainside to the half-empty reservoir.

"Do you know what that means?" Stella quizzed them.

"That God will never again destroy the world with a flood," said Calvin, and they all sighed with relief.

It was dark by the time they reached San Francisco.

"The Grateful Dead!" exalted Calvin in front of Winterland. "You know what I like about the Dead? Everything they sing is about me."

"Everything anybody sings is about him," Sam explained to Stella.

Being at Winterland warmed her to yarning about the golden age of San Francisco music: the Fillmore, Chet Helms and the Family Dog, "two dollars a ticket to hear three bands, the Airplane, Big Brother, Blue Cheer. We never went to hear the Dead. They played for free in the streets and were they ever terrible!"

The Dead weren't terrible that night though. In fact, they were great. Jerry Garcia looked cherubic, like the happiest creature on God's brown earth, just standing there grinning and playing. And it felt to Sam as he listened with his body, the music gliding curiously from passages of unanswerable sweetness to cunning discordancy, that a lot of gunk that had been collecting about his self was getting worked loose, was suddenly not quite as heavily compacted as it had been a few dry hours, a few dry days, a dry year or two or three back. This went on piece by piece, nearly until midnight when the concert seemed to reach either Sam's, or its own, moment of truth. By which time he was in full agreement with Calvin that whatever anybody was singing was about him. The Dead gave forth with a medley of "He's Gone" (and nothing's gonna bring him back), "Stella Blue," and a song Sam had never heard before that Bob Weir introduced over the medley's connecting instrumental riff by suggesting, "Don't guess anybody's looked outside?" The lyrics began as a plaintive litany of the troubles in the singer's life, but then swung into a joyful chorus whose only three repeated lines were, "It looks like rain, it feels like rain, here comes the rain . . ."

A memorable electric shock cut its unquiet way through Winterland, but there was a certain natural electric order to it. Spaces in the crowd got larger, and then people began to dance back into the hall, soaking wet.

Outside, ticket stubs and paper cups were washing across the sidewalk into the street and there was a very sweet smell to San Francisco.

"Do you suppose rain is general in California?" asked Sam.

"I wouldn't be at all surprised," said Calvin, sniffing the wind.

"Hey you guys, I wanted to hear the Dead," protested Stella.

"But it's raining!" Sam told her.

"It looks like rain, it feels like rain, here comes the rain," Calvin agreed.

"The Dead are judged by their works!" cried a naked young man running past Winterland.

"We're going to the beach," Sam decided.

"But what about the Dead?" persisted Stella.

"Leave the Dead to b-b-b . . ." Sam told her before he sneezed.

"Are you getting sick?" she wanted to know.

"Not before I get to the beach," Sam determined.

Taking off his own clothes and running through the rain into the waves along The Great Highway that night-morning did not, as it turned out, do Sam's health much good.

"You guys are crazy," Stella informed them sensibly. She crawled into a sleeping bag in the van and told them to try not to drown.

Redwood City was awakening to a grey miserable wet wonderful day when Sam drove up to the train depot. Calvin hoisted his pack and exclaimed "What a long strange trip it's been!" He gestured thumbs-up and ran for the train.

The stop at the DMV branch in Mountain View to get his California Driver's License was not an action Sam could have explained very sensibly. It had to do with an earlier vague realization that he really did live in California, and was likely to be there for a while, and with an equally vague resolve to stop the next time he went by that place around opening hour when the lines wouldn't be too long. He put down Stella's parents' address as his own, since it was the closest thing he had to a home. He stood in front of the camera in the Grateful Dead T-shirt he'd bought at Winterland that night, and grinned.

Stella's parents were having breakfast. Sam was ready to let himself be sick and sleep it off in the van by then. "They'd never allow that," Stella informed him. "This dope went swimming after the concert," she explained through his sneezes.

"And what did you do?" asked Maria. "Where's Calvin?"

"I slept in the van while he caught cold. Calvin's on his way back to Montana."

All of which appeared to be within the normal course of events to the Orientis.

"Can I put Sam in my room?" asked Stella.

"Where you gonna sleep then?" her mother wanted to know.

"On the couch in the living room."

"Put him to bed," Anatale ordered her. "Make him some

tea. Ma, get a hot water bottle and some aspirin."

"Our prayers were answered," added Maria as she left the room.

"Haw! For awhile!" laughed Anatale.

And soon afterward, aspirin dulling the pain in his throat, the taste of cough syrup on his palate, hot water bottle at his feet, in Stella's bed, rain spattering the patio outside the window, and he feeling rather good considering how sick he was, Sam found himself in a state somewhere between belief and disbelief, grateful that he wasn't dead yet, and not likely to be in the foreseeable future, happy to have beheld a thing revealed, and to be drifting to sleep.

Driftwood Suspects

. . . numbers add up to nothin'. . .

I

They are doing it again.

"Driftwood?"

"Five, four-fifty, five, six-fifty, five-twenty-five, six, seven-fifty . . .

Claude leans worried over his calculator. "Thirty-nine-seventy-five," he reports.

"Just like the time before and time before that," says Burton. It is almost as though he's enjoying it.

"J-j-jaimie?"

"Five, five-fifty, six-fifty, seven . . ."

A cloud races down the mountain, stops directly over the plastic cookshack, and spatters it.

One by one, Claude calls their names and they repeat themselves. Every time the numbers are the same. Claude writes and adds, and hands the calculator to Burton. "You t-t-t-try it," he suggests.

Burton's long hair falls like a viewing hood around the little instrument. "Four-forty-four," he reports, shakes back his hair, and grins in knowing perplexity.

"Add the daily totals again," says Bomb.

The answer is always the same. They have planted exactly

forty-four thousand, four hundred trees.

"It c-c-can't b-b-be," Claude insists to himself. "It can't b-b-be."

Thad sits seriously at the far end of the table. "I don't trust those things." He seems to mean the calculator. "Let's all add them in our heads, or at least on paper."

Claude tears nine pages from his notebook, writes laboriously on each in a large uneven hand, passes them around. There aren't enough pencils, so it takes time. As heads rise in completion, he calls their names yet again.

"Driftwood?"

"Thirty-nine-seventy-five."

As always.

"Jaimie?"

"Forty-two-seventy-five." The forty-two is fawty-two in Texas drawl.

"L-l-lauren?"

Subdued. "Forty-one."

"Burton?"

"Forty-one-fifty."

"R-r-robin?"

"Sixty-one, it comes out exactly, Claude . . ."

"Morris?"

"Forty-eight-fifty . . ."

"N-n-n-no, that's wrong. You add it Robin . . ." A further pause.

"Forty-nine-fifty," she reports. "You forgot to carry one, Morris."

"D-d-damn," murmurs Claude. "Thad?"

"No question, fifty-six-fifty."

"B-b-bomb?"

"Fifty-six . . ."

"B-b-brain?"

"Fifty-six, same as the Bomb."

"Add them Burton." Claude hands his own sheet over.

"Four-forty-four," Burton reports to no one's surprise.

II

"Why . . ." wonders Lauren, dreamy bewilderment in her wide eyes. "Why don't we just tell Murphy there's been a mistake?"

Burton shakes his head in disbelief. "Because he'll say mistake, schmake. The Forestry doesn't make mistakes. Planters make mistakes . . ."

"Everything's too p-p-p-p-p . . ." Claude loses the word, and they all wait until he finds it in flying saliva. "Perfect."

Tomorrow they were going to finish by planting six thousand trees to bring their total to fifty thousand four hundred – a number whose unroundedness has to do with the fact that the trees come six hundred to a box. Unrounded and all, it is the amount specified in their contract. The Forestry supplies the stock. The contractor counts the boxes and signs the inventory. The trees are twenty-five to a bundle, twenty-four bundles to a box. Six hundred each, in all. Unfortunately, they are in possession of a few more than six thousand trees. Six thousand more than six thousand, to be precise, and no idea where they came from. It is a little hard to imagine Claude, or anyone, miscounting the boxes by ten to come up with eighty-four of them when there were really ninety-four. Unless some strange numerological necromancy was having its way with his generally sober and dependable wits.

"Well what else can we do?" Lauren persists.

Even Driftwood, a treeplanter for all of a week now, knows what they can and probably will have to do. If he knows, Claude has to know too. Even Lauren must know.

"All those people out of work, and we have extra trees we can't plant," Thad laments.

III

That is the sad part. They are the only treeplanters actually planting trees for miles around. For some reason the stock at Red Rock Nursery could not come out on schedule. The highways for two hundred kilometers in every direction around Prince George are lined with out-of-work planters. Their own contract is near one of the highways, the Alcan, and they've been getting visitors. This ought to be the height of the season, and people are losing not only their wages but a percentage of the unemployment they hoped would see them through the winter. Even Driftwood, in Canada for all of two weeks now, understands. Understands from what Claude told him at the airport, and from the faces of the visitors asking about work. Claude has to tell those visitors no, that all he can give them is supper for one night, and that over the objections of their cook.

He said it the first night. "It isn't a rich contract. I wish we could p-p-pay ten cents a tree. B-b-but we're lucky to have the work at all . . ."

IV

Although the ironic sadness of their situation is real, and they feel badly enough about it, and certainly regret what will have to be done, the most powerful emotion circulating in the cookshack is a palpable hunger to figure it out.

"I hate t'bring somethin' like this up," Jaimie does quietly. "But me'n Wren was on this contract coupl'a years ago people done a whole lot'a stashin'. Not us, y'know, but . . ."

V

Driftwood hasn't heard that word stash since arriving in Canada, but knows immediately what Jaimie means. It occurred to him early that first rainy day when wet, bone-weary, and physically miserable in a manner beyond any he had remotely imagined, he thought he couldn't possibly plant another tree and wondered whether anyone would ever miss a few here, a few there, in a rotten stump, or buried back in the woods. He even asked Jaimie between runs. "How, er, does anyone know how many we, er, take?"

"Ya'll keep track fer yerself," Jaimie replied.

"But what . . ." tugging his sou'wester down over his brow against the rain. He bought the hat just before leaving England because he remembered Claude's delight at finding one in the Oxfam in Saint Ives. "That's exactly what you need for planting in the rain!" Claude had exalted then. "And they're fifteen-twenty bucks in Vancouver. Only a pound?"

Before leaving, Driftwood paid two for his own in London. "But what . . ." he repeated to Jaimie. He knew he was going to work in the rain, but somehow expected it to be like gentle south-country summer rain, not this icy wind-whipped northern storming. "But what if you make, er, a mistake."

"Hey man," Jaimie shook his head solemnly. "It ain't that hard. If yer really worried, j'st hang on t' the twine from the bundles. Count 'em at the end'a the day."

"It's not stashing," declares Robin. "That's not possible.

I would have had to stash every tree I planted to account for that many."

It was only last night that he had the one bit of comfort available. Her, beside him in her tent, he surprised that anyone who worked that hard could feel that soft.

"So?" she rose on an elbow, and cocked an eyebrow. "Don't your women ever work?"

"No one works in England," he replied in only slight exaggeration. "There isn't any work to do. I even had to borrow money for the plane ticket over here."

"There's treeplanting in England," she answered him. "I read a story about it."

Her strength has everything to do with her planting six thousand trees in seven days, and not because it is such immensely difficult work. Already, Driftwood has learned that brute force is not necessary to the planting itself. That act is more a matter of coordination, stamina, and an almost preternatural spiritual peace in the face of physical discomfort, of chilling rain one day and searing heat the next, of rubber boots squishy with sweat, of biting insects in a dozen miserable varieties, of plants and branches dead and alive that stab, stub, trip, scratch, and cut, clothing that chafes, and one's individual consciousness that would rather not put up with any, let alone all, of those things. To deal with it necessitates some special emotional grace. He has felt it dawn upon him three specific times at three specific moments, and it was a feeling so foreign and blissful that the first time it frightened him. The second time he accepted it, and the third time positively reveled in it. He has been trying to create it on his own ever since and found that to be impossible. Robin carries herself as though she possesses it all the time. Since Day 3 they have had to lug whole boxes of trees into the site by hand. What once was logging road suppurates into quagmire in wet weather, and desiccates into impossible crevices of rut in dry, and there isn't the remotest hope of getting the toughest four-wheeler through it, let alone the automatic transmission pickup Claude rented in Vancouver and in which he and Driftwood drove nine hundred kilometers north together. Most of the crew is limited to planting six hundred trees a day by the simple fact that that is how many are in a box, and once they've carried one, picking their way through the ruts or splashing through the quagmire, and then made the effort to plant what's in it, there's not even foolish hope of going back and getting more. But Robin stuffs eight bundles into each of her bags, ties a full box to her pack frame with rope, and sets off like a Sherpa. Yesterday, she planted a thousand. And today, on hardly any sleep at all, another thousand.

VI

It was Day 6, yesterday morning, that Morris contemplated the pile of boxes, raised an eyebrow in Claude's direction, and said, "There's more than three days worth of planting here."

"N-n-nah," Claude dismissed him. "This-s-s-s's about right." And then had not bothered to start adding things up until after supper tonight. To learn that things were not so OK after all.

"On the other hand . . ." Burton begins in again. "Maybe it isn't just one person. Maybe everyone's doing it. Say three people were stashing a hundred a day."

That is just plain in bad taste, but, then again . . . "Three people stashing two hundred a day?" he recalculates. "Four people . . ."

They plant in groups of three, two, and one. Two three-somes: Driftwood and Jaimie and Lauren, Thad and Bomb and Brain. Robin was the one who nicknamed the last two the Killer Bees. They are blond as the beach at Brighton, and benignly bonkers, Thad's friends and welcome foils to Thad's more seriously obsessive barminess. Burton and Morris plant partners. Robin plants solo. Claude doesn't plant at all, just hobbles through the slash leaning on his curly ram's horn handle blackthorn cane, watching them and attempting to sweet-talk Murphy about the plots.

Thad rises immediately to the bait. "See here," he insists. "I don't care for being . . ."

The two of them have been at it since Day 1. Thad and the Bees plant with shovels instead of mattocks. The Bees don't seem to care one way or other, but Thad believes in those shovels and has enough along for everyone. He's been pushing them like a drug, but Burton resisted with "thanks, but no, real planters use mattocks."

"So live in the stone age!" Thad snapped back. It happened the second day at the site, and most of them heard, but it was just one of those things.

Morris takes off his glasses and begins to clean them. "Stashing can't have anything to do with it," he informs them all. "If trees were being stashed they'd still get used up. We have too many trees not used. Someone would have to be claiming to have planted trees they never took out of the box. It would have to be so many that they haven't planted a single tree yet. And the only person with six thousand is Robin. And we've all seen her plant."

Morris and Burton tried to follow her the first two days.

VII

"Your name's not really Driftwood, is it?" was the first thing she asked him in the tub.

He had remarked to Claude, not twenty minutes before, that treeplanting was just the thing for his libido. It was gone.

Claude laughed and told him, "you should have been at Bella Coola," and said it not as though it would have changed his mind, but as though they could have used him there.

The only thing he knows about Bella Coola is that that was where Claude was working before he met him at the Vancouver airport stumbling along on crutches. Crutches since replaced by that curly ram's horn cane, a sure sign Claude's a fast healer. "Good thing I got hurt," Claude said. "You'd never have found me. I'd still be up at Bella Coola."

One of the peculiar things about Claude's stammer is that it never seems to trouble him when he's alone with Driftwood. "I found your letter when I got home," Claude went on. "I guess I didn't really imagine you might come."

"Well, there, you offered me a job. No work in England."

"You should have been at Bella Coola," Claude told him again, but didn't explain. Then he changed the subject. "There's great coals down there and the water's hot. Go have a soak. You'll feel loads better."

He was lolling in the steaming water, watching the trees sway in the wind above him and enjoying the light spray of rain filtering through them, when she came down the trail into the ravine. Everyone must wash in the stream before climbing into the tub, and as he watched her it occurred to him that he might have a libido again after all. When she was through, he made a motion to rise, partly to escape a developing physical manifestation, partly because it was, after all, her turn, and he was, after all, a gentleman.

But she said, "take your time," and approached. He pushed up to climb out, but she stopped him. "There's room for two," was all she said. The wooden seat turned out to be a little bit narrow for the both of them, and she found her way quite pleasantly into his lap.

In her tent, she brought out the packet about the time he was wondering. "Well, I see we're prepared," he joked coolly.

"Brother," she said, "I guess you haven't heard about Bella Coola."

"Not very much," he admitted. "So what did happen at this Bella Coola?"

"Don't even ask," was all she replied as she slipped it over him.

VIII

"The only thing I can come up with," Morris has decided, "is that the boxes must all be short trees.

"Hey!" Brain shakes his head. "We been countin', every last suckin' box."

"And?" inquires Claude.

"Six hundred, every suckin' one."

"Everyone else c-c-counting?"

"I am," says Burton.

"Sometimes," says Jaimie.

"Most of them," says Robin.

"Me too," says Morris, "But that's all I can come up with."

"S-s-shit," says Claude.

Driftwood has been saving his twine each day as Jaimie

suggested, and his boxes all come out twenty-four bundles to a box, six hundred each, in all.

"The thing is," Morris continues, "the plots have been good. How many have too few trees? I mean, it would show up in the plots."

Murphy, the Forestry checker, is quite simply the toughest any of them has ever had to work with. They all say it. And their plots have been good anyway. They're all proud of the job they're doing. The contract isn't rich, and it's been tough lugging all those trees back into the slash, nobody's making much money, but it has been, they all say, together. They have a lot to be proud of. And now this.

"Claude," says Burton. "Who else is planting around here?"

"No one," replies Claude.

"No, I know, it's a ways away, but who's got the only other working contract anywhere near here?"

"Oh brother," realizes Claude.

"He'd do something like that too," mutters Robin. "Either him or his crazy brothers. After what happened . . ." She stops before she says it. "And he was pissed at us for leaving," she adds.

"I was hurt," Claude reminds her.

"He said you wanted to get hurt. He said you created your own reality. He said it after you left."

"F-f-f-frans, even if he is p-p-p-p-pissed at me, he-he-he wouldn't do so-so-so-something like that," Claude protests.

Even Driftwood has heard of Frans. Everybody has.

Thad shakes his head and shifts his sharp grey eyes up and down the table. A quick burst of rain pops against the roof. "Kind of a warped thing to do," he figures. Behind the cloud, to the west, through the trees, Driftwood can see a streak of blue sky.

"So less j'st bring 'em back to'm!" The obvious answer as far as Brain is concerned.

And Bomb agrees. "That's right! Load 'em up and get 'em outta' here."

"N-n-n-no, h-h-hold on you two," Claude struggles for control. "We don't know that's what happened." He turns to Maureen, the cook, who is watching them from the kitchen counter, hard face set, cigarette on lip gun-moll style, too good to be cooking for the likes of them, but with her own reasons, like that she borrowed an Alfa in Vancouver without telling the owner and wrapped it around a telephone pole and didn't have any insurance. "Has anyone c-c-come up this road while we're n-n-not here?" Claude wants to know.

"Nobody," she says. "I've been here all along."

Driftwood looks at Jaimie because they both know it is simply not true. They came back early on Day 5, tired out, and she was nowhere to be found, and then came roaring back into camp a few minutes later in the BowMac rent-a-truck. No water hauled or groceries from Mackenzie or anything. Just out joy-riding as far as they could tell.

Jaimie stares solemnly back at Driftwood. Are they going to call Maureen on this? Does it matter? She certainly didn't do it. Is guarding the camp part of her job? The food didn't taste too good tonight. Robin is not real fond of her. They look a little bit alike, except that Maureen's hair isn't red, and Robin's face is softer and rounder, with those freckles. Neither smiles much. Robin says Maureen does less and less work every day. And Claude agreed to pay her way too much in the first place. She's making more than any of the planters except maybe Robin herself, and everybody knows that cooks shouldn't make more than good planters.

IX

Thad is pursuing an earlier train of thought. "This Frans, I mean, I've never actually met the guy. Would he really do a thing like that?"

Claude shrugs. "I s-s-s-spose he might do nearly anyth-th-th-thing."

"But what," Thad insists, "does he gain by it?"

Burton speaks. "It's six thousand trees he gets paid for and doesn't plant. His own contract is so big they'll never miss them. He gets a good laugh every time the story gets told. And he settles the score."

"I don't suppose," says Thad, "that anyone wants to tell me what the score is."

"I don't," says Burton.

Driftwood suspects by now that it may have something to do with Bella Coola.

Lauren has been watching silently and intently and finally speaks her piece. "I know it would be a lot of work," she begins, "but I think we should plant them. Tell Murphy that there was an error, and just plant them."

Which might be the right thing to do. And they don't stash. And they have a lot to be proud of. But no one, including Driftwood, particularly Driftwood, wants to plant trees for free. And yet, there's enough respect for what she's suggesting that no one hoots her into the woods. Although Maureen does ask, "If you all work an extra day for free do I get paid to cook?"

Claude looks from face to face. "Even that won't w-w-work," he explains. "See, if-f-f-f we tell Murphy about it he's going to g-g-get all the checkers in the area out here d-d-doing plots over again. They d-d-don't have anyth-th-thing to do r-r-right now either. If we don't make a hundred percent payment, we're at least g-g-going to be c-c-close, as we stand right now. We c-c-can't af-f-f-ford to have them c-c-come through here taking p-p-plots all over again. And if we stay h-h-here an extra d-d-day you not only p-p-plant for free, it c-c-costs us money, like for f-f-food, you'll all g-g-get less p-p-per tree on the rest." He sighs at having gotten it said.

"He's right, you know," Robin tells them all.

"Trees are living things," insists Lauren.

"Everything dies sometime." Burton shrugs his shoulders.

"We'll take care of it," the Killer Bees offer in unison.

"No," says Claude, "I'll take care of it."

X

You can say this for Claude, he's taking care of it himself, at least trying to. Although he does bring Driftwood along. The Bees wanted to come too, jumped up from their fire where they were drinking beer with Thad as they do every evening in the long daylight, stopped the truck as Claude and Driftwood drove down from the site with the ten boxes of phantom trees under a tarp in the bed, and stood there by the window grinning. "We know just the place," Bomb told Claude, shaking his blond head eagerly.

"We're good at this kind of stuff," agreed Brain, but Claude turned them down.

"So now what?" wonders Driftwood as they pull out onto the highway. It is a relief to be able to talk. Originally, Claude warned him about talking when Forestry people were around, lest they hear his accent and start asking about things like work permits. Driftwood even feels a little guilty

because of all those Canadian treeplanters on the road and
the fact that he is displacing one of them, so he has been
practically voiceless in the camp, talking to Jaimie as they
work, to Robin in her tent last night, but mostly cautiously
quiet. Immediately, they spy two planters hitchhiking, a man
and a woman, and Driftwood imagines from the worn wanting look visible in their eyes as the truck nears them that they
must be finally discouraged and headed back toward Prince
George and eventually further south, where long choruses of
planters' blues will be sung all summer long. Under normal
circumstances, Claude would certainly pick them up, but
tonight is anything but normal, and Driftwood can read the
surprise in their faces as the truck roars toward them, as
they focus on its cab and realize that Claude and Driftwood
are two of their own tribe who, incredibly, have no intention
of stopping. Driftwood turns to watch them recede, dazed
looks on their faces, maybe contemplating raising an arm
in contemptuous gesture, but thinking for what? and not
making the effort.

"It's not that I don't trust them," Claude begins, and it
takes Driftwood a moment to realize that he's talking about
the Bees, not the hitchhikers. "It's just that we only need the
two of us."

They met in Plymouth, where Claude was busking on
the street with his banjo, and collecting a fair crowd with his
flat-picking and northern transatlantic ballads. Claude also
never stammers when he sings – old sea chanteys, lumber-
jack tales, his own compositions about trees, about planting
them as well as just being in them – in a worn husky voice.
Driftwood listened for an hour until Claude pocketed his
take, closed his banjo case, and asked Driftwood for directions to the nearest real-ale pub.

They found one together, closed it down that night, and

set out across Dartmoor the next morning, the countryside mint-green and grey in late summer, spattered with the
yellow and purple of gorse and heather. Claude was carrying
a copy of Mysterious Cornwall, and chasing ghosts. Driftwood was only one step ahead of some less public ghosts
of his own, and the two of them found an appropriate pace
together. After Robin last night, Driftwood figured he might
have widened his lead on the ghosts he hadn't shaken on that
moor, but now he wonders about that, wonders if maybe they
might not catch him yet after all.

"You realize if we get caught, we'll be fined so bad we
won't make a cent?" Claude explains to him.

Which would truly be silly, to have done all that work
and not get paid. "So what do you think really happened?"
Driftwood returns.

"Some sinister force is at work," Claude allows. "We
covered it all in the cookshack."

The northern sun is beginning to sink against a sky
awash in disintegrating cumulus, what is left of the rain
that fell earlier against their roof. The show of light and
color, right down to a double rainbow, is extraordinary, and
daylight will hang on for most of the night, with new dawn
hard on its trail. In a week, Driftwood has practically grown
acclimated to it. Long summer twilights are not that foreign
to him in the first place, even if the huge open sky and landscape are.

"A sinister force, eh?" he asks, talking Canajun. "Does
it have a name?"

"It does," is all Claude answers him.

"Frans."

Claude shakes his head a nervous "yes."

Driftwood must ask. "What happened at this Bella
Coola anyway?"

The name comes between them in a fashion that reminds Driftwood oddly, and then maybe not so oddly, of the feeling of Robin against him. And the fact that the condom was sheep gut rather than latex. "It's natural," she had explained as she applied it. He remembers wondering if vegetarians use sheep gut prophylactics.

What he still wonders about is why it was him. He had not been seeking her, and at least one other, Morris, pretty obviously was, although pursuing too awkwardly, ogling, she complained to Driftwood, at the creek and in the tub, and trying to keep pace with her in the slash when she took off her shirt on the two hot days they'd had. And between her and Claude there is obviously something she isn't talking about, something which made her peek out her tent before Driftwood left in the morning, to make sure no one was watching to see.

"He wants to show me who's boss," Claude goes on. "That's important to him."

Two different things are on their two different minds, although both attach vaguely to the matter at hand, the criminal stashing of six thousand trees, and it is from that matter that the intensity, the one might even call it terror, begins to well in Driftwood's own gut. Claude's knuckles white on the wheel and his tuneless bud-duh-bup-pup-bup singing suggest his own fear.

"Do you know where we're going?" Driftwood wonders aimlessly.

"I sure do," mutters Claude. They are entering Mackenzie; the stupid little town springs at them suddenly from the bush.

"Not to his camp?" Suddenly, Driftwood understands. Claude has to have an awfully good reason to risk driving through this particular town. They pass the hotel where the beer parlour is just now closing – pickup trucks differing mainly in color exit randomly from the parking lot. "Good, I don't see any of his vehicles," Claude mutters distantly and swerves by, giving the pickups, all headed in directions other than theirs, wide passage. "The beer parlour is off-limits to his crew," he tells Driftwood.

"What happened? Did they tear it up one night?"

"No, no," Claude whispers hoarsely as though back there in the woods somewhere Frans might be listening. "Nothing like that. He declares it off-limits to them."

Driftwood finds his own voice dropping as well. "What if we see him, or someone from his crew, on the road?"

"I don't know," Claude frets. "See, it's probably a test. He doesn't really want to shut us down. He just wants to put us in a position where we could be shut down. And then see how we respond. There's no right thing to do, what I mean, there are several. Some better than others. If we see him and he knows what we're up to . . ."

"He wouldn't turn you in to the Forestry?"

Claude reacts in shock to that suggestion. "He'd never do that!" he declares.

Driftwood isn't so sure. "Would he make you plant them?" he wonders.

"On his own ground!" Now Claude does seem to think he understands, and it becomes very important not to encounter Frans or any of his crew. Ahead through the woods, past a bend in the road, a flash of white light appears. Claude throws the truck into reverse without even stopping, cuts their headlights and backs in reckless haste for several hundred meters, peering wildly over his shoulder through the rear window until he finds a side road, slams the truck back into forward gear, and barrels into the bush, eyes alight with fright. Both he and Driftwood turn in time to see the battered yellow panel truck race past. "That's one of his." Claude is convinced.

They sit and wait. No more lights, no more vehicles. It may be as dark by then as it is going to get, which isn't very, a darkness defined more in terms of the silvery luminance to it than by the absence of light. "If we had to, I guess we could outrun him," Claude imagines.

Driftwood doesn't find that very convincing. He surveys the bush. "Pretty thick," he suggests, "Why don't we just dump the trees right here?"

Claude may be considering it. "Evidence," he is all he can come up with. "Who knows who'll come in here. We did. Someone else might too."

"Then," realizes Driftwood, "we can't just dump them anywhere."

Claude considers that too. It is what each of them would dearly love to do. "No, we can't."

So the real fun begins. Claude pulls out of the bush and drives as a human being possessed up the gravel road. Indicates to Driftwood the turnoff for Frans' camp, and seems relieved to have passed it. "Now, if we can find one of his sites."

Which, of course, they cannot. Claude's desperation seems to increase as he drives; by this time they are a good fifty kilometers north of Mackenzie and more than a hundred from their own camp, and it must be past midnight. It will be growing lighter again soon and they really must do something with the trees.

"I planted here last year for him, you know," says Claude, "but, I mean, the sites will be different now . . ."

There are side roads every three or four kilometers. Claude turns up one of them. They encounter a wide plain of logging slash, get out of the truck for a moment and contemplate it in the soft grey glow. "I think we planted this," murmurs Claude, which means that half-forgotten habit, not chance, has brought him back. Which means that they can't just leave the trees here because consciousness is involved, and the same habit might well bring Frans himself upon this very place at any time.

Nonetheless, Driftwood tries to find his way though the maze into which Claude has led him. Tries to get through the walls with clarity, acuity, he tells himself, as though even groping for words suggesting hardness, mental hardness, will get them out. "Why can't we just leave the trees?" He faces Claude in the greyness. "Wouldn't everyone think they're just his trees?"

"He'll know," Claude tells him simply. "It would be against the rules. He'd get me, us, all of us, back."

"But if we leave these trees with his trees, that's OK?" Driftwood is beginning to catch on.

"Yes, that would be best. That would put an end to it." Although Claude doesn't say it in words, Driftwood understands. That would be passing the test. Any other solution is a form of failure.

"And we can't just drive them into his camp, and leave them there?"

"No! He wouldn't like that at all."

"You know, we could drive around all night long and not find where he keeps his . . ."

"And ours just up the road. I made it so easy for him . . ." The old create-your-own-reality syndrome.

"Let's get out of here, huh?"

And they do. Claude keeps the lights off until they get past the turnoff for Frans' camp, and then flips them on and screams toward Mackenzie.

"We have to put them somewhere nobody will ever find

them . . ." A plan may be forming.

Driftwood asks no questions, is dead tired, but with a heavy nervous edge to his weariness, although that part of it seems to melt a bit as they get further away from whatever that was back there. And the thing is, it was a something, a presence. Claude is plainly spooked, and it's hard to sort out what is just his sensitivity to that, and what his own realization that it, whatever it is, was there. But, oh brother, it was, and it doesn't really matter, Driftwood suspects, whether he felt it through Claude or all by himself on his own.

XI

Claude stops the truck on the bridge where the highway crosses the Parsnip River and turns off the headlights. This, Driftwood realizes, is the purest form of madness – the highway is the fucking Alcan, the most heavily traveled road in that whole part of the world. There's a restaurant, a gas station, and a general store, all within sight of this bridge by daylight. Which it may as well be, the sky is already lightening in the north, Driftwood can practically see the westerly motion of the wine-red glow along the immense horizon there. "Let's do it now," rasps Claude and frantically they pull box after box from the truck bed and turn them over the bridge's guardrail, all ten. The little bundles cascade down in dusty sworls, and splash audibly over the rush of the river as they land. The two of them fling the empty boxes back into the truck and cover them with the tarp. "These we can burn," declares Claude. "Let's get out of here."

But once he has driven off the bridge he stops, and takes a flashlight from the glove box. Driftwood too is so utterly relieved that the deed has finally been done, just wants to be back in camp, asleep in his tent, or Robin's, and at the moment hardly cares which, and what's this? Claude gets out of the truck, steps to the side of the highway, and trains a beam on the bridge's understructure, and what is that? A single bundle of twenty-five trees, caught in the cleft of two curving girders.

"No, Claude, forget it, no one will know," Driftwood calls after him. "No one will ever notice it . . . your leg . . ." His own shrill voice echoing back from a forested hillside, borne on a summer breeze over the rush of the Parsnip, a hundred feet below.

And there goes Claude, ram's horn cane in hand, flashlight in his mouth, and climbs, cane as a sort of runescape climbing hook, jeez you have to hope that piece of horn is securely fixed to the blackthorn stick, flashlight throwing a twitching silver shaft through the girders against the tumbling river and mossy chasm walls. Gropes his way along the understructure and finally reaches forward with the cane and pushes the dark drooping object from between the bridge's legs. The flashlight drops as well, sparkling like firefall, and then gone beneath the current. And for that moment as Driftwood's eyes try to move up, out, and down it is not at all apparent to him that the vision of a body dropping to the river below is hallucination of weariness and shifting light, and not his friend Claude following the trees and the flashlight on their final journey to the Arctic Ocean.

But, he realizes vaguely, as he adjusts to his hallucination, that a figure is scrambling through the girders, cane still in hand, and then Driftwood is racing toward the place on foot but already Claude has chinned himself up, cane hooked on a railing, and good leg kicking up over it. Then standing, then hobbling toward Driftwood with the look of a man reborn on his face. "Let's get out of here," Claude pants as he runs.

XII

It is all but daylight when, nearing the turnoff back to their camp, they see the two hitchhikers again, one sprawled in a sleeping bag just off the shoulder of the highway, but the other, the man, still standing there trying.

"Shall we stop this time?" wonders Claude.

"We're going the other direction," Driftwood points out to him. "And we're not going anywhere except back to camp."

"No, and we can't offer them work," Claude decides. "If they're still there day after tomorrow when we leave, we can probably find a place for them to ride." He slows a little while he considers it, but then speeds up and passes them by. Driftwood tries to read the hitchhiker's face in the mirror as the image recedes. Although he can't see it well, it does not look happy.

XIII

Claude parks the truck by the cookshack, sighs deeply over the steering wheel, and says, "Well, that was a night's work. Guess we better get a couple of hours sleep yet, if we can. We really do want to finish today."

"What time is it?" Driftwood isn't wearing a watch.

Claude pulls his from his pocket. "Three-forty-five. Doesn't give us much time does it? They have been arising at five and hitting the slash at six on the days it doesn't rain, which it does not look very much like it will do in the next few hours. "I think you and I can sleep a little longer this morning if we want, though," Claude decides. And heads into the cookshack for something or other before hitting his sack.

Her tent is on Driftwood's way to his own, and he is wondering whether he ought to peek in and pauses for a moment outside it, only to have her poke out her tousled red head. "I thought that must be you," she tells him. "Where did you go?"

"Everywhere," he sighs.

"Want to come in here?" she offers. "I have to ask you about something anyway. And besides, your bag's in here, remember."

That's right. He remembers. He expects her to ask of their long night's exploits, but she has a question about another long night, the one before. "How many," she begins, somehow, it seems, a little sheepishly, "the other night, how many, uh, you know, times did we, you know . . . ? Do you remember?"

It wasn't as though he was counting, but it shouldn't be that hard a thing to recall, and he thinks he does, well enough. "Four, right? Somehow, that last time was the best."

She looks at him quite strangely. "Well that's what I thought too, but, uh, this is so weird, I just happened to count, and we only used three of those things. I mean, there's still nine left in the box and it doesn't say anything about extras . . ."

"That last time," he pauses for fuller recollection. "You know when you . . ."

She blushes. Driftwood can see it through the early morning light filtering through the thin skin of her mountaineering tent.

"Did we maybe . . ."

"But I thought we . . ."

"How strange," is all he can conclude. And reaches to touch her for reassurance. "But, you know how that is, the first is the strongest, I wouldn't worry too much, it's not very likely . . ."

"No, no," she replies. "You don't understand. That's not what I'm worried about. I'm not worried about me, I'm thinking about you. You aren't the one who was at Bella Coola."

Bella Coola: Calvin's Tale

... I hear the mountains are doing fine ...

Day One
Wet cloud
Fine mist
Light mist   Ocean spray mixed with
Dreary mist   fine mist. Where one
Full mist   begins and the other ends?
Drizzle (Fine through full, & etc)

(? Although dreary doesn't parallel fine, light &
full. As in IQ tests. Find the word that doesn't
fit. Dreary. Emotive content. How many kinds of
mist, drizzle, rain are there?)
(And why must I experience them all?)

The Inuit, sz someone should know, have more than 50
words for snow, each meaning a different kind of snow. That
fact sometimes cited to prove the superior wisdom of the
aborigine.

I think it may have more to do with the power of language
to shape reality. The X-country skier, fr eg, knows how
many? Kinds of snow, that is. By types of wax: light green,
green, blue, purple, red, yellow, the whole range of clisters.

Each may be applied, say, light, medium, heavy, with or as kicker. So four values for each up to clister renders 24 kinds of snow. Not counting snow so cold a good base wax on pine tar will do (25) and all the various levels of rot you might use clister on.

Although I wouldn't know about those anyway, always being up some godforsaken coast by that time of year planting trees.

Is my intelligence inferior to that of the savage? A moot point.

Hillarie Hillarie Hillarie. I'd rather be here on this grey mountain than anywhere with you. (Brave words.) Where was I?

Rain
Squall
Downpour
Deluge & etc

Day 3
A brutal day. Tore my rain gear. Boots leak. I still do not understand F's triangularzation scene. He and Marty and Lattice and who else? mainly them, badgering the rest of us about it.

> Why am I hear, here, I mean
> Who else pays 12 cents a tree
> Question? Answer
> Goodnight sweet
>   dense
>   fog.
> Hillarie I
> would like you
> and the rest

of the world
to go away
nights like
this one

(And, oh dear, the food. No rotten tofu, but . . . Am I the only person in the world who finds burned mushy zucchini a little bit unpalatable?

(Just asking . . .)

#4 It may be one of those contracts.

Lattice, who is not necessarily the sweetest-tempered person in the world, is suddenly so bright and cheerful and just plain alive whenever Abram's around. Honest Abe. But what about Pete? He watches her changes as though he doesn't see them. He spent the whole winter in the same cabin with her. Claude sz Peter's religion is against jealousy. And against good sense, as far as I am concerned. Who could spend an entire winter in a cabin with Lattice? Although maybe she's different in the Kootenays. Maybe horses fly there. Burton warned me about this one.

And this must be day six. Didn't write last night. Why not? Claude and his banjo. Singing rain songs. He doesn't stammer when he sings, it's amazing really. Actually, he hasn't stammered much at all up here so far. Sz he has finally accepted the meaning of his stammer and has stopped caring whether he does it or not. I write tonight only to remind myself of time's passage. Tomorrow is our Sabbath. The Hebrew in Frans.

Frans told Claude the rain was depressing enough without his rain songs. I kind of like them myself, one in particular he says he learned off a tape from an old Grateful Dead concert.

7. Things have changed. For one thing, the sun came out. Frans and Jesse, Marty, Lefty, a couple of others decided to go plant, Sabbath or not, since it is our first relatively clear day.

And I can write at the cookshack table instead of scrunched in my tent. Run-off still trickling through the cookshack, has made its own channel across the flattened boxes. The rain was heavy snow further up the mountain but we hadn't seen it because of the clouds. Now, very impressive. That sawtooth splendor above the site. How steep the mountains are. How precariously we cling to this miserable road. But in the mist and rain – I hardly dare mention it while it happens. How the grey sky lowers into this valley. The sensation of being in some sense in the sky as it – defined by the mist that fills it – flows down the mountain.

Today, in clearer weather, I can look down and realize that, yes, there is a bottom to this slope, down there, somewhere. But before . . . well, the day we arrived, on a barge with the crummy. The road climbed steeply from the inlet. You know you're going up a mountain, but in turning and switching back I, at least, lost track of the shape of the thing, except climbing, always climbing (Jacob's ladder?) & where we are, the place we are, now, we turned a definite corner to get here, and there was a sense of valley below, but no revelation as to its contour or depth or what lay at the end. And now, to see it, helps in some way. ie. it is deep, & steep, & the other side would seem to be about the same as this one except no road, thus no logging, thus no slash. At the top, a sort of mildly spectacular glacier. And to think it goes on like this, this coast I mean, hundreds and hundreds of miles of it, far enough for me at least to conceive of as forever.

How precariously we cling to this mountainside. I and the people I am with.

Robin comes in, gives her hair a good shake and takes off her shirt. Smiles, at me, I guess, asks where Claude is. Is he planting today? No, I don't think so? Sleeping in? She ties the shirt around her neck by the sleeves and heads up the road to find him. One of those contracts. There isn't a whole lot to do except plant. Unless one scribbles as I do.

Ed, Cheryl, Weena, Jackson, a couple of the others are sitting around talking about whether or not to build a new cookshack. This one being about half as big as it should be. And there are at least twenty of us. Very cozy in the rain.

Speaking of cozy, Ed has this big umbrella tent and Claude tells me that both Cheryl and Weena are sleeping in there. With him. As in WITH him? I wonder and Claude just sz, Well, you know . . .

They, those others in here, decide that a new cookshack is a bit much to tackle, but that a drying hut would help. Which is a good idea, & I will have to help. But now they also decide we should dig a trench around the cookshack to divert the water. Also a good idea. They decide I should do this since I'm not doing anything anyway. I tell them I'm writing. They don't seem to think that is much of anything.

Later, same day: or night by now. The people planting met a bear on the slope. No harm to any of them or to the bear. Ed & them built the drying hut. A neat little plastic shack with a fire pit in the middle. Pretty amazing how much wet clothing was hanging on rocks & logs up and down the road today. My own tent has twice the room with mine all dried and packed. Room for two. These Sabbaths make sense.

I ask Claude if Robin found him. He grins.

Frans sz Happyjack is making it in sometime this week. Probably tomorrow with the Forestry. Who live down on the inlet. Fly in and out on weekends. They've repossessed a cabin in the old logging camp from the gulls and squirrels. Glad Happy is arriving because he's funny. We need a laugh. Frans mainly concerned to have his chalk, sz HJ better remember it.

9. HJ arrived with F's chalk. Eight different colors. Triangularzation on the blackboard yet last night. Makes no sense that I can figure, but here it is . . . Sz Frans, here's Area B (A already finished) on our (camp's) side of the road, further up the mountain than A. The point is, sz Frans, to think of his drawing not as a map (seen from above) but as a picture. Seen from where we see what we see. (What does that mean?) He draws one rough triangle, the mountain. A road cuts up it with three switchbacks. The point being

the mountain

is triangle

the switchbacks

make triangles,

and we are supposed to think triangles.

Whatever that means! I catch Claude's eyes. He rolls them, as though, Dat man crazy.

HJ watches it all real serious and looks worried, like maybe he shouldn't have brought that chalk after all. Wondering what he came here for, besides Gretel. But everyone listening hard and trying to understand. As though it means something.

On the sacred blackboard the mountain is green, the switchbacking road brown, the four sectors of Area B red. Then all of our names on the board coded by color. Like so:

```
Jesse
Lefty          blue
Abram
- - - - -
Marty
Pete           yellow
Lattice
- - - - -
HJ
Gretel         purple
Jackson
- - - - -
Cheryl
Ed             orange
Weena
- - - - -
Claude
Robin          pink
Calvin
- - - - -
```

Triangles, five each, each of those colors worked into the mountain. Well, it is colorful, I don't deny it. And he is so excited about it, pointing at the board, waving his hand with the chalk in it, mumbling fervently, although I can't remember a word that I understood.

The thing is, today, planting, I did work with Claude and Robin, all just like he wanted, all day. I have no idea whether we were indeed planting the area he meant with that pink triangle, but Claude seemed to think we must be. Really curious, the force his suggestion has. At any particular moment I would have sworn we were planting the way we always do, but, there it was, we finished that first sector in one day.

- - - - - - - - -

There is something wrong, either between or with, either HJ and/or Gretel. HJ's humor strained. Did his And Now for the News CBC imitation this morning, mainly about his arrival in camp. And was trying too hard. I don't imagine I'm the only one noticed it.

Late this afternoon, as the day wore down, the clouds began piling up the valley again. It is, of course, by now, raining.

Day what? How long since last writing? Three? Four? Could figure it out. And do. Is three because we finished the three sectors of Area B. One a day. The triumph of triangularzation.

In the rain. The drying room pretty much a success even if all our clothing smells of smoke. Funny to see how my body runs dirty to clean from hands and feet to torso. Little rivulets of muddy stain trace past my elbows. Dirty tracks from neck to chest. Feet all wooly blue from lining of calk boots. Grey stripe around belly. Still no sauna. Apathy or weariness or whatever against it. Maybe next Sabbath which is, what? three days yet. Took off my clothes and soaped on the road. Raining hard, so rinsed in no time. Sat in the drying hut. Is something like a sauna, and now I smell like smoke. Just like my clothes.

Next day. Something strange. HJ and Gretel.

The Second Sabbath (day 14). Raining real hard. Just as well it is the Sabbath. We can work in the rain, we do work in the rain, but is no damn fun at all. Not at all. Depressing. And wet and cold. I keep trying to patch my rain gear and it keeps ripping out. Heavy needle and threadwork today and don't expect it to last half a day tomorrow. What a way to live.

Am all but alone in the cookshack. Ditches from last Sabbath holding up pretty well until now but now those little rivulets are starting to flow at my feet. People either out walking or working in this, or holed up in their tents. Probably the latter. That is all.

The rain was harder yesterday than Sunday. And harder than that today. Writing this, on my elbow by flashlight in my tent with the rain drilling it and myself dry and warm for the first time since waking up, it doesn't seem so bad anymore, but while it happened . . . The funny thing is, just at this moment, I am liking this weather. Such life and motion in it. But it takes most of what you have, to live in it, and that doesn't leave much for planting trees, triangularzation or no triangularzation.

The drying hut blew down in the wind and hasn't been rebuilt. Which is trouble if the weather doesn't break. I was walking down the road realizing that for the first time on the contract I was truly miserable: feet wet and cold, fatigues drenched what with all the holes and tears in my raingear. Hands, ears, nose, all cold. Physical discomfort actually a kind of stimulus. As long as you keep moving you stay warm. Wet, but warm. And as I come around the bend in the road where we get our first sight of camp coming down the mountain the drying hut just goes down. The wind hit the wall facing up the mountain like a sail and twisted the whole structure like a thing being screwed, as though it might fly and then, instead, just crumpled in a heap. And everybody's clothes wet and have to hang dry and the only place for that the cookshack again. I took some hardtack and cashew butter and headed here dressed only in rain gear. Wasn't worth even trying to eat in the crowd. Real happy to have a good tent and downright comfortable, just now, toasty warm in dry cotton and wool.

Speaking of comfort. Claude asks me today what it means if you feel like you have to piss all the time and can't. I say it's from too much sex, joking of course, but he didn't seem to think it was funny. I mean it being so wet and cold I even feel something like that and too much of anything not my problem at the moment. He seemed worried, though.

The last couple of days I have an interesting sense of myself as not here, at least not in the sense that the rest are here. What it signifies I am not sure. Remember GT talking about solipsism in connection with Wordsworth, The Prelude, Book 1, school days, mine and his. How it was a thing for the poet to confront and overcome. As I remember, the passage has to do with trees and touching them. What I feel may be like that, except the question not whether the rest of all this is here but whether I am. Which I sort of have to gather I am. And am writing this down. To tell the story. But what story? Except that we are here on this bare coastal mountain planting trees in the rain. An occurrence both exotic and common.

A phrase in my head for the last day, just under consciousness, and now found. Biblical, I believe. "I alone am left to tell the tale."

But what tale?

What tale indeed. If I'd been in the Kootenays this winter I might have caught on earlier.

It seems that at least some persons on this contract are either suffering, or think they are suffering, acute discomfort involving either their reproductive or urinary systems. No one besides Claude has mentioned symptoms to me, but there seem to be an awful lot of standing and squatting figures at the edge of the bush between runs in the slash. They stay that way a long time and return with pained grimaces. It would seem to be a bit more than cold feet making them look that way.

And here is what happened tonight.

Supper was about over, the rain still peppering the shack, and I getting myself together to go to my tent and bag, the one dry place available to me, and Frans stands up at the head of the table and tells me not to leave, that we are going to have a meeting.

Not only have I never heard of a meeting on a Vander Grove contract before, I have never heard Frans use the word. Even the blackboard triangularzation was Frans talking to whoever might be listening, which was not all of us. I watched that because it was interesting, in a funky obsessed sort of way. But it wasn't directed at us all, at one time. This, his stopping my leaving and saying that word meeting, was something else.

We have a problem, he sd.

We have a problem, and we have to see what all is involved, he sd.

I figured it was going to be about plots. So did Claude. P-p-p-p- plots? he stammered.

The plots are fine, sd Frans. It's not the plots.

He stood there like he didn't exactly know how to say what came next, but finally began: We, uh, we have to figure out who's uh been uh with who . . .

Which surprised me, but it was as though I was the only

person it did. Little noises of recognition around the table. He picked up the red chalk and went to the blackboard, which is now nailed to the cookshack frame. He wrote:

    Frans ↔ Marty

Then he wrote:

    Pete ↔ Lattice

Then:

    Claude ↔ Robin

and looked for confirmation in Claude's direction. Claude looked puzzled, like whose business is this anyway? but he didn't deny it. Then:

    HJ ↔ Gretel

Then Jackson sd: Now, on this contract, or before?

    F: Before too.
    J: How long before?
    F: I don't know. Three months?

And Jackson looking like he's counting on his fingers. Then looking at Lefty.

    Frans wrote

    Jackson ↔ Lefty

on the board. Come on, everyone, he insisted. Ed and who?

Cheryl?

Ed shrugged his shoulders. And Weena, said Cheryl.
The three of them together in that umbrella tent. I wonder if
they all fall asleep in each other's arms.

Cheryl ↔ Ed ↔ Weena

wrote Frans.

Jesse ↔ Agatha

he wrote.

What about Calvin? said Lattice, it seemed to me nearly
unfriendly.

And Frans wrote my name. And then sd to her, What
about you and Abram. And then I sd: I don't see how it's
anyone's business, but no, not anyone, I was in Vancouver or
back east all winter. I haven't, not with anyone. Ask them . . .
I mean, there was, but she's not here. And I haven't seen her
since way last fall. And besides, she doesn't plant!

And Frans puts a question mark by my name. People
keep shifting position to get out from under the multiplying
leaks where the plastic is nailed to the roof. Abram? Marty
asks Frans as though surprised. And Frans writes Abram's
name on the same line as Pete's and Lattice's and picks up
the blue chalk from the table. Pete shrugs. Lattice glowers.
Abram sits off in a far corner looking almost pleased with
himself. C'mon big brother, fess up, Jesse calls down the
table. I thought he was talking to Abram, but Frans, without saying a word, inscribes another double pointed arrow
between his own name and Agatha's, as though trying to
sneak it by.

Frans! sd Marty softly.

I thought I heard Jesse chuckle.

Frans looked at Marty with a superior smile, and dropped another arrow between her name and Happyjack's. Before we came up here, he sd. I know about that.

At that point something quite wonderful happened. The ditch I had dug around the cookshack overflowed at the entrance. We heard the sound of water on gravel, and one rivulet, then two, then three, cascaded across the floor. People scrambled to stand on the bench by the table. The atmosphere in the place had become so thick that such a genuine if minor disaster was welcome. I led the charge out the door, grabbed a mattock from the pile and went to work. Claude and Robin came with me.

This is the strangest damned thing I've ever seen, I told them over the rain. Why is he doing it? What's the point?

Well, Claude told me, We're all infected. Everyone but you . . .

Rain streamed off Robin's red curls. Come with me tonight, Calvin, she suggested. You can have it too.

You all are, I mean . . . ? I sd. How do you know?

We f-f-feel it, sd Claude.

There's no point pretending they aren't the only people here I care much about at all. The only ones I can talk to.

What about you? You going to play? She asked Claude with grim humor.

What ab-b-b-bout me? he answered her.

When we got back into the shack Claude's name was connected to Gretel's by another of those tell-tale double arrows. He recognized this amendment. He raised his eyebrows and cocked his head. Robin whispered to him, and he shook it.

Cheryl had her hand in the air like a child in school.

Jesse, was all she sd.

My, you do get around, sd Frans over the sound of the rain.

He takes after his big brother, grumbled Marty.

An entangled conclusion began to emerge. It was weird, as though there was an imperative, as though a pattern in which each of the seven lines of two or three names was going to be connected to at least one other. Two more confessions, Abram, in silence, getting around to Lefty. Frans' other brother with Marty's sister. Symmetrical, if bordering on incestuous. And then Cheryl, to Jackson, no doubt while Lefty was in Abram's tent. Like so:

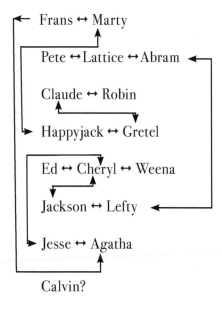

Calvin? My dreams tell me what I feel. Last night in bed with both Robin and Hillarie. Felt like the real thing. Fucking Hillarie but with my hands all over Robin's body, then at the point of coming Hillarie pushing me away and Robin spreading before me, pulling my head between her breasts, my hands beneath her, and then I wake, with a genuine wet dream soaking my longjohns. One of the dubious pleasures of treeplanting celibacy. Perhaps all this triangularzation is not as weird as it seems. If it's in our dreams? If we can imagine it we can do it? Right? Calvin? And we need a plague to tell us this?

Down to the cookshack, but no one there. I wonder what they're all dreaming. That blackboard still nailed there in for now mute witness. No more connections. Still raining and the drying room not rebuilt.

Lattice comes in just then with her sleeping bag wet over her shoulders. What are you doing? she demands. Writing, I tell her. Well cut it out, she snaps. And then adds, under her breath, Pervert!

The blackboard has still not been erased after two solid days. No more connections. The rain falling and the drying room not rebuilt. Wetness and coldness and, I have to assume, a fair amount of suffering both physical and spiritual. Hardly anyone ever in the cookshack anymore. Only to eat, fast, joylessly. Agatha's disease infecting all our diet. All the area near the airtite overhung with grungy awful treeplanter clothing. No one sz a thing, just keep looking at that board with each entrance and exit.

It is all but Transylvanian in this landscape. Wind and rain and the occasional sharp ring of mattock on rock in the slash the only sounds.

I get a chance to talk to Claude and Robin as we work, almost as though I were the third point to their triangle. Claude can't speak a sentence without stammering anymore. T-t-t-two years of Reich-ch-ch-ch-chian therapy down the t-t-t-tubes, he laments between trees. Are you really sick? I ask. I m-m-m-m-ust be, he replies.

What about you? I ask Robin, realizing the question is a little bit personal.

I'm all right, she tells me. Poor Gretel, though, I think she's going to have to fly out tonight with the checkers.

Today is Friday, it would appear, the nineteenth day. Which means that when the checkers leave tonight we will be at our own mercy until Monday. I wonder what they know, or think. They can't help but see the blackboard. Fun and games in the old north wet woods.

And our own mercy comes to this. Tonight after supper, another meeting. Frans stands by the blackboard and sz: Well, I guess we're all in this together . . .

Except for Calvin, sz Lattice.

Well, yes, we'll see about that, sz Frans, and then proceeds to ask them all, one by one, if they've ever been "intimate" with me, recently. When he thinks it might have been, I can't imagine. I was in Vancouver or Michigan all winter. It would all be hilarious if it weren't so wet and abysmally heavy. And to judge by their expressions, I don't think most of them care too much for me, not that way anyway.

Lattice: Are you kidding?

Weena: Well, really now . . .

Agatha: I should hope not!

The best I get are non-committal shrugs. Only Robin is the least bit kind about it. Not recently, she smiles, although the answer is of course, not ever. Except in my dreams.

If I hadn't been so completely curious I might have left and gone to my tent but, c'mon Calvin, face it, yr a bloody damned voyeur. And there may be, if not an end here, or a point, a something coming. I can feel it.

What we need to know, sz Frans quietly after I would

seem to have been absolved of whatever it is, What we need to know, he sz, is whose fault this is.

I've been looking over this chart, he goes on. It had to start somewhere . . . we can find the what do you call it . . . who brought this here . . .

We weren't having any problem were we? He looks to Marty. So it can't be either of us. So I must have . . . gesturing toward Agatha. Or you from . . . he turns back to Marty. But that was before we left, right? Slow sheepish nods from at least the parties who think they should be concerned. Erases the blue line marking two connections and redraws it in yellow. And then sz: OK, yellow's clean. And from us to . . . He erases the blue line from Agatha to Jesse and Cheryl, redraws it in green, circles the Ed ↔ Cheryl ↔Weena triangle in green, takes the line from there to the Pete ↔ Lattice and Abram triangle by way of Abram, in green. Green's clean, he sz. Stern now. Declares that blue is unclean. Only blue line remaining from Gretel to Claude.

See! cries Lattice. See! Pete hasn't done it with anyone but me and unless Robin is lying it is him. See! See!

Right, sz Marty. So Claude gives it to Gretel who gives it to Happyjack who gives it to me.

When were you and Gretel together? Frans turns to Claude.

That is none of your business, sz Claude without stammering.

Gretel? demands Frans.

She's not here, sz Marty. She went out with the checkers.

That's right, realizes Frans.

At that point I half-expect them to just up and sacrifice Claude like their Jonah. Old Testament vibes all the way, or is it just old news. Anyway, they had what they wanted.

Claude spoke: What b-b-b-bullshit, he sd calmly and

left. Just got up and walked out. You stay here, Frans shouted after him. Claude spit on the ground.

Well at least we know, Marty and Lattice cried in unison.

I wonder about a lot of things. I find myself watching and also trying to figure out who is responsible, not for the infection, but for the event. Wondering what makes this necessary. Only three of them really seem to want it: Frans, Marty, Lattice. Frans because of who he is. Marty more-or-less ditto, her identity linked to his. And Lattice from simple bad nature. All of which can hardly be the whole show. The thing is, the rest are letting it happen. The rest of us. Although I am beginning to think I am beginning to know why I am not attempting to prevent it.

They shake heads in disgust and mutter back and forth and study the chalkboard like a sacred text and shake their heads again. It's stopped raining, Robin propositions me. Let's go for a walk.

Which it has. The stars actually peeking from the clouds overhead in the narrow strip of sky between our two rows of mountains. The glacier glowing a little in starlight. Want to know something funny, sz Robin. Claude's never fucked Gretel. Never even got in a bag with her.

That stopped me right there. You mean . . . ? So who drew that line . . .?

Who do you think?

I can guess, but I don't know. I know it wasn't Claude or you or me.

Exactly.

And why didn't Claude contradict him?

I asked him that myself.

And he said?

He said he wanted to see what happened next . . .

Come on!

Seriously.

Why didn't Gretel contradict him?

I don't know . . . Square it with Happyjack? Ever seen *Jules et Jim?* Happy's a pretty charming guy when you get right down to it. I mean, who knows. It was just an impulse. Why do you think I'm a little cautious about Claude right about now. For his sake, is what I mean. And Gretel really is sick. Or at least thinks she is.

And Claude?

I can't tell you how Claude feels, it could just be wet feet and a cold. He says he's fine. I think he's OK. Obviously. I feel better. I mean, I guess I better get some lab work next time I'm around a clinic.

So this disease business . . . And you?

If you aren't actually feeling what someone else is feeling in her body there's no way to know, is there?

The sky kept clearing, revealing more stars. We need a full moon, I suggested, not exactly changing the subject.

No, she replied. No moon at all.

What happens now? I wondered.

The contract's nearly finished. They can all go home and think about things.

About their sins.

One word for it.

And Claude, and you, and me?

Here's what I really want to know. Can they finish without us?

Frans always finishes. Even if he has to plant them himself. He's the mountain king.

She laughed there on the road. That's something like what Claude said, she told me.

4-22, Bella Coola

When Claude called me in Vancouver, he said we were going to plant trees in Bella Coola. It's funny how contracts are always named for a place which as likely as not you never actually see. Well, today I saw Bella Coola. Funny too, how every town of a certain size in British Columbia looks the same. I've never been in Bella Coola before, except driving through that Sunday morning on the way to the barge to get to the site. There's a little hospital & Gretel's in it. Sick all right but not with what some of them probably thought. Hepatitis, is the story. Bad water and a bad diet in the Kootenays probably, sz the doc. The doc sz we should all be tested. I told him I'd been in Vancouver and back east all winter and he sd the test wouldn't hurt, just to be sure, it could have got around the camp. Well, if any one thing was pure on that contract it was the water, so I'm not too worried.

Robin, on the other hand, all but dragged the doc around a corner where she could talk to him privately. I was more than happy to head for the hotel, or more specifically, the beer parlour there.

And, as that turns out, tomorrow, the long hitchhike up the Bella Coola Chilcotin Hiway to Williams Lake and the Fraser Canyon and Hope and then Vancouver. For me. Robin stays until Claude is out of the hospital. Right, he's in the hospital too.

They got their human sacrifice, or something nearly like it; Claude offered himself up, or down, as the case may be. Down over the side of the road, sd he was going fishing, started down the hill toward the river and missed a step. Bone sticking out his leg and blood everywhere. Never seen a compound fracture up close and real life before. A fairly gruesome sight. Robin and I carried him back up.

Worried – needless to say – about the blood and no way

to get him to town on Sunday. Lattice wanted to tourni-
quet him up, but 24 hours of that and you can lose a leg. We
managed to control the bleeding with cold compresses and
there he lay on the cookshack table, eating 222's like candy,
and not overly unhappy it seemed, everything including the
bone sticking out of his leg considered. But worried, natu-
rally.

And what finally happened was pretty crazy, but beautiful too in its own strange way. Claude's gritty courage, and
Robin reacting like a champ. The crummy broke down the
second day but we hardly needed it anyway because the camp
was so close to the site and what with all the rain no one bothered to try to fix it. Frans just muttered about Jake not being
there like he should have been . . . So now, when we could use
it . . .

Let's run, she sd. It's downhill. The checkers have a radio,
she told me. They always do. Jesse, she sd, get Claude's pack
together for him. I'll take the tent out myself.

So we ran. Six or eight miles, in all, but it was the Sabbath
and we were fresh, not having been working. Both worried,
of course, but there was also that kick of doing the necessary right active thing, the only thing to be done, knowing
that we were running well, in stride, that we were going to
make it, that even if one of us tripped and got hurt ourselves,
or pulled up lame, or something, that the other was going
to make it. No point to panic, and no matter what trouble
Claude was in, we were doing exactly the right thing. So
we loped along, stride for stride, breathing deeply on that
terrific super-oxygenated forest air.

The derelict logging camp on the little bay by the end of
the road. The Forestry truck by the ramshackle cabin with
four-ply plastic spread over the roof, and inside, housekeep-
ing arrangements for two men in the bush, and their radio.

I assume it's tuned to the Forestry frequency, she sd. I hope the batteries are good.

She switched on the power and the air crackled. Hope someone's monitoring, she sd, contemplating the microphone. She pressed the button at its base and the crackling stopped.

Forestry, hello, is anyone there, help, emergency! Words barked urgently but without panic: Do you read me.

Stood there with the mike in her hands.

Over, I sd, say over, and let go of the button.

Forestry Bella Coola, squawked the box. What seems to be the problem?

Neither of us even knew the name of the little bay we were on. But we told them it was where Larry and Curly were the checkers and they said they knew where that was. We told them about Claude and they said someone would be there as fast as they could.

So we had a big hug there in the cabin. Spent a few minutes looking for the keys to the truck but couldn't find those. Started wetly back up the road. We hadn't taken our raingear, and hadn't even noticed the rain coming down because we were running, but we were wet by then, and going back up walked briskly to stay warm.

Perhaps halfway back to camp we heard a roar behind us and there came a helicopter overhead. It landed just past us on the road. The sky so low that to find the camp they were following the road. We got in and took off, flying a few yards off to the downslope side of the road, a strange feeling, to be traveling beside a road in a helicopter.

Claude was pretty weak and pale by the time we arrived but the paramedics strapped him to a stretcher and got an I.V. running. We threw his pack in the copter after him and they swooshed off. Robin and I collapsed at the cookshack table.

How much time before dark? I asked her.

Three hours?

If we can get back down to the logging camp we can fly out tomorrow on the plane that brings in Larry and Curly, I suggested.

Just what I was thinking, she agreed.

Got that much left?

How about you?

We nodded to each other.

Jesse came by as I was tearing down my camp. Long walk in the rain, he sd.

We'll be OK, I told him. Have to see how Claude is. You guys can finish without us, can't you?

Sure, the rest of us will just make a little more. One extra day, y'know.

Frans was erasing the blackboard when we checked in at the shack to let him know we were on our way out. Everyone else was there and it was crowded.

You know anyone quits a contract doesn't ever get hired again, he told us. If we have a problem at the end I'm going to dock you both.

We just shrugged. Whatever you say, boss, Robin told him.

Pansy asses, he growled.

We both had a good laugh about that as soon as we passed the first bend out of camp. Pansy ass! she chortled. Is that supposed to be an insult?

I think he's impugning our sexuality, I speculated. Of all the weird things to impugn, considering what's been happening up there.

The thing is, she sd. I think less was going on than they think.

You mean?

Well, I hate to even have paid attention to it, but listen, most of that stuff happened before we got here, get it? It's all Kootenays stuff. The long grey winter, get it? It's just we all end up here . . . I remember the magnificent gesture she made at that point, stopping on the road in the rain and spreading her arms as far upward to the misted mountain as the pack on her shoulders would allow. And then continuing. And after a long winter cooped up in the Kootenays we're all cooped up again in tents and rain, and it's supposed to be April, but we're so far north up the goddamned coast it's still winter. Get it? And the only real news to come out is that Frans and Marty are fooling around. I mean like the thing with Ed and Cheryl and Weena has been going on forever, and none of them is complaining. So big deal. Huh? If it weren't for Frans and Marty it wouldn't matter, would it?

So what about you and Happy?

Just something that happened. No big deal. I'll get checked. Promise.

Is that why I was out of it? I asked her without really thinking. Because I wasn't in the Kootenays this winter?

She laughed: You would have wanted to be in it, Calvin? You would have? No, listen, you spend so much time writing in that notebook you don't play the game. You don't just end up in a bag with someone. Not even in the Kootenays. There is the game, get it? And you aren't in it.

I find myself wondering about that game. It turned out to be a great walk down the mountain. I was tired, and my legs really hurt today, a day later, but we talked and talked, and not about the game. We dropped that soon enough. About the wet grey sky, and books, and what the natives – the real Bella Coola – must have felt about this country two hundred years ago. Forgetting wet and cold, just walking and talking, that hard.

The point being that I'm getting to know her, as one does, spending whole days with another person.

There was that moment, though. When we got back to the cabin, near dark. Very wet, raingear and all. The cabin with an airtite stove and a lantern and she lit the lantern while I fired the stove. Both of our teeth chattering. Without saying a thing we undressed and stood together naked as close to the hot tin as we could without burning our skin. It was, no other word for it, sexy, her strong red-fleeced body glowing in lantern light, and yet there was, after all that gaming and triangularzation and talk and grimness a something saying to me, no, hold back, take this like you might a great painting to look at but keep it between you and the thing itself, don't make it between you and a person. As she was, of course, by then, a person for me. We did touch hands and smile, and I think a thing was understood. When warm and dry, we arranged our clothing and gear so they could dry as well, and climbed into our respective bags in Larry and Curly's respective bunks. Ooooh, does this feel good, she exclaimed in a sort of voice I think Keats might have had in mind when he wrote about a woman making sweet moan.

Today, clear and beautiful, so changed. Suddenly, in a day, springtime arrives. We flew from the checkers' cabin to Bella Coola in a single engine Beaver. The inlet calm and blue beneath us. The peaks glistening with white. The Queen Charlottes on the far horizon, black ridge like a dinosaur's back.

I think I'll go ski in Garibaldi when I get back to Vancouver. Look this over and see if there is a story, or if it just seemed like one at the time. See if it happened. Maybe chase girls.

One other thing. At the hospital Robin asked Gretel why she let the line stand there on the blackboard between

her name and Claude's. And Gretel sd she never saw it! Was
really surprised, and highly pissed off, to hear it was there.
Actually, almost seemed to disbelieve that it had been there.
Although she sz her memories of that night are not so good.
Sz she wasn't feeling too good.

Robin up in the room, tired, she sd. Me in the beer parlour, writing more than I'm drinking. Something absurdly
gratifying about writing in a beer parlour, although I do
get some pretty strange looks. It's a good thing I'm a tough
in-shape treeplanter just out of the woods. Can defend
myself.

I have decided that I am here: I know this because I see
my reflection in my beer glass. For some reason it reminds me
of something that happened in school, before I quit. Something I never wrote down before. There was this seminar
with a distinguished guest professor from Toronto who was
all shook up about some French writers he said were solip-
sists. For example, he sd, gesturing loftily at the window in
the seminar room in the tower: We can look outside and say
with certainty that it is not raining.

On a grey cloudy March day. Riding the bus through
the Endowment Lands to class I could see the squalls were
moving off the Island toward the lower mainland. The
squalls still hadn't arrived when I got to the campus, but the
moist greenness all around. I considered suggesting to the
distinguished guest professor that it would probably be raining soon, asking how he defined the difference between rain
and mist, suggesting that it pretty certainly was raining at
that very instant somewhere, probably not very far away, telling him about the 50 different kinds of snow the Inuit can
name. It might have been a great moment, I would have either
wowed everyone in the seminar room or inflamed them
with jealousy. And didn't do it. Didn't say a thing. Let those

other people argue and flatter him. Watched as tiny droplets began to mist against the window as he gestured grandly once more and intoned in a sure deep voice: We can say with certainty that it is not raining.

There is no point to arguing about reality with someone who isn't looking.

My own certainties are less grand but, it seems to me, more true, if qualified.

I am certain, for example, that I am in a beer parlor. If I were transported around the globe a few times, put to sleep with the heaviest of drugs, and woke up here, I would know it was a British Columbia beer parlour. The damn things are unmistakable.

I am certain that it is in Bella Coola, based on one day's experience of being here.

I am certain I never want to work for Frans again, although not certain I never will.

I am certain I intend to leave in the morning, but you never know.

I am certain that I would like to sleep with her tonight, but pretty certain I will sleep on the floor instead.

Pretty certain that if I were to join her in the bed up there we wouldn't do anything.

Certain I am becoming intoxicated, although not necessarily drunk.

Certain that I learned some things this month, although not at all certain, as yet, exactly what they are.

Certain that me and a bunch of people will be thinking about this for some time to come.

And also certain I couldn't really say without a window to look out, this weather being what it is, whether it is raining, or not, in Bella Coola, just now, at this precise instant.

AFTERWORD

When I was courting my wife Chris she once let slip that she had dreamed of living with a writer. Once we were actually living together, she realized that wasn't necessarily a good dream. Fact is though, none of this writing would have ever gotten done if it weren't for her.

I owe nearly as great a debt of gratitude to the late Bernard Van't Hul. My first encounter with Bernie was at, of all places, Calvin College in Grand Rapids, Michigan. As a sophomore there I took Bernie's History of the English Language course. In essence, Bernie applied his native instincts about how language works, Darwinian evolutionary theory, and rudimentary Chomskyan linguistics, to an insistence that language was not a sacred trust to those who use it, but an ever-changing form of practice. (I later learned that it was the first and last time he was allowed to teach the course.) It was probably the most important I ever took in four years at Calvin.

When I re-engaged with Bernie as a grad student at the University of Michigan, some eleven years later, he was engaged in his own practice on that institution's ongoing Middle English Dictionary and mentoring us graduate teaching assistants.

In my first semester there I found myself unwittingly

directed toward the department's entirely new-to-me focus on "critical theory" (think Derrida, Roland Barthes, et. al.).

It wasn't so much boring or uninteresting, in fact some of it was downright fascinating in a perverse sort of way, but it had little to do with where I wanted to journey as a writer. Although there are both grudging homages and derisive sendups to such fortunately short-lived, at least as far as my experience with it, theoretical practice in these stories, by the second semester I had determined that I was a writer, not an academic scholar.

Among the reasons I had applied to the U of M in the first place was that I wasn't getting accepted into any prestigious MFA program, needed a graduate assistantship to pay my way, and as a Michigan native knew about the Hopwood Awards. Thing was, I found out once there, you needed to be enrolled in a creative writing course to enter the contest. And the Hopwood Director/Creative Writing Chair (who shall remain nameless here) turned down my application to take his class.

Bernie, who didn't much care for this fellow (and of course by then neither did I), agreed to take me on for a one-hour credit creative writing independent study, which enabled me to submit the first four stories in this cycle. I'm not sure who got the most pleasure when the aforesaid unnamed Director announced at the awards ceremony that my four stories had been granted the largest cash award up to that point in the contest's history. But it may well have been Bernie Van't Hul.